Rules for Rule Breaking

♡

Talia Tucker

Kokila

KOKILA
An imprint of Penguin Random House LLC, New York

First published in the United States of America by Kokila,
an imprint of Penguin Random House LLC, 2024

Copyright © 2024 by Talia Tucker

Visit us online at PenguinRandomHouse.com.

Library of Congress Cataloging-in-Publication Data
Names: Tucker, Talia, author. | Title: Rules for Rule Breaking / by Talia Tucker.
Description: New York: Kokila, 2024. | Audience: Ages 12+ | Audience: Grades 7–9. |
Summary: When Korean American teens Bobby and Winter reluctantly go on a college visit
road trip together, the sworn mortal enemies discover they might actually be a perfect pair. |
Identifiers: LCCN 2023019229 (print) | LCCN 2023019230 (ebook) | ISBN 9780593624753 (hardcover) |
ISBN 9780593624777 (ebook) | Subjects: CYAC: Automobile travel—Fiction. | Interpersonal relations—
Fiction. | Korean Americans—Fiction. | LCGFT: Romance fiction. | Novels. | Classification:
LCC PZ7.1.T8225 Ru 2024 (print) | LCC PZ7.1.T8225 (ebook) | DDC [Fic]—dc23LC record available
at https://lccn.loc.gov/2023019229 | LC ebook record available at https://lccn.loc.gov/2023019230

ISBN 9780593624753
1st Printing
LSCH

This book was edited by Joanna Cárdenas, copyedited by Kaitlyn San Miguel, proofread
by Margo Winton Parodi and Jacqueline Hornberger, and designed by Asiya Ahmed.
Joohee Baik was the consultant for transliterated Korean text. The production was
supervised by Tabitha Dulla, Nicole Kiser, Ariela Rudy Zaltzman, and Caitlin Taylor.

Text set in Glosa Text

In loving memory of Kenny Moon

♡

Winter Park

1. WE WILL NOT BE FRIENDS

The term "family friend" implied said friend was a friend to the entire family; therefore, the term was decidedly a bullshit one. At least as it applied to Bobby Bae and Winter Park, nemeses since the ninth grade. Or first grade if you ask Winter.

They were the only two Asian kids in their school, so they were frequently on the receiving end of comments like "I didn't know you were allowed to have more than one kid in China"—which was problematic because one: They were not related, and two: They were Korean. It was either that or the ever-persistent assumption they were dating.

Winter hated spending time with someone as uptight as Bobby Bae. Yet, when she asked her parents if she could visit MIT over summer break, he was their first choice to accompany her.

"No," Winter said plainly. "Just because you and Bobby's family are best friends doesn't make *us* friends."

Their parents had met when Bobby's family moved from New Jersey to North Carolina. It was during a back-to-school night when Winter's parents, who had formerly been the only Asian parents in the PTO, spotted the Baes from across the room and adopted them as their so-called family friends. Since then, it'd been all sunshine and Melona bars for their parents. However, for Winter and Bobby, if their relationship had a mascot, it'd be an eye roll.

Winter's father wrinkled his nose. "You both are too competitive. It's always something with you—class rank, attendance, even marching band."

"Because he's such a try-hard for no reason," Winter huffed. "And what's wrong with a little competition?"

"You're usually on the same team," her mother replied. "We don't need to have this conversation again. We're well aware of your rules."

Of course her parents knew the rules, but Winter feared steam would come out of her ears if she tried to hold in the reminder *and* refrain from further slandering Bobby. Multitasking wasn't one of her strong suits. She took in a sharp breath and was not surprised when her parents' voices echoed her own. "We will play nice in front of our parents. We will not be seen talking to each other at school. We will not meet outside of school," the three chanted in unison.

"It's a legally binding contract!" Winter said. Bobby had even tried to get it notarized at one point, but the notary refused on account of it having been written in crayon.

"Then your mother and I can sue because you gave up on rule number one years ago," Appa said. "And how many amendments have you added since then? Forty?"

Winter's shoulders tensed as she said in a defeated tone, "I would rather walk to Massachusetts than be stuck in a car for eighteen hours with *Bobby Bae*."

Bobby was, for lack of a better word, boring. He spent all his free time padding his college résumé with any and all extracurriculars, and it was unclear if he had any interests of his own other than making sure people thought he was a saint. Plus he was dating Jacqueline Charlotte "Three Names" Turner, who, like Bobby Bae, always seemed to be thinking of her next quip rather than actually listening to what anyone was saying.

"You're being dramatic, Soon-hee," Winter's mother said as she idly flipped channels, not bothering to look up. "You can't walk that far."

"Not true, Umma. Frodo did it, and he wasn't even wearing shoes," Winter retorted.

Umma looked up for the sole purpose of rolling her eyes. Sarcasm was lost on Winter's mother, who was the most literal woman in the world. Winter was named Winter because she was born in, well, winter. Umma didn't mince words, and she didn't entertain Winter's theatrics. She was a hard-looking woman with a pin-straight graying bob that was customarily clipped to the side and a revolving door of floral blouses and sensible black shoes.

"Bobby is a nice boy," Appa chimed in. "I don't see why you don't get along. You have so much in common."

Winter bristled at the word *boy*. If she were a boy, her parents probably wouldn't be hassling her about being too competitive or begging her to be more polite so a *boy* would like her. Bobby's parents never gave him grief about anything.

"What do we have in common other than being Korean?" Winter asked.

With a sigh, Umma replied, "You both get good grades, play instruments, are involved in student council, have good heads on your shoulders; you're kind, family-oriented, want to go to school in Boston, maybe a little stubborn—"

"Okay, I get it," Winter interrupted.

"Why do you need to visit the campus anyway?" Umma asked. "You are going to school to learn, not look at buildings."

"I'm not going to move into an entire school sight unseen. I'm not a Property Brother."

Appa breathed in slowly. "Bobby is visiting several schools on the way to Harvard. Go with him. He's a very good driver. He took lessons with your appa. We've already discussed it with his parents, and they would feel better if you went with him."

"No, Appa," Winter whined.

"You can go with Bobby, or you don't go at all," Umma said, and she changed the volume on her Korean drama from background noise to uncomfortably loud. "And I don't care if you wear shoes or not."

"You don't care if I wear shoes? That's a bald-faced lie. We're Asian," Winter said loudly, trying to be heard over the TV. "I'm in the National Honor Society, my robotics team has made nationals every year since I joined, my school had to create an AP Latin course just for me, and I'm one of two students taking classes at community college this year. But who cares, right? As long as Bobby Bae is my boyfriend."

"You've proven your point, Winter," Umma said.

"Have I? Will you show some interest in my education and take me to visit MIT?"

"You know it's our busy season," Appa said. "Your mother and I are *essential workers*, Soon-hee. We can't pick up and leave our practice so we can fly all over the country with you."

Appa was very proud of their dermatology office, which they affectionately referred to as "our practice." This was something that both amused and embarrassed Winter. Sometimes their work involved finding cancerous lumps, but most of the time they were popping pimples and extracting ingrown hairs.

It seemed that no one wanted to visit Boston with her. Not her best friend, Emmy, and not even her own parents. Emmy had the valid excuse of preparing to move to Germany early next month, but

Winter's parents were choosing lancing abscesses over their only child.

"Ugh!" Winter groaned as she stomped upstairs to her bedroom.

She changed into a T-shirt and jeans, making sure to put on her dirtiest pair of tennis shoes. Then she looked in the mirror. Winter was satisfied with the way she looked, though she knew from everything she understood about Korea that she would have been considered plain if she lived there. She thought herself to be of average height, rounder in some places, her eyes hooded and untrusting. And even if her straight black hair could do nothing but fall limp over her shoulders, she still probably wouldn't have done anything with it. There was no section on her transcripts for looks. There were other ways of expression that she enjoyed more than fashion.

Winter grabbed her phone and stomped back downstairs.

"I'm going to visit Halmeoni," she called to her parents, making a show of tap-dancing across their hardwood floors in her beat-up Chuck Taylors.

Her parents raised their eyebrows at her but didn't say anything.

Halmeoni lived in an elderly community, which was about a twenty-minute walk away. Winter found herself marching over to Halmeoni's apartment often, mostly when Bobby Bae had won something at school Winter believed she deserved instead and when she needed a Chanel Eau de Parfum-scented shoulder to cry on.

"Tell your grandmother hello for us," Appa said.

"She's *your* mom. Call her," Winter retorted, and walked out the door. She then stuck her head back inside and said, "I love you both. I'll definitely tell her you said hello."

Her parents smiled, and she headed out into the hot North Carolinian day, where there were dads in golf shorts mowing their lawns, happily sipping on cans of Cheerwine.

♥

Bobby Bae

The Baes sat down for dinner on the terrace at precisely six p.m. Though their patio wasn't bigger or nicer than the Reynolds', their neighbors, the Baes liked to eat out there as much as they could. Dinner alfresco was a win in *The Book of Bae*.

"Bobby," his father, Robert Sr., said, nudging his son hard in the shoulder.

Bobby refrained from soothing his shoulder and looked up from his plate. "Yeah, Dad?"

"I heard a joke today. Want to hear it?"

Bobby sighed. "Sure, Dad."

"What does a robot do at the end of a one-night stand?"

"What?"

"He nuts and bolts." Robert Sr. laughed jovially, making his beer belly, which hung over the top of his khaki golf shorts, jiggle.

Bobby's mother, Diana, laughed at her husband despite herself, but Bobby remained stone-faced.

"My handsome boy. You never smile," Diana said. "Lighten up, son."

Bobby smiled, but he did not lighten up.

He took a piece of sangchu from the bowl in the middle of the table and filled it with a perfectly round dollop of rice. He then aligned the meat next to the rice, spread some spicy soybean paste over the meat, and rolled the entire thing into a perfect little bite without breaking the spine of the lettuce. He chewed quietly as he watched his parents joking and laughing, often with their mouths open and food inside.

Bobby always prided himself on being the perfect son. He did exactly what he was supposed to without being asked, so his parents rarely had to parent him. Nevertheless, Bobby thrived on structure, so he often parented himself. And, if nothing else, Bobby Bae was the best at everything he did, so he parented himself at an excruciatingly high standard. He got perfect grades, was in all sorts of extracurricular activities, including volunteering with animals and the elderly, and made his own pocket money by participating in online gaming tournaments. He was tall and slim, with a head of thick hair that he often tossed out of his face while bent over his game controllers.

"Bobby, we have to talk to you about something," Diana said, suddenly getting serious.

Bobby wiped the condensation off the bottom of his glass and put it down on the cedar patio table. "What is it?"

He didn't like conversations that started like this. They always ended with some terrible news, like their family dog, Kimchi, having to be put down, or Winter Park beating his SAT score by ten points. He looked at his mother anxiously. She had long hair that she lightened into a brassy burgundy color, and she always wore the mommiest of mom shoes.

"Have you spoken to Winter lately?" Diana asked.

"No, of course not," Bobby answered harshly. "Why?"

"Well," Diana said, taking a deep breath. "You know how we're supposed to drive up with you to Massachu—"

"No," Bobby said, more forcefully than he meant to. "If you're about to ask me if it's okay if Winter comes with us, the answer is no."

His parents exchanged glances.

"Actually, we were going to say that we think it's a good idea if *only* you and Winter go to visit Harvard. She's interested in the space program at MIT."

Bobby's mouth fell open.

Winter was his rival at school, and she had this annoying quality about her that he couldn't quite pin down. She always wore big cable-knit granny sweaters that basically went down to her ankles, and she usually had a cup of hot tea in hand. At lunch she always had her nose in some cozy mystery novel instead of studying everything on—and off—the test like Bobby did. But it wasn't like she was reading because she didn't have anyone to eat with; she was comfortable and content all the time. Not that comfort was inherently annoying. But her nonchalance and effortless intellectuality infuriated him to no end. She loved space, and it was clear that was where her head usually was. He wanted her to come back down to Earth and be miserable and stressed like him and everyone else.

"Why don't you guys want to come with me anymore?" Bobby asked his parents. "We were going to visit Dad's old stomping grounds in Boston and the Smithsonians in DC. There might even be few fun tourist T-shirts in it for Dad."

"You know I love souvenir shirts, but you'll be at school for four years."

"So?"

"*So*, there will be plenty of opportunities to shop for a T-shirt. And it's not that we don't want to go with you. This could be a chance for a good old-fashioned American road trip. I drove up the coast with my little brother when we were about your age." Bobby's ears perked up. His dad never mentioned his brother, Eugene. Robert Sr. seemed to notice his slip and quickly tried to cover it up by saying, "What I meant to say is that you could have a good old-fashioned American road trip like in the movies."

Bobby's upper lip tightened. "Which movies, specifically?"

"How about *Green Book?* That was a good one."

"I think you missed the point of that movie, Dad."

"Maybe, but wouldn't you have more fun with somebody your own age?"

"She's not my age," Bobby huffed.

"Exactly. She's younger than you, and for whatever reason, she hasn't gotten her license yet, so you should take care of her," Diana said. "It'd be a very nice thing for you to do."

Bobby knew that it would be nice. He was always nice, and he would do anything his parents asked him to, but not this. He didn't want to spend a second with Winter, much less days.

"I know what you're doing," Bobby said, his arms folded and his nose turned up.

Robert Sr. narrowed his eyes. "What are we doing, son?"

"You just don't want me to go with Jacqueline. I know you both don't like her."

"That's not true, sweetheart," Diana said. Her voice was like a cup of sugar. "We just noticed we haven't been seeing her around as much lately. We thought you may have broken up."

Bobby picked up his glass and plate and stood up. "May I be excused?"

"Fine, but think about it. Okay?" Diana asked.

Bobby activated all the muscles in his face that were used to form a smile, but he was not smiling inside. Maybe he was his parents' son after all. The two of them always seemed to have a certain

9

melancholy, like they were lost in thought, thinking about something or, more likely, someone. For Mr. Bae, Bobby assumed that person was Uncle Eugene, since he was the only living relative he knew of. Just yesterday, Bobby had come home to his father drowning the plants with the garden hose. When Bobby called to him, he pretended like he'd meant to do it even though he'd overwatered one of his mother's raised garden beds so much it overflowed and her Thai basil plant floated away. And Diana was someone who sat for hours holding knitting needles but not actually knitting. The sun would set and there she would be in the dark, unsmiling, with the same unfinished scarf in her lap night after night. Bobby turned the lights on for her every afternoon and knitted a row for her every night after she went to bed. Her entire family still lived in Korea, and her contact with them had dwindled in the years since she had decided not to return after college. The Parks were their replacement family, much to Bobby's chagrin.

Bobby dumped his dishes in the sink and mentally grounded himself for not washing them immediately. He ran upstairs, slammed his door shut, grabbed his phone, and dialed Winter Park.

It rang twice.

"Why are you calling me?" Winter said as soon as she picked up.

Bobby clenched his fist. "You just had to try to be better than me at something again, didn't you?"

"What are you talking about?"

"*What am I talking about?* I'm talking about you wanting to go to MIT. Since when is that a thing? You know Harvard is my top choice."

Winter let out a noise to indicate that she was disgusted. "Not everything is about you, *Bae*. I want to major in aerospace engineering, and MIT has one of the best programs in the country."

"You always have to take everything away from me," Bobby said, tight-lipped, as he sank into his bed. "First it was that dinner with the governor. Now it's Massachusetts. My father went to Harvard, and the plan was always to follow in his footsteps."

"You're not the king of Massachusetts," Winter spat. "And I didn't steal that dinner from you. It was a dinner *for women*."

"You're the one who suggested it only be for women just so I couldn't go. What if I want to become a politician one day? Now I may never know."

"I'm hanging up now."

Bobby sat up straight. "Wait. Why do you even *want* to come with me? You realize I'm not only going to Massachusetts, right? I also plan to visit a few other schools. And if I'm not going with my parents, I should at least be going with my girlfriend."

"Trust me. I don't want to go either, but my parents said I can't go unless I go with you."

Bobby clutched his phone harder. "Look, where are you? We should talk about this in person."

"I'm visiting my grandma now, but—"

"I volunteer at her community center sometimes. I'm on my way. Don't leave."

"Wait, no—"

Bobby hung up the phone. His chest puffed as he grabbed his keys and sprinted out of the house to his car.

♡

Winter Park

3. WE WILL NOT HAVE PRIVATE CONVERSATIONS

Halmeoni was from the generation that still believed in getting dressed to impress every single morning. Even though she'd been slowed down considerably by arthritis, Halmeoni always had at least two rings on each finger and gold bangles that chimed every time she moved. There was always a gold brooch over her heart, either in the shape of a flower or a bird, and her hair was short and immaculately feathered and maintained. Winter admired her outfit for the day: a bouclé jacket, slacks, and velvet horsebit loafers. Winter enjoyed that Halmeoni always wore stockings under her pants even though the only place they could be seen were the tops of her feet. Halmeoni really cared about detail, whereas Winter was lucky if she remembered to shower.

In the middle of Halmeoni's gated elderly community was a senior center where Winter was meeting her grandmother for tea. Many of Halmeoni's neighbors from other apartment units met there to have meals, chat with one another, and attend special events. It was the social hub for the fifty-five-and-older community. One whole wall of the building was made of windows from which residents could see family members marching up the lawn for visits. All the seniors would place bets on whose children and grandchildren would visit on any given day. Because of Winter's frequent visits, Halmeoni was often a safe bet. However, Mrs. Fowler had six children and fourteen grandchildren, so she was usually the hot ticket based on numbers alone.

Winter got off the phone with Bobby and slammed it down on the table, causing her and Halmeoni's barley tea to slosh over the sides of their teacups.

"What's wrong?" Halmeoni asked in Korean. Winter only spoke Korean with her grandmother. It wasn't perfect, but even with her limited vocabulary, she used the words she did know to their full extent. When she saw Halmeoni, it was like a switch turned on. She loved how they could speak freely in Korean without fear of repercussion. Not that they gossiped often, but the senior center could get spicy at times.

"Bobby Bae," Winter replied, her voice thick with disdain.

Halmeoni took the napkin out of her lap and wiped the table where the tea had spilled. She then folded it up neatly and put it to the side. "What has he done this time? It's your summer break. You're not even in school."

"I'm trying to figure out where to apply for college, and Umma and Appa won't take me on visits. They think it's pointless. But I want to see the campuses and where I'd be living for four years if I get in. That could affect my decision," Winter replied. She pushed her hair behind her ears. "They want me to go on college tours with Bobby Bae. He's on his way over here right now to talk about it."

Halmeoni contemplated her words for a moment. "Maybe that's good. You should have more friends, like I do."

"Bobby and I *are* friends. Family friends. We just don't like each other. Plus I don't need more friends. I have Emmy."

"Then where is she?"

Winter looked down. "With her dad, probably."

Emmy's dad was in the military, so they moved around often.

Sometimes in the United States. Sometimes not. Every year of her childhood, Emmy would spend the summer with her grandmother—Năi Nai—who had lived in the same senior community as Halmeoni until she passed away about a month ago. Now Emmy and her dad were staying in Năi Nai's old condo, cleaning it out and readying it for the next inhabitants.

Halmeoni pursed her lips. "Emmy and her father will be stationed in Germany. Once she leaves next month, who will you have? You should try to make other friends, Soon-hee."

"Most of our friendship has been long distance," Winter said. "And Emmy is going to come back for college. She's kind of artsy. I could see her going to Emerson if they have a dance program. Then we'll get to live in the same city for once."

"Did she tell you she wants to go to Emerson?" Halmeoni asked, arching one brow. "College is an important decision. You need to let her make her own choices."

"Well, no. But you know how she is. I'll probably have to do her applications for her. And what is this lecture? You're the one who won't even talk about Năi Nai. I miss her too, you know."

Winter smiled as she remembered how she and Emmy would run around and play together while their grandmothers watched from the senior center, communicating in an odd mix of pidgin English and hand gestures because Năi Nai only spoke Mandarin. Both women were widows, and because they never forced the other to talk about their husband, they grew close. Their bond was built through shared grief, on a strong foundation of peace and quiet.

"Only you young people act like you are constantly in confession. I don't need to talk about every single feeling I have."

Winter stiffened. "Can you at least start coming to Sunday dinner again?"

14

"If I step into that house, your father will never let me leave."

"He's just worried about you living alone now that Năi Nai is gone."

"I don't live alone. I'm in a community of people my own age."

This wasn't Winter's battle. Truthfully, she liked that Halmeoni had independence. But, with Halmeoni aging, Appa wanted her to move into the house. It only bothered her that Halmeoni had begun skipping Sunday dinners to avoid Appa, and Winter missed having the whole family together.

Not wanting to provoke Halmeoni any further, she asked hopefully, "Can you take me to visit MIT, then?"

"I can't sit on a plane for that long. And I have things to do here," Halmeoni replied.

Winter looked around, trying to figure out what her grandmother could possibly have to do. The senior center was a sea of gray hair, flesh-colored orthopedic shoes, and newspapers enjoyed over muddy cups of coffee or watered-down tea. Winter didn't even know where you could buy a newspaper anymore. She didn't want to offend her grandmother, so she didn't inquire about her plans. "Bobby is best served in small doses, and our parents are constantly forcing us together," Winter said instead. "He's so . . . uptight."

"*You're* uptight, Soon-hee," Halmeoni clapped back. "You need to relax and stop trying to control everything. If you want to have a terrible time, you're going to have a terrible time."

Winter clutched her metaphorical pearls. "Halmeoni!"

"You and that boy never relax. It's always a contest with you. I admire your hard work, but you're sixteen and it's your summer break. After you graduate, those next four years will be hard. Don't start now."

From everything her father had ever told her, Halmeoni was not the type of parent to tell anyone to relax. She was the kind of parent to shame her children into doing things by telling stories about waking up at five a.m. to feed chickens. To this day, Winter didn't know if that was true. She couldn't imagine her grandmother in a chicken coop with all her expensive handbags and silk scarves. Although she was a doting mother by all accounts, Halmeoni had been strict on her children when it came to academics, particularly Appa, her oldest son. So much so that he went to med school to be a dermatologist rather than a veterinarian like he wanted. Halmeoni didn't think that veterinarians were real doctors. Harabeoji had been the more lenient one, but he passed away when Winter was only six. According to Appa, Harabeoji's death took a toll on Halmeoni, and she softened up considerably.

"I'm happy the way I am, Halmeoni," Winter said after a little while. "I can have fun after school, when I get the job I want."

She did admit that at times she wished that not every minute of her day was accounted for—the band practices, club meetings, competitions, debates, tournaments, and whatever else she packed her calendar with. But if being uptight would get her into MIT and bring her closer to the life she wanted, then so be it. As long as no one saw the effort she put in. Especially Bobby Bae. She didn't need to give anyone any reason to doubt she deserved her spot. Unlike Bobby Bae, she didn't have the luxury of being an insufferable workhorse and know-it-all with his hundreds of tutors and bread crumb trails of flash cards and tears wherever he went.

Halmeoni pursed her lips. "Okay, Soon-hee."

Winter anxiously bounced her leg as she awaited Bobby's arrival. She half expected him to spring out of the ground and immediately launch into one of his self-aggrandizing rants about Winter's "laissez-faire" attitude. Halmeoni put her hand on Winter's leg to stop her.

"You'll shake out the luck," she said.

"What if I shake out the bad luck?" Winter replied, and kept on bouncing.

She took a long sip of her bitter tea, and her gaze settled on the gigantic windows. It was then that she spotted Bobby Bae. He haphazardly pulled into a space in the black Nissan SUV his parents had given him for his seventeenth birthday. He hopped out of the car and tossed his hair back out of his eyes as he was known to do. Winter didn't see why he didn't cut it. He'd hurt his neck one day. Not that she cared. It just seemed impractical, and Bobby Bae was the most practical person she'd ever met. He didn't seem vain enough to care about something like hair. He wore a different variation of the same outfit every day like he was Steve Jobs's more neurotic twin.

They locked eyes, and the theme song that plays in every Western cowboy movie when there's about to be a showdown started in Winter's head.

"Be nice," Halmeoni warned as Bobby entered.

Bobby located his target and came right up to her.

"Winter," he said.

"Robert."

Bobby scrunched up his entire face until he had a Pangaea of features glaring back at the girl in front of him. "Why can't you call me Bae like everyone else?"

Winter had only recently learned that *bae* actually stood for something. It was an acronym that meant either "before anyone else" or "before anything else." But she couldn't imagine putting Bobby Bae before anything except a speeding bus.

"Aren't you going to say hello to my grandmother?" Winter asked, ignoring his request.

Bobby reddened. "Yes, I'm so sorry." He turned to Halmeoni and bowed low. "Hello, Halmeoni. How are you?"

"Did you just bow?" Winter laughed.

Halmeoni swatted Winter with the back of her hand. "I'm fine, Dae-seong. How are your parents?" she asked, still speaking Korean.

"English, Halmeoni. Bobby doesn't speak Korean," Winter reminded her.

Bobby's posture was rigid. Halmeoni, who spoke English almost as perfectly as she spoke Korean, though with an accent, repeated her question. Bobby relaxed slightly.

"They're fine. Thank you for asking, Halmeoni," he replied.

"And how is business?"

"Uh . . . fine, I think."

Halmeoni nodded approvingly, and Winter laughed. After several years of her grandmother asking this question, it became clear to Winter that Bobby Bae had no idea what his parents did for a living.

"What do you want to talk about, Robert?" Winter interrupted.

"Can we speak privately?" he asked, taking Winter by the arm.

Winter looked down at Bobby's hand and raised an eyebrow at him. He immediately let go. She turned to her grandmother. "We're going to talk outside for a minute. I'll be right back. Ignore any screaming or police sirens you may hear."

Halmeoni nodded, and the two went out to the courtyard behind the senior center. There were bright pink azalea bushes and the smell of freshly cut grass. Winter inhaled deeply as the two of them walked down the stone path to where there was a little bridge over a creek, which was more like a trickle of murky water passing over a few stones. Winter leaned her back against the railing of the bridge and looked at Bobby expectantly.

"So, no offense, Winter, but I don't want to go on a road trip with you," Bobby said plainly.

Winter folded her arms. "Well, full offense, Robert, but I don't want to go with you either."

He sucked his teeth. "Please stop calling me that, *Soon-hee.*"

Winter glared. "Ew. Only my family calls me that."

"Do you realize how far Boston is from here? We'll be trapped in a car together, sharing hotels, being forced to . . . talk. It goes against all our rules. Maybe you can fake sick or something," Bobby said. "How good of an actor are you?"

"The worst. Do you remember my audition for *Fiddler on the Roof* in ninth grade?"

"I remember you tripping during your musical number and then eating almost a gallon of fudge brownie ice cream."

"Exactly."

"My girlfriend won't like this," Bobby said, biting his lip and swaying from side to side.

Winter rolled her eyes. "I can't believe your girlfriend likes *you.* How is Jacqueline anyway?"

She didn't understand how it was that Bobby had a girlfriend. He was tall, sure. Smart, fine. His hair was bouncy. She would give him that. But the way he craved everyone's approval was exhausting, and the temper tantrums he threw when he came second to her didn't exactly steam her dumplings.

Bobby shot Winter a dirty look. "Jacqueline is fine. We spoke a couple days ago."

"A couple days ago?" Winter's smile grew. "You guys don't talk every day?"

"No."

"When was the last time you saw her?"

Bobby turned bright red. "The last day of school."

"Is she on vacation?"

"No."

"Have *you* been on vacation?"

"No."

Winter laughed so hard she snorted. "So what makes you think you're dating?"

Bobby folded his arms and huffed. "It's none of your business."

"She doesn't live that far from you. I think you could walk to her house."

"Drop it already. Why do you care so much?"

Winter mimed zipping her mouth shut and dropped the subject even though she still had so many thoughts. She couldn't imagine Bobby as a boyfriend. Freshman year, he petitioned the band director over and over again because he wanted to be first chair for trombone. But there was a kid named Ethan who was far better than he was, so Bobby, wanting to be the best, switched to flute and became first chair instantly because that whole section was a tragedy. But Bobby was so miserable he claimed to have lost his flute and switched back to trombone. Winter still maintained that Bobby lost that flute up his ass.

Bobby's girlfriend, Jacqueline Charlotte Turner, wasn't any better. She thought that because she had opinions on everything, everyone wanted to hear them.

"Anyway," Bobby said in an "I'm changing the subject" kind of way.

"What are we going to do?"

"Well, we're not going together. That's for sure. We'd kill each other within an hour."

"Within a minute."

"Stop arguing with me."

"I'm not! I'm agreeing with you."

"Fine. Whatever," Bobby huffed.

The sun was setting, and Winter had fresh mosquito bites on her arms and legs. They had always been especially drawn to her for whatever reason. Her doctor told her eating a lot of garlic and onions would help, but he would have known that wasn't an issue if he had ever tried Korean food.

"Soonhee-yah, come help me. Daeseong-ah, you too," Halmeoni called from the door.

Winter threw up a peace sign at Bobby and headed inside. He immediately came following after her like a lost puppy. His shadow obscured hers in the doorway. Halmeoni instructed them to set up the room for the weekly bingo game. It was going to start soon, and the seniors were already filing in.

Halmeoni pointed to the supply closet where the spinning bingo apparatus that held the balls was stored. The bingo cage alone might not have been so horrible to move, but because it was connected to a clunky cart, it had to be maneuvered by at least two people. Together, Winter and Bobby rolled the bingo cage out of the closet. They had to stop when it caught on the door threshold. Instead of redirecting it, Winter pushed it harder, which made it jump up over the threshold and roll over Bobby's foot. He cursed loudly, drawing the attention of several elderly ladies who were probably mentally adding his name to the tops of their Sunday prayer lists. Winter wanted to make fun of him further, but he did such a great job of embarrassing himself all on his own.

They parked the cart next to the stage by the windows, then went to set out the food on the tables in the back. They were mostly things you could get at Costco in bulk, such as a thousand cookies in an impossible-to-open plastic container and a punch bowl that had been filled with a sugar-free powdered drink that tasted a lot like cold medicine.

Winter watched Bobby lay out the napkins in perfect little piles. He looked too pleased with himself, so she took the top napkins off each stack and folded them into origami bunnies. Bobby scoffed. He attempted to fold his napkins as well, but he didn't know how to do origami and ended up turning them into wads of nothing. He threw his failed attempts in the garbage can, and Winter smiled to herself.

"Soon-hee, Dae-seong. Come here," Halmeoni said in a tone that made Winter feel like she was in trouble. The two of them walked over, shoulders hunched.

"Yes, Halmeoni?" they said in unison.

"You disappoint me."

Winter and Bobby didn't have much in common, but the one thing they knew they did was that they didn't like to disappoint.

"Did we do something wrong?" Winter asked. She had never been in any real trouble before. She didn't know what to expect. Her worst infraction to date had been the time her parents invited their church's pastor to dinner, and when asked about what she was learning in school, she used the term "galactic bulge" one too many times. Umma and Appa grounded her for approximately twelve minutes before feeling bad and calling it off.

Bobby's mouth dropped open. "Is it the napkins? I can learn how to fold them."

"No, Dae-seong. It's you," Halmeoni replied. Bobby's eyes got wide. "It's both of you. You both are so young, and you're here, at a senior center, on summer vacation, setting up for bingo."

"I like visiting you, Halmeoni," Winter said.

"I know you do. And I love that you do. But when I was your age, do you know what I would have done on a trip without my parents? Who cares who you go with?" Halmeoni's mouth curled into a dark smile. "Why do you think your parents let you do this?"

"Because our parents trust us," Bobby said.

"Yes, and you know why?" Halmeoni raised her hand to the two confused teenagers, not letting them answer. "Because they know you will try not to have fun. You only care about school. You are already the best. Try to be something else."

"Like what?" Winter asked.

"Kids."

"Why didn't you say all this *before* we set up the room?"

"Because my back was killing me," Halmeoni said. "Break a few rules. Your parents trust you. Take advantage of opportunities, as I just did."

"We would only be visiting colleges," Winter said.

Halmeoni clicked her tongue. "You have no imagination." She looked around at the nearly full room. "Now it's bingo time, so I have to go. Stay or leave. That's your choice. But our games get intense."

Winter snorted. "Intense? What, do you put money on it?"

Halmeoni smiled.

"Wait, how much?"

"Enough. We put money in, and whoever wins gets the pot."

"You gamble in here?" Bobby asked. "Do you have a permit for that?"

"Our age is the permit."

Bobby was such a stickler for the rules. He was probably going to leave the center and head right over to the police station to report them all. Winter rolled her eyes.

"How much money do you guys put in?" Winter asked her grand-mother. "Like, five bucks?"

Halmeoni shook her head.

"Twenty?"

"It's a one-hundred-dollar buy-in," Halmeoni conceded.

The teenagers' mouths nearly hit the floor.

Bobby mentally counted all the seniors in the room with their bingo boards and markers. "Halmeoni, there are, like, fifty people in this room. That's a lot of money."

"I know," Halmeoni replied. "You have to break rules once in a while." She smiled sweetly. "I have to host my event. If you want to stay, that's fine, but you should do something fun. It's Friday night."

Halmeoni had a beaded bag that hung from her shoulder by a thin, twisted cord. It was very chic. She popped open the clasp, pulled out her equally sparkly wallet, and handed Winter forty dollars. She then walked away without saying another word.

"Did she just wink at us?" Bobby asked.

"What the hell just happened?" Winter looked down at the money in her hand. "And what the hell am I supposed to do with this?"

The two of them sort of wanted to stay, but they feared the judgment they would receive from Halmeoni. Bobby offered Winter a ride home. She knew it was only because it was the gentlemanly thing to do, not because he cared if Winter got eaten by a coyote if she walked.

They sat in the parking lot in silence for a while, watching the seniors pop bottles of champagne, whooping and hollering every time a number or a letter was called. The teenagers couldn't hear anything, but it looked like Halmeoni's neighbor, Mr. Joe, was about to hit someone with his cane for cheating. Halmeoni was right; they did get intense during bingo.

"I'm so confused," Bobby said.

For once, Winter Park agreed with Bobby Bae.

"Me too. Just drive. We need to talk."

Winter buckled up, and Bobby pulled out of the parking lot to get on the main road toward her house. They were quiet and awkward next to each other, upset that something had happened that they were supposed to bond over. They didn't want to bond. That was Bobby's entire reason for going to see Winter in the first place.

The sky was pink and red as the sun finally set behind the trees. It gave a little reprieve from the heat, but it was still excruciatingly hot. Winter felt like her skin was boiling, which was worsened by all the mosquito bites she couldn't help but scratch.

"Can you please stop that?" Bobby asked, his face pinched and judgmental.

Winter scratched harder. "No, I'm so itchy, and it's all your fault."

"*My* fault? You're the one who asked me to go outside."

"I know. Shut up." She made an effort to stop scratching but quickly gave in. She spotted the Village Park to their right. She pointed to the parking lot and said, "Stop there."

"The park is closed. We'll get in trouble."

"It's open for another fifteen minutes. We just need to stop somewhere for a second so we can discuss the logistics of this trip. Halmeoni is right; we've never done a bad thing a day in our lives."

Bobby looked offended. "Speak for yourself."

Winter gave him a side-eye. "You have never broken a rule, Bobby Bae." She pointed at the speedometer. "Look, you're going exactly the speed limit. There's literally nobody around."

Bobby lightly tapped the gas and went one mile per hour over the limit. "There."

Winter put her hands up in false surrender. "I'm mistaken, you're such a badass. Now pull into the park." She added a *please* when Bobby didn't immediately do it.

Bobby pulled into the parking lot and cut the engine. They were right in front of the basketball courts and the picnic area. The park was completely empty, but there was evidence that people had just left, probably because of the mosquitoes. The trash cans were stuffed to the brims with the remnants of picnics and cookouts.

Winter often walked past this park to admire the stars at night. Since she was a little girl, she dressed up as famous astronauts instead of princesses. When she was a kid, her uncle gave her a gigantic LEGO castle set. She used it to make a life-sized replica of the Mars rover instead, which sparked her lifelong love affair with robotics. There was something almost spiritual about the vastness and unknowability of space. It was the perfect marriage between science and poetry, messiness and order, everything and nothing at all. Winter delighted in knowing that she was a small part of that chemistry.

She looked up at the sky. It was too cloudy for stars. *Figures*, she thought to herself. That had to have been Bobby Bae's fault too.

"What kind of rules are you trying to break?" Bobby asked. "I'll tell you for certain I am not going to start some kind of underground gambling ring like Halmeoni." He flipped his hair out of his eyes. "You always try to one-up me. You're probably going to go straight for, like, a Ponzi scheme or something."

Winter eyed Bobby and then looked out over the deserted park with miles and miles of woods. "Or maybe I'll plan the perfect murder."

"You and your mysteries."

Winter ignored him. "Maybe we don't have to commit felonies. We could just do typical rebellious teenager stuff. We could maybe go to a college party or something. I've never drank before. Have you?"

"No, I haven't."

"Let's do that, I guess. And . . . I don't know what else."

Winter knew that her uncle had given Bobby a shot of soju at one of their shared family dinners once, and she appreciated that he didn't bring it up.

Bobby was thoughtful for a moment. "Well, if we do this trip together—and I'm not saying that I've invited you yet, but if we do— why don't we do stuff we've always wanted to do? They don't really have to be bad or illegal things."

Winter's ears perked up. "Like a bucket list?"

"Yeah, I mean, is there anything you never got a chance to do?"

Winter thought for a moment. "I've always wanted to play chess outside, like on one of those chess tables that are in parks sometimes. That seems really relaxing."

"Like Magneto and Professor X?"

"Uh . . . yeah?" Winter said, not sure of why she'd even said that. "What about you?"

"I've always wanted to try a Philly cheesesteak. I put UPenn on the tentative itinerary."

Winter grimaced. "Because you're lactose intolerant? Halmeoni was right. We *are* boring. Let's just make some ground rules for our trip and call it a day. I think the *how* is more important than the *what* anyway."

"You want us to make rules for our rule breaking?" Bobby asked. "I still haven't agreed to let you come with me."

"What else are you going to do, go alone? Or go with your non-girlfriend girlfriend? Just give me some paper. I know you have a notebook in your pocket."

"Or am I just happy to see you?" Bobby shook his head. "I'm so sorry. My father's perverse sense of humor is rubbing off."

Winter raised her eyebrows. "Rule number one is clearly 'No making jokes.'"

Bobby feigned being wounded. "I guess a few Geneva Conventions couldn't hurt."

He opened the center console and took out an engraved leather-bound notebook, which was more of a leather sleeve with several small notebooks inside. His parents had given it to him when he started high school, and it appeared he'd replaced the notebooks inside several times since then. They'd given Winter one too, but she lost it somewhere in her room about a week after receiving it.

Winter grabbed for the notebook, but Bobby yanked it out of her grasp.

Bobby pursed his lips. "Please don't touch it."

"What's with you and notebooks anyway?"

He was constantly writing things down. She didn't know what exactly. Every time she got close enough, he snapped it shut. Because of him, she knew what A6s were and had actually picked up his penchant for sugarcane paper. There were fandoms for everything, but this was by far the most random one Winter had ever heard of.

"Are you genuinely asking, or are you just trying to make fun of me?" Bobby asked.

"I'm genuinely asking."

Winter was willing to listen to anyone talk about anything so long as they were knowledgeable about it. And she did want to know what it was that Bobby was writing all the time. She didn't take him for a diary person. Bobby never did anything worth writing about. If it were a diary, it would probably have been planning its escape from Bobby the moment he first wrote, "Dear Diary."

Bobby hugged the notebook to his chest. "There's something very classic about pen and paper. A6s are my favorite because they fit in my pocket. I have a few for jotting down random notes, as well as a planner and bullet journal in here. I also enjoy a good Japanese-made pen. When you write old-school, you can't get hacked in the cloud."

Winter had no idea what sort of private thoughts Bobby Bae could have written in there that would make him concerned about getting hacked in the cloud. She regretted asking. Now she was imagining him scribbling manifestos.

They contemplated each other for a moment. That was probably the most civil exchange they had ever shared. Winter thought about continuing it or perhaps calling him a nerd and moving on, but Bobby was right, the park was closing soon, and she didn't want to get in trouble for being there after-hours.

Bobby turned to a clean page in his notebook. Winter tried to see what was written on the other pages as he flipped through it, but she couldn't. She thought she saw a few pages covered in Hangul, but he was flipping too fast for her to know for certain.

They took turns jotting down whatever rules came to mind in the few minutes before the park closed. The scratching of pen and paper was the only sound to be heard in the car. Winter became self-conscious of her breathing and tried her best not to disturb the silence. With two minutes to spare, they leaned back to inspect what each had written.

Winter's contributions included: *We will not abuse moratoriums, we will stay out of each other's business, we will not tell anyone details about our trip.* She scanned Bobby's additions. Most of what he wrote was acceptable: *We will respect the itinerary, we will not discuss personal matters, we will prioritize college visits.* Though, there were a few he crammed in at the end that gave her pause.

"Why did you write, 'No venting about your girlfriend'?" Bobby asked. "I wouldn't do that with you."

"Why did *you* write down, 'No physical contact'?" Winter replied, answering his question with a question. "*I* wouldn't do that with *you*."

"I'm trying to be respectful of Jacqueline."

Winter's witty comeback caught in her throat, and her cheeks went hot. The fact that he felt the need to put that in writing struck her as odd. Who was he worried about lacking restraint: Her or himself? She looked sideways at him, and he mindlessly licked his lips, his focus still on the list in her hands. Her face went hotter. Physical contact could mean a punch in the face. *I'm probably overthinking it,* she thought.

"Why did you—? Maybe this was a stupid idea. Let's just forget it," Winter said. She slammed the notebook shut and thrust it back at Bobby.

"You're giving me whiplash, Park. Do you want to come with me or not?"

"I . . . I don't want to do anything to offend Jacqueline. I'll take a virtual tour of the colleges or something."

Bobby shook his head and let out a long breath. "You're probably right. This would be bad optics."

He stashed his notebook in the console and pulled out of the park in time for it to close. He drove a few more blocks to Winter's house. They both knew Winter's parents would be watching from the window, so he got out and opened Winter's door for her. He then waved at the house, and once Winter was safely inside, he drove off.

♥

Bobby Bae

Bobby was distracted as he drove home. Something Winter had said had resonated with him. It wasn't anything to do with breaking rules; he knew he never had and probably never would. Doing anything wrong even for a second gave him severe anxiety. When he was seven, his mom had a pair of ornate vases she'd brought from Korea. Bobby accidentally knocked one over and cracked it. He turned the crack toward the wall so no one could see it, and it was like that for approximately two hours before Bobby snitched on himself. His mother was so impressed with his honesty that he didn't get in trouble and was instead rewarded with a new skin for whatever game he was playing at the time. He had been chasing that high ever since.

The thing that was bothering him was what Winter had said about Jacqueline Charlotte Turner.

Bobby called Jacqueline over Bluetooth. She didn't answer the first time. Or the second time. She answered on the third try. "Sorry, Bae. I'm hanging out at Carly Bishop's house. What's up?" she said.

He rolled his eyes. She knew that he knew that she and Carly Bishop weren't friends. The only reason anyone ever went to Carly Bishop's house was because her parents never noticed when bottles went missing from their extensive collection of liquor.

Bobby cleared his throat. "I wanted to see if you wanted to hang out. We haven't seen each other in a while."

"Uh . . . sure, you can pick me up now."

"Okay, I'm nearby. I'll see you in a few minutes."

The Bluetooth disconnected, and Bobby smiled to himself. Being able to prove Winter wrong put him in a good mood, although the drive to Carly Bishop's house threatened to ruin it. He didn't much believe in the supernatural, but if werewolves existed, he'd bet any future scholarship money that they lived along the dark, twisty roads it took to get to her house. The crickets screeched into the night, giving the summer its melody, and the yellow light of the streetlamps exposed thousands of swarming gnats.

When he finally pulled up to the dimly lit house, Jacqueline was standing outside trying to figure out how to put her crossbody bag over her head without letting go of her phone. Her usually kempt ash-blonde hair was suffering from whatever she'd put it through that night as it hung in several different curl patterns around her face.

Bobby put the car in park and ran around to open her door, but Jacqueline had already gotten in. He pretended like he was playing a game of chicken and ran right back around to the driver's seat, jumping in smoothly and refastening his seat belt in one continuous motion. He leaned over to give Jacqueline a kiss, but she turned her head.

"I've been drinking," she said simply. Her voice wasn't as commanding and robust as usual, and her eyes were half-closed. "Actually, no. Motion to strike. I had three drinks."

Bobby reached over her into the glove box and retrieved a spare contact lens case and solution. She popped out her contacts as Bobby drove off.

"Did you have fun?" he asked.

"Mm-hmm."

"Do you want to find somewhere to look at the stars? It's a nice night tonight."

Jacqueline leaned her head against the window. "It's cloudy, don't you think? And you're slouching, Bae."

Bobby stiffened. "Ice cream, then?"

"May I remind you that you're lactose intolerant?"

"Italian ice?"

"I'm tired, Bobby. Would you be angry with me if I asked you to take me home?"

So what makes you think you're dating? Winter's judgmental voice filled Bobby's ears. He could imagine what her smug face would look like if she were there. Bobby chewed on the inside of his cheek. Imagining her while he was already agitated wound him up further, and he was afraid he'd say something to Jacqueline he'd regret. He debated simply asking what was wrong, but if he did that, she might actually tell him.

Bobby sighed in defeat and silently took Jacqueline home. When they arrived, he didn't get out of the car. He didn't open her door. He didn't even try to kiss her good night. Jacqueline didn't seem to mind. She grabbed her things and left, blowing a kiss at Bobby before she slammed the front door behind her. Through the windows, he watched each room light up and go dark as Jacqueline made her way through the house to her bedroom.

"I should have walked her to her door," Bobby muttered to himself.

The palms of his hands tingled, and he gripped the steering wheel tightly, trying to distract himself from the sensation. Heat crept up his body and into his face, and he suddenly felt stifled by his own clothing. He yanked his tucked-in shirt from his waistband and cranked the air conditioner to its highest setting. With his eyes closed, he took in several deep breaths until he felt well enough to drive.

When Bobby got home, his parents were already asleep, so he quietly snuck into his room and gently closed the door behind him. If he slammed it too hard, it made all the medals and trophies he had on his walls rattle. He didn't want to wake his parents, who worked in . . . maybe finance or some kind of consulting? Bobby wasn't absolutely sure what his parents did for money, and it was embarrassing to ask at this point, but he did know they woke up very early. At the very least he knew his mother worked around lawyers but wasn't one herself.

In the bathroom he stared long and hard at his reflection in the mirror. He hadn't had a panic attack in several years, but he remembered that when he was younger, sometimes he almost wouldn't recognize his own face afterward. He would whisper his name over and over while looking in the mirror until he knew himself again.

Bobby lathered his face with cleanser, then violently scrubbed it off, eager to get back to his reflection. "Bae Dae-seong, Bae Dae-seong, Bae Dae-seong. Robert Dae-seong Bae Jr.," he muttered, before slapping toner onto his face and finishing the rest of his before-bed routine. All the while, his phone stared at him from the bathroom counter.

There was a nagging voice in the back of his head telling him he'd handled the night entirely wrong. It wasn't lost on him that the voice sounded a lot like Winter Park. He finally gave in to its taunting and texted Jacqueline Charlotte Turner.

Bobby: Hey, Jack. What was that earlier?

He saw the three bouncing dots of death appear and then go away. His breath caught when they reappeared, but then they were gone again. He shook his head at his impatience. He then slid down the bottom of his bed onto the floor and flicked his PlayStation on so he could therapy-play Mortal Kombat.

After nearly an hour of this, Jacqueline finally replied.

> **Jacqueline:** I'm sorry. I was just tired and maybe slightly inebriated.

Are we still dating? Bobby typed out, then erased.

> **Bobby:** Are we okay?

> **Jacqueline:** Where is this line of questioning coming from?

> **Bobby:** Could you answer me, please?

She replied instantly.

> **Jacqueline:** Bobby, I really like you but...

Bobby started to sweat. Who ended a text message on a "but"? The bouncing dots were taunting him. He gripped his phone tightly and didn't even care that he was losing his game, which was still playing in the background. It offered a nice upbeat soundtrack to his impending heartbreak.

> **Jacqueline:** I don't think we have a single thing in common anymore.

Bobby and Jacqueline originally belonged to a bigger group of friends when they were in junior high, but friendship at that age when everyone is discovering themselves and building their personalities is strange. You would go away for winter break or summer vacation one year, and when you came back, it was a toss-up whether you would resume those friendships or never speak to one another again. A few cycles of this happened until Bobby and Jacqueline were the only two left. They sat next to each other in math class, and Bobby would hold the door open for her every single day and walk her to her next class even though his was in the opposite wing. In sophomore year of high school, she asked him out, and they'd been together ever since.

Although he didn't want to, Bobby couldn't help but agree. They really didn't have anything in common. They probably never had. She'd spent her evening at a party, and he'd spent his at a senior center. Still, that didn't mean they couldn't be together. At least to him.

Bobby: So you have been avoiding me.

Jacqueline: I don't think that accurately depicts the situation.

Jacqueline: And why didn't you make these feelings known earlier? We just saw each other. That's the problem with you, Bobby. You indebt people to you by acting so nice, like everything is perfect all the time. I've been trying to get you to argue with me for months, and this is the first time you've said anything at all.

> **Bobby:** You've been mistreating me on purpose to see what I'd do? That's cruel, Jack.

> **Jacqueline:** Look how long it took you to say something. Honestly, I thought things would fizzle out and we wouldn't have to suffer a formal breakup.

Sitting on the floor made his back ache, but Bobby was rooted to the spot. He considered requesting a probationary period so she could reassess the relationship and revisit the conversation at a later time, but Jacqueline was probably still drunk and wouldn't care. A million terrible things to say raced through his head. He wanted to say all of them to Jacqueline Charlotte Turner, but what he settled on was:

> **Bobby:** Thank you for letting me know. Enjoy your summer.

That was brief, he thought to himself. He'd never been broken up with before, but that seemed excruciatingly short-winded. Most breakups were novels, but this one was a tweet.

He untucked the sheets and blanket from the bottom of his bed and crawled into the center, where he settled into a little ball and cried. He didn't like to admit it, and people rarely saw it, but it didn't take very much to get a tear or two out of Bobby Bae. A birthday card was enough, as was any video online that had to do with injured animals or people reuniting after having been separated for almost any reason, and he could no longer watch singing competition shows because the sob stories of the contestants made him do just that. Most embarrassingly, he couldn't watch *Star Wars* without breaking into a full-out ugly cry every time Luke looked out over the Tatooine desert at the two suns with his theme song playing in the background. As soon as the horns dropped out and the string section swelled, Bobby Bae would completely lose it.

Bobby stayed like that for a little while, wiping his tears with the back of his hand. He opened up his phone and looked at his text exchange with Jacqueline. *She's kind of an asshole,* Bobby thought. *Who breaks up with someone over text?*

He kicked off his blanket and looked at his awards wall. He always wanted to be the best at everything, and that included being the best boyfriend. And Jacqueline had seemed to genuinely like him—at least at first. She could be pushy at times, but she was one of the smartest people he knew. They made sense together. They looked great together in the yearbook.

Bobby smacked himself internally for being so boringly superficial. He wasn't even sure that he had ever liked her back. Maybe *he* was the asshole.

"Bae Dae-seong, Bae Dae-seong, Bae Dae-seong. Robert Dae-seong Bae Jr.," he whispered to himself, thankful that another wave of what hit him earlier didn't get him again. "You need to stop pretending you're good, Bobby Bae."

He covered himself back up, and before he went to sleep, he sent one more text. To Winter this time.

> **Bobby:** Jacqueline and I broke up. If you still want to break some rules, I'm in.

♡

Winter Park

5. WE WILL NOT DISCUSS EACH OTHER WITH OUR FRIENDS AND FAMILY

Winter wasn't much of a packer. Her family rarely went anywhere except Korea every few years, but Winter always deliberately under-packed a too-big suitcase so she could fill it with sweaters there and bring them back.

Winter lounged on her bed, completely devoted to a letter she'd received that morning, as her mother balled up socks and folded pants for her.

"You won an award. Why are you moping?" Umma asked.

"Because it's a recognition award for being a girl in robotics. It's meaningless."

"It's all meaningless when you get as many awards as you do."

Winter scowled. "I'm serious. Brandon Long was given an intern-ship. They didn't think that the only girl on the team could benefit from an internship? Brandon and I are partners. It's not like he out-performed me. But I only get a letter, and he gets an internship?" She put the paper over her face and blew it up into the air before watching it float gently to the floor.

Umma retrieved the paper and placed it on the dresser. "You asked me to help you pack," she said. "Why am I doing everything?"

"Because you're good at it." Winter hopped to her feet, opened her dresser drawer, and grabbed all the T-shirts on top, tossing them recklessly into her bag.

Umma took the shirts out and refolded them. "Sit down," she said, and Winter threw herself back onto the bed. "Stop complaining about winning awards and focus on your trip. I got lunch with Mrs. Bae yesterday, and she told me Bobby has been very down since his girlfriend broke up with him."

"Really? I didn't even think he liked her."

"You two haven't spoken?"

The only time they communicated since Bobby said he was "in" was when he sent Winter an itinerary and told her he'd allotted fifteen minutes in total for bathroom stops. She chose which rest stops she wanted and then sent the doc back, having changed the font to Papyrus to annoy him.

Winter rolled over onto her stomach and played with some fibers on the carpet. "You don't think he's going to be annoying, do you? He's probably going to cry the whole time."

"It's normal for a young man to cry."

"Not as much as he does."

Umma sucked her teeth. "Well, then, make it your job to cheer him up."

"My job? I don't remember putting in an application for that, but it'll probably be the only job I get since I haven't completed any internships."

"He's a very nice boy."

"So you keep saying. What does that even mean?"

"It means he's available now," she replied, as if that answered her question. "Bobby is smart and handsome. If you both go to Harvard or MIT, then you—"

"Please don't finish that. I'm not dating Bobby Bae. Not now. Not ever."

"Mind your tone, Soon-hee."

Winter hid her face and mouthed all the things she would say to her mother if she wasn't such a good daughter. Umma brought up her dating Bobby all the time as if he were the only "nice boy" from a good Korean family in the world. Winter didn't understand why they moved to a town with barely any Koreans if Umma wanted her to marry one so badly. Or maybe she didn't know she wanted that until she saw Bobby and was seduced by his man-bangs and lack of a personality. Now it seemed to be her life's mission to unite the Parks and Baes by marriage.

"Umma?" Winter asked. "What if I never date anyone?"

Her mother looked up from the suitcase. "Why don't you want to date?"

"I'm not saying I don't want to. I'm saying what if I never do? I want to accomplish so much, and I don't want to be distracted or not taken seriously. Being a successful woman is lonely. I should get used to the idea now."

Umma went back to folding. "I'm a doctor, you know, Winter. I may not be a NASA scientist, but I did go to medical school and still managed to marry your father."

Winter didn't want to share a career with her husband like her mother did. Perhaps Winter was a product of the idealism of her generation, but she wanted something that was only hers. Umma must have sensed her dissatisfaction with that answer, so she said, "Angela Merkel has a partner, and she's one of the most powerful women in the world. She probably got her fair share of recognition awards too."

"Her husband is a quantum chemist. What are the chances I get a quantum chemist to fall in love with me?" Winter asked, her eyes narrowed. "My personality is sort of an acquired taste."

"Your personality tastes fine. You will find someone one day," Umma snapped. "You young people only want butterflies in your stomachs. But butterflies don't help you through hard times. When you have your career, you're going to want a partner."

Winter sat up. "But what makes you think that person has to be Bobby Bae?"

Umma frowned. "You may or may not like Bobby one day, but if you don't give people a chance, you will never like anyone. I don't know why you're so determined to be alone."

The closest Winter had ever come to having a proper crush was in the tenth grade with the new kid, Anthony Nichols. He sat behind Winter in band, and it quickly became evident that he didn't know the meaning of *pianissimo*. And despite her hesitancy, she was roped in to a double date with him; her stand partner, Lucy; and Lucy's boyfriend, James. Anthony was way too loud in class and way too loud in life. He talked through the entire movie and then didn't ask for Winter's consent before stealing her first kiss. She swore never to date again unless she met someone who was worth attaching her name to, and Lucy became her *former* stand partner.

Winter often fantasized about having a love like Ann Druyan and Carl Sagan's. They worked together to send a golden record into space with sounds and images from Earth in case some alien neighbors happened to find it and were curious about what humans were all about. It included people speaking in over fifty languages; the sounds of whales and birds; music, including jazz and classical; and a recording of the brain waves of a woman in love—Ann Druyan. She'd proposed to Carl Sagan only days before, and their love was immortalized on that gold disk, which was designed to last over a billion years. Winter couldn't imagine Anthony or anyone being able to give her that.

Winter gave her mother a hug and then shut the suitcase before Umma packed her bed too.

"People are different when they're away from home, Soon-hee," Umma said. "I think you'll have fun with Bobby."

"Yeah, maybe."

Once Umma left the room, Winter got comfortable among the plushies on her bed. She lay down for a long while, staring at her copy of *Jamaica Inn*. She had only read the blurb on the back even though she and Emmy had chosen it for book club in March. When she opened the book, her note cards from AP Bio fell from where she'd hidden them. She could feel Bobby's eyes on her at lunch sometimes, willing her to fail with his mind, so she studied while pretending to read.

Winter threw the note cards and book onto the floor and video-called Emmy. Winter was surprised Emmy answered. They'd been playing an elaborate game of phone tag all summer.

Emmy took a second to adjust herself in the camera, giving Winter a moment to admire her friend. Emmy was the main charac-ter of her own life. She was strong and athletic from years of training in contemporary dance. She often forewent real clothes, choosing to remain in her black or nude leotards with jeans or flowy skirts on top. Emmy's mother left when she was a baby, so she spent most of the time with her dad, save for the summers she stayed with Năi Nai. Yet, it didn't stop Emmy from being the girlier of the two, having learned to mother herself at an early age with a uniquely feminine protectiveness that she extended to Winter, who she viewed as a little sister despite Winter being a few months older.

Emmy poked out her lips and threw her long, perfectly straight ponytail over her shoulder before asking, "How's my favorite unnie?"

It was nice to see Emmy in a good mood. Talking to her lately made Winter feel like she was walking on eggshells. Winter wasn't quite sure how to meet her friend at these feelings, and sometimes she opted to keep things light. Occasionally it worked. Other times it backfired. She took a chance.

"Anxious," Winter replied. "I'm going on a college-visit road trip with your least favorite oppa, Bobby."

"Stop it," Emmy said, the corners of her mouth slowly turning upward. "You're not serious. Is his girlfriend okay with that?"

"Why does everyone assume she wouldn't be okay with it?" Winter retorted. "And it doesn't matter anyhow. They broke up, and apparently he's taking it hard. I'm going to have to deal with his moping all week, and Umma says I have to try to cheer him up."

"You can ask him to get ramyun," Emmy replied, running her tongue over her teeth.

"Gross. No. Never. Please stop."

Emmy shrugged. "The only way to get over someone is to get with someone else."

With a snort, Winter said, "Getting his first girlfriend was a fluke. You want me to find him a second one?" Emmy looked at her like she had a million heads. "What is that face for?"

"I know this is going to be painful for you to hear, but it wouldn't be that hard. Bobby is hot."

Winter's face scrunched up in confusion, and she feared it would stay like that forever if somebody didn't clue her into what the hell Emmy was talking about. Maybe she was coming down with that disease where people can't see faces. Face blindness. Either that or she was really into guys who looked like car-dealership air dancers

44

whose best chances at getting tans were from the blue light emitted from computer screens.

"You're kidding, right?" Winter asked.

Emmy laughed. "Bobby kind of sucks, but he's a beautiful Asian man. Plus he's going to be, like, the next Warren Buffett or something."

Winter looked all around her to see if anybody else had stepped into the twilight zone she was currently in. "But you . . . okay, no. I'm not helping him find another girlfriend. And I thought you were on my side! You can't in good conscience be calling him hot in front of me."

"Okay, whatever. All I'm saying is that he has a hot girlfriend."

"Bobby *had* a hot girlfriend," Winter corrected.

Now that Winter thought about it, Jacqueline Charlotte Turner was one of the prettiest girls in their grade. But she'd always assumed Jacqueline had had a serious lapse in judgment that lasted for . . . a year and a half. There had to have been more to this. Winter wanted to write a think piece: "Is Bobby Bae Hot? An Investigation."

"Did you think Bobby was hot this whole time and you never told me?" Winter asked.

"You would have burned me at the stake!"

"Of course I would have, you witch!"

Emmy snorted. "Look, Winnie. I never wanted to tell you this, but I had a gigantic crush on Bobby when we were kids."

Winter's shoulders sagged. "So all those times you were making fun of him with me?"

"Desperately in love," Emmy admitted. She applied a clear gloss to her lips, considered her reflection for a moment, then wiped it off with the back of her hand. "I even drew Punnett squares in my journal to see what our kids would look like. Spoiler alert: They would have had black hair and brown eyes."

"I feel like I don't know you anymore. Like, why do you keep adjusting yourself? And are you putting on makeup? Do you even still like *Cosmos*?! Or board games?"

Emmy's smile disappeared.

"It's possible to enjoy all those things at once, you know," Emmy said, annoyance in her voice. "Anyway, why don't you come over to Năi Nai's? We can go for a walk or something."

"I just got into bed. Can you come over here? We can watch a dumb movie and be lazy together," Winter replied.

Emmy got suddenly serious. "I always come to you. Just come over here. I want to talk to you about something."

Winter felt the eggshells under her feet again.

"Is everything okay?" she asked.

"Yeah. Everything is fine. But we should talk in person."

"Okay, I'll see you in a few, then," Winter said, and hung up.

The synapses were firing in Winter's brain, but they weren't making any connections. What could Emmy possibly need to talk about in person? Ninety percent of their friendship happened over the phone.

Winter walked down the community center path toward Năi Nai's old condo. Emmy was sitting on the edge of the open patio, waiting for her. She had on one of her customary leotards, nude this time, and her shoulder was bound in neon green athletic tape. She must have been in the dance studio that day.

Winter took a seat next to her best friend, and they let the awkwardness linger in the air for a moment.

Winter felt small under the canopy of the evening sky. Stars appeared, seemingly one by one, twinkling, daring the next one to shine brighter. Lightning bugs also slowly made themselves known. They burst into flashes of light, then disappeared, adding magic to the community courtyard lined with trees that were only silhouettes against the recently set sun.

"How is your dad?" Winter asked finally.

"I'm used to seeing him grieve, but it's different this time. Năi Nai can't come back, and I think a part of him has always thought my mom might. He seems a little better every day, though," Emmy replied. "Maybe once we get out of here and aren't living in a shrine of his mother's stuff, he'll be able to grieve properly."

Winter winced at Emmy's eagerness to leave her behind.

"So are you going to tell me what's up?" Winter asked. "What's with the lip gloss and the clandestine meeting?"

Emmy averted her gaze. "I was going to wait to tell you, but a scout at a modeling agency saw some of my dancing videos and wants to sign me, so I'm going to Raleigh soon to get some headshots taken. If this works out, I might try to move to Milan or maybe Paris after I graduate."

Winter froze. "I don't understand any of those words. What about college?"

Emmy sat back and folded her arms. "School is your thing. It's never been mine. This could be *my* MIT."

In truth, Winter could see Emmy as a model. She had all the stillness of a ballerina but the fire of a performer. Emmy was effortlessly pretty, charismatic, and one of the most talented people Winter knew. This just went against everything she had always imagined for their future together.

"Your dad is okay with this?" Winter asked.

"Surprisingly, yes. He just wants me to be happy."

Winter scoffed. "Since when?"

Winter knew, of course, that not all people went to college. She understood that skipping college wasn't inherently bad. But it was what was supposed to happen after high school. She and Emmy had heard this since before they could speak. Winter had a hard time believing the memo had only resonated with her.

Emmy waved her hands in front of Winter's face, and she came to.

"Sorry, you're dumping a lot of information on me. I'm still stuck on the Punnett squares," Winter said. "I'm happy for you, though, Em. This is incredible."

When Winter skipped eighth grade, she left behind all her friends and was never able to recover from the loss. She kept her head down for a year, waiting for her friends to join her in high school. However, when they did, they were all so different, and Winter felt like she was on the outside of an inside. Her visits to Halmeoni increased, she and Emmy became closer over the phone, and she threw herself into schoolwork.

She knew she couldn't take Halmeoni to college with her, but she thought that at least Emmy would be by her side, something that had only ever happened in short bytes for the entirety of their friendship. There were so many things she wanted to do with Emmy in Boston, like shop on Newbury Street, visit the Harvard Museum of Natural History, and drink tea by the harbor. With Emmy so far away, their friendship could only remain as strong as the Wi-Fi signal.

The entire four years played out in Winter's head like a movie. She imagined riding tandem bikes alone, intertwining her own arms together with ice-cream cones in each hand, and looking longingly at empty chairs. The loneliness she had always felt in Emmy's absence was only tolerable because she thought there was an end to it. But now it seemed it would be permanent. Real.

"Are you sure you're not mad, though?" Emmy asked. "You'll be okay in Boston without me? Because I'll hop on a plane if any of those little STEM boys steps out of line."

"I'm just a little bummed. I thought this was our chance to finally live in the same city," Winter admitted, resting her head on Emmy's shoulder. "We've always talked about how we'd be Halmeoni and Nǎi Nai one day. I don't see how that's possible if we're never together and never on the same page. Is this why you didn't want to visit MIT? Is it because you always knew you weren't going to college with me?"

Emmy took a deep breath, and Winter's head rose and fell with it. "Win, I've never expressed any interest in going to college or even coming back to the States for that matter."

"Why didn't you say anything?"

"I did. But you always told me I was having cold feet," Emmy replied. They sat, embracing, in silence for a moment, watching the sky darken and more lightning bugs flicker in the distance.

"Are you absolutely sure this is what you want to do?" Winter asked.

"No, but it's the only thing I've been excited about since Nǎi Nai."

Winter was speechless for a moment. When Winter's grandfather died, all the adults in her life were so sad and treated Winter like she was sad as well. At the funeral, Winter held on to her father's pant leg and looked up at all the somber faces. The only time anyone met her at her level was when they knelt into deep bows. She had no idea what was going on. She'd seen Harabeoji only a week before, maybe even a few days. And then soon after, Halmeoni packed up the house and moved into the senior community. Sitting on a curb alone, Winter watched boxes of Halmeoni's stuff, and only Halmeoni's stuff, enter the apartment. Winter felt like she should search for Harabeoji but didn't know where. That's when Emmy came along, offering Winter a chocolate-dipped biscuit stick. Together, they ate Pocky and looked for Harabeoji until the streetlights turned on. Even though the girls were only six, Emmy somehow knew what Winter needed in that moment; she needed to see for herself that Harabeoji wasn't anywhere Winter could find him so she could finally understand the sadness around her. With it being her turn to be there for Emmy, Winter didn't even know what to say. Everything she could think of was either too morbid or too cliché.

Winter looked out over the apartment complex, which used to seem so much bigger when she and Emmy were small. Now that she was soon off to college and leaving her childhood and her home behind, the world was growing too large too quickly. She feared this place she used to believe was her universe would shrink into nothingness. She was desperate to cling to the memories the two had created here.

"Do you remember how Nǎi Nai used to have us step on her back when we were really little?" Winter asked.

Emmy laughed. "Yeah, and she'd bring us a new snack every ten minutes."

"But then she'd pinch the fat around my ribs. She didn't know a lot of English, but she did know the word 'chubby.'" Both girls giggled at the hypocrisy. "I really miss her," Winter said.

"Yeah, me too."

"I'm going to miss you too."

"Nothing is going to change," Emmy said, but by her tone, Winter could tell she barely believed her own words. Winter had already started to feel something was off. Usually when Emmy was in town, they would have to be unzipped from each other. But this summer they had only hung out a handful of times.

The two uncoiled from each other and remained quiet for a long while. Winter wrapped her arms protectively around herself as she figured out how to make eye contact with Emmy, who had similarly tensed up right next to her. Emmy suddenly reached over to Winter and pulled their bodies together again. It made Winter tear up. She nestled into Emmy's collarbone, and Emmy hugged her tighter.

Finally, when the mosquitoes started to make their appearance, Winter and Emmy said good night and went their separate ways.

♥

Bobby Bae

6. WE REALLY WILL NOT DISCUSS EACH OTHER WITH OUR FRIENDS AND FAMILY

It had been two weeks since Bobby Bae's girlfriend dumped him. The first few days, he barely left his bed. He'd watched three full seasons of *Riverdale* with his blackout curtains drawn. After that, he did get out of bed occasionally, but only to take comically long showers. He'd lean his forehead against the wall under the hot stream until it turned cold. Because of the excessive bathing, his eczema flared up, so he was back to lying in bed, in the dark.

Mr. and Mrs. Bae left him to it at first. They had always known their son was a . . . deep-feeling person with emotions perhaps more accessible than their own. Space usually did the trick for them, but Bobby rarely went even a day without talking to his friends. A full two weeks mourning a relationship with a girl they didn't even particularly like was where they drew the line, so they called in reinforcements.

"Bobby," Diana said as she opened the door slowly to her son's room. "What are you doing, honey?"

Bobby was lying flat on his back in darkness.

"Netflix asked me if I was still watching *Riverdale*," he replied.

"You finally got tired of it?"

"No. I can't find my remote." He sighed deeply. "Do you think I'd look good with red hair?"

"What are you talking about?"

"Don't worry about it."

"Okay, well, Dakarai is here to see you." Diana opened the door the rest of the way, and Dakarai, or Kai as his close friends called him, stepped inside. Kai was Bobby's best and sometimes only friend. "I'll be downstairs if you need anything," Diana said before she disappeared.

Typically Bobby got over his moods quickly, and Kai knew to give him his space. But this time it was different. He was grateful Kai came to his rescue. He'd meant to call him, but he'd kicked his phone under his bed a few days prior and couldn't summon enough energy to find it.

"Hey," Kai said in a cautious tone. "How are you holding up, man?"

Bobby didn't answer with words. He scooted over on his bed, and Kai lay down next to him. The two of them stared at the ceiling for a while, completely quiet. It was nice to have someone to share his solitude with, and Kai was capable of such marvelous silence. Some people knew when to talk and when not to. Kai was one of those people.

He was tall and lanky, and he slouched so people could hear him because he always talked in a low drawl. He dressed like one of the kids from *Stranger Things*, and he rode around on a Huffy bike like one too. Kai was also extremely spiritual, which he mostly attributed to his Nigerian and Creole heritage. The energies of his ancestors provided him comfort and protection, and he transferred this same feeling of solace to everyone he loved.

"Do you want to talk about it?" Kai asked after a while. Bobby shook his head, so Kai reached into his pocket and pulled out a vape. "Do you want to get high about it? It's Tropicana Cookies."

Kai believed that animals' stress chemicals transferred to him, so he followed a strict anti-inflammatory vegan diet. He also employed other plant-based methods to manage his anxiety—one of them being vaping. But Bobby had his own ways of coping.

Bobby turned his head away. "Kai, you know I don't smoke."

"All right. I thought it would be rude if I didn't offer. You're always going on about your manners and etiquettes or whatever." Kai pressed the button a couple of times until the vape lit up, and he took a long pull. "Look, dude," he said, with the hit still in his lungs. "You know that song 'No Woman, No Cry'?" He blew out and smiled as he watched the smoke dance in a sliver of light that the blackout curtains failed to keep out.

"Uh . . . yeah. Bob Marley?"

"Most people think that song is about a man getting over a woman. That just because you don't have a woman, you shouldn't cry. But he was actually telling a woman that *she* shouldn't cry because everything was going to be all right."

Bobby contorted his face in confusion. "Yeah? So what?"

"Well, it's uniquely relevant right now because I want to tell your goofy ass both things. Nuh cry, woman. And especially not over Jaqueline Charlotte Turner," he replied. Bobby smacked him with his pillow, and Kai giggled deep in his throat. "But seriously, dude. You good?"

"Yeah, I'll be fine. Maybe I just need to get up. Should we go do something?"

Kai took another hit. "There were some planes outside leaving those lines in the sky, dropping hella chemicals. You know how I feel about that. Let's chill."

"We've only got one iota of courage between the two of us. It's supposed to be your turn to have it," Bobby said.

"I don't want it anymore. I've been thinking about asking out this guy who always comes into the bookstore during my shift. Depending on how that goes, it may be my turn to watch *Riverdale* soon."

Bobby looked at his friend, and an immense feeling of gratitude took him over. Kai was like a hermit crab. He could crawl into any shell and make it his home. Everything about him, from his height to his personality to his twists, made it impossible for him to fit in where they lived, but somehow he always found the tiniest crack and nestled right in.

Bobby held out his hand. "I changed my mind," he said, realizing his own anxiety-management tactics, for the most part, had never worked. Perhaps trying something new wouldn't be the worst thing in the world. "I do want to smoke about it."

Kai laughed. "Good-Boy Bobby wants to smoke? You for real?"

"Yeah. Why not? I don't think I'm Good-Boy Bobby anymore. Plus I was recently told I'm boring."

Kai had a boisterous laugh when he thought things were genuinely funny. It sounded fake, and you could almost spell it: *Ha. Ha. Ha.* But Bobby knew it was real.

"Who dared to call you boring?" Kai asked sarcastically.

"Winter Park's seventy-year-old grandmother."

Kai clutched his chest and rolled side to side as he laughed. "That's amazing."

"That and Jacqueline breaking up with me are the only reasons I agreed to go on this trip with Winter in the first place. I'm not going to lie; I'm regretting it a little bit. She has it in her head that we need to use this trip to become Bonnie and Clyde or something."

"I like Winter. I don't see why you been sleepin' on her. I like her way better than Jacqueline. I'm sorry, bro, but Jacqueline sucks. She always wanna argue with somebody. It's exhausting."

"She wants to go into political journalism."

"I'm not Tucker Carlson. She doesn't have to argue with me."

Bobby looked at his best friend sideways. He felt like arguing with him right then, but he was right. He sighed. "It's hard to explain, but Winter . . . I don't know. Everything seems so easy for her, while I work my ass off. We get the same grades, and I've never even seen her study. And she goes around speaking Korean, throwing it in my face that I can't. My parents are completely obsessed with her. *She's the perfect Korean daughter.*"

His parents had never attempted to teach him even a word of Korean. Every time he asked, they told him they didn't remember how to speak the language. He figured they wanted him to assimilate, but they didn't know how much shame it caused him, especially seeing how they celebrated Winter for doing the exact thing they'd refused to teach him. It was all very confusing. And being the dutiful son he was, he didn't want his parents to feel like they failed him in any way, so he kept the shame to himself.

Kai shook his head. "Look, man. The only culture my parents shared with me is fufu and Sunday service. It's not your fault," he said, and Bobby laughed. That wasn't necessarily true, but Bobby appreciated his friend's attempt at trying to console him. "But why don't you tell her you're trying to teach yourself Korean?"

"No, I can't. That'd be humiliating."

"I can't read or write Korean, but I'm pretty sure those little hieroglyphs in that notebook of yours are wrong. You're going to mess around and summon a spirit. Winter is the perfect person to help. I don't see why you hate her so much."

"I don't hate her. She hates me."

"Whatever, Bae. I'll never understand you two." Kai handed over his vape. "Here."

Bobby took it and rolled it around in his fingers. "If I smoke this, will I understand some of the crazy shit you say better?"

"Couldn't hurt."

Bobby pressed the button and inhaled deeply. He thought it'd be more pomp and circumstance if he ever gave it a go. He thought a SWAT team would descend from the ceiling and take him away. It was something for other people, like Kai, who looked natural and at ease when they did it. Not for someone like him who was incapable of relaxing or stepping a toe out of line. But it was shockingly easy . . . and tasty. Kai didn't typically do it in front of him. He figured now he had means and motive. Bobby took another hit before Kai took the vape from him.

Bobby fixated on the ceiling where some light peeked over the top of the curtains. There was the shadow of a tree branch in it, and every time the tree shook, the light flickered. The ceiling suddenly felt closer, and he reached out to touch it, immediately feeling foolish when he grasped only air.

"You know when you lose your train of thought?" Kai asked.

"Yeah?" Bobby was surprised by the sound of his own voice.

"Where do you think it goes?"

Bobby wanted to explain neural processes, but his own weren't working, so all he could manage to say was "To the giant rail yard in the sky."

Kai nodded slowly. "Word."

Bobby wasn't sure if he was feeling anything, but things did seem slower. At that moment, Bobby felt there was something else even smaller than the smallest unit of time, wedged between the nano- and milliseconds, pushing against them, forcing him to be more present. That something was him. A person was only entitled to a few perfect moments in their lifetime, and Bobby, with his best friend at his side, felt that this was one of them. Maybe doing "bad" things, as long as no one was getting hurt, was okay sometimes. He felt more at peace with his decision to allow Winter to come along on his trip.

He moved his head from side to side, and his vision lagged like an old cartridge video game. Kai laughed, and it startled Bobby. He almost didn't recognize his best friend's face. He'd never gazed so intently and deliberately at him. He looked back to the spot of light on the ceiling, and it had transformed into a peachy glow. As a matter of fact, everything seemed to be tinged in pink—heightened. It was beautiful, ethereal. It was almost too much to handle, so Bobby did what he always did when he was overwhelmed—he cried.

"Let it out, Bae," Kai said.

Bobby sat up and shook his head. "I've made a mistake. I don't think I like this."

"Mistakes are all part of the process. Just breathe." Kai took Bobby's hands in his own and massaged the pressure points with his thumbs. "Do you need me to find your medication?"

"No, I don't have any."

"Just count with me, then."

They slowly counted to thirty together, taking deep breaths between each number. Bobby calmed down somewhere around nineteen, but Kai's baritone voice was hypnotic in his altered state.

"You're okay," Kai said. "You hungry?"

"Kind of," Bobby replied, wiping his face with his shirt.

"Want to get vegan burritos?"

"No . . . but yes."

Kai clapped him on the back. "All right, Bae. Let's go."

♡

Winter Park

7. WE WILL RESPECT THE ITINERARY

Winter wanted to spend some time with her grandmother before she and Bobby left, so she walked over to her place early in the morning. The sun had barely risen, so it was cool outside, though still very humid. She skipped along her empty neighborhood. She only saw one person—an overly ambitious jogger—on the way over. The senior center, on the other hand, was nearly full. Many of the seniors were enjoying their black coffee and cinnamon-raisin toast as they gossiped and read the paper.

Winter crossed the parking lot to her grandmother's apartment. It was on the first floor in a building of four separate units. Halmeoni was sitting on her patio, drinking her customary cup of tea.

Winter's Korean-language switch flicked on. "Halmeoni, jeo wasseoyo!"

"Don't sit down," Halmeoni responded in Korean. "Let's go for a walk."

Winter helped Halmeoni to her feet, and they started along the sidewalk that formed a circle around the entire complex. They passed Mr. Ahmad, who was strolling with his hands clasped pensively behind his back. He nodded as he walked by.

The two also passed by Năi Nai's old apartment, but Winter didn't say anything so as not to upset her grandmother. Halmeoni and Năi Nai had exercised together, gardened together, shopped together.

They didn't speak the same language, but they took the time to create their own unique form of communication. That was a best friend, unless Winter completely misunderstood the term. Winter wondered if her own best friend was inside. They hadn't spoken since Emmy told her she wouldn't be returning to the US after graduation. Every time Winter typed out a text, she ended up deleting it and doing something else instead. Winter hadn't even told Emmy that today was the day she was leaving.

Halmeoni trudged along, refusing to look at the apartment.

"Can I ask you something?" Winter asked.

Halmeoni took a sandwich bag full of stale bread out of her purse. She took a piece of the bread, crumpled it, and threw it at the birds. "What is it, Soon-hee?"

"What did you think of Harabeoji when you first met him?" Winter watched the birds devour the little pieces of crust.

Halmeoni threw some more. "Where is this coming from?"

Winter idly kicked a few pebbles off the sidewalk and back into the street, frightening off some of the birds. "I don't know. You never talk about him, and something Umma said got me thinking. I was curious."

Halmeoni paused in front of the community garden. It was adorned with benches donated mostly by children of deceased former residents. They were arranged around a pergola, which looked like it was being swallowed whole by the bed of petunias in which it sat. Halmeoni bent down and touched the petals of the closest flower. "Your grandfather and I were introduced by our families," she said. "We knew each other for five months before our wedding."

"But what did you think of him?"

"He came from a good family, he worked hard, and he always took care of me. That's all I needed to know."

60

"Was it love at first sight?"

"Yes and no." Halmeoni kept her attention on the petunias. "Being alone then was different than it is now. My parents worried about me. But I don't worry about you, Soon-hee."

Winter could tell her grandmother didn't want to talk about it anymore, so she changed the subject. "So you're not Team Bobby like Umma and Appa are?" she asked.

"It would bring me comfort knowing you have a friend in Boston. We don't all have the luxury of *choosing* to be alone," Halmeoni replied. "Could you at least try to be his friend for your parents' and my sakes?"

Winter hated to imagine Halmeoni being alone. The two had only become close after Harabeoji died. Now that Năi Nai was gone and Winter would be going to college, Winter feared what effect it would have on Halmeoni's health. She suddenly felt guilty for having only considered the consequences of her leaving on her own life. And truthfully, having someone in Boston whom she knew would be nice. Even though that friend was supposed to be Emmy.

Winter sighed. "I'll try."

"Good. Now help me dig up some of these flowers."

Winter thought her ears were broken. "What?"

"I need some flowers for my flower box. Help me."

Winter looked all around. "What if we get caught?" she asked in disbelief.

"Then we get caught. If we don't, then we have petunias."

Winter stared at Halmeoni. She wasn't sure if she was being serious or not. But in all the years Winter had known her, she hadn't been one to play pranks. Winter saw that her grandmother had fresh flowers in her flower box at all times and always wondered who took her to the nursery to buy them.

Winter crouched down next to her grandmother, and they

looked at each other for a moment. Halmeoni's eyes seemed tired, but not because it was six a.m. and she was fully dressed, fed, and halfway through her day. She appeared worn down in a way Winter had never noticed before. She supposed Halmeoni was aging, and because Winter herself had been getting older so quickly, she failed to notice they'd been doing it together.

Winter stuck her hand into the freshly laid mulch and scooped out one pristine red petunia in honor of Năi Nai. Red had some negative connotations in Korea, but in China it was lucky. Năi Nai complimented Winter whenever she wore the color.

Winter liked how the dirt felt on her hands. Being a bookworm, it wasn't something she felt often. But it reminded her of when she was younger and she and Halmeoni would grow fruits and vegetables in the backyard of the house she and Harabeoji used to live in together. She would grow lettuce and peppers, but her favorite was hobak. They would pick the Korean squash and then fry it up and eat it with sauce or turn it into something delicious, like soup or pancakes. Those were some of Winter's happiest memories. She was sad when Halmeoni couldn't maintain the house anymore and had to sell it. But it was a blessing in disguise because she lived so much closer now.

Halmeoni scooped up a white petunia, and the two of them walked back to her apartment as fast as they could, giggling like they were both teenagers. Winter grabbed the flower box off the patio floor and put it on the table. They each took a finger and made a little hole in the dirt and deposited the roots of their flowers inside. They covered them up and stood back to admire their work. The long flower box looked a little silly with only two flowers in it, but Winter liked it. To her, they represented Năi Nai and Harabeoji. She took a picture of it with her grandmother in the background giving a thumbs-up with her dirt-covered hands.

When they were done, Halmeoni opened the door to her apartment. The smell of fresh, hot rice and the garlicky, spicy, vinegary aroma of kimchi of meals past hung in the air like an afterimage. Winter breathed in deeply and smiled. Halmeoni's apartment always smelled the same.

Winter kicked off her shoes, washed the dirt off her hands, and threw herself onto the couch. It was hard and very unlike her grandmother because it came with the apartment, but it did smell like her signature perfume. Halmeoni busied herself in the kitchen and came back with a Yakult. Winter stabbed a hole in the top of the red foil lid with her fingernail and downed the entire yogurt drink in a single gulp. It tasted like her childhood. Except when she was younger, she would freeze them and then crush up the tiny plastic bottle with her teeth trying to get the frozen drink out of the small opening. She would always cut her mouth, but it was the only way to enjoy them, in her opinion. It was all part of the experience.

Winter's phone buzzed, interrupting her peaceful morning. It was Bobby Bae.

I'll be at your house in ten minutes, the text said.

"Crap!" Winter yelled.

"What did you say, Soon-hee?" Halmeoni asked from the next room.

"Nothing, Halmeoni. But I have to go." Winter ran into her grandmother's bedroom, where she was fixing her hair in the dresser mirror, and gave her a kiss on the cheek. "I promise I'll call you from the road."

"Don't worry yourself. Have fun."

"Saranghaeyo, Halmeoni!" Winter yelled as she tore out of there in the direction of home. Bobby considered timeliness next to godliness. They hadn't even left yet, and he was already going to kill her.

Bobby Bae

8. WE WILL NOT HAVE MUTUAL FRIENDS WITHIN TWO DEGREES OF SEPARATION

Bobby planned out his morning so that he would arrive at Winter's house at exactly 6:30 a.m. He put everything in the car, programmed all their stops in the GPS, and had his father do a twenty-one-point check on the car the night before.

He was wearing his most comfortable but respectable outfit because he knew that he would have to talk to Winter's parents for a considerable amount of time before they would be allowed to leave. He allotted exactly thirty minutes in the schedule for this purpose. What he did not plan for was for his parents to follow him in their own car so that they could see him off. Kai was also in that car because he had fallen asleep with his vegan burrito on his chest the night prior, and Bobby hadn't had the heart to wake him and send him home.

As Bobby pulled into the Park's driveway, Winter came running up to the window, panting and sweating. She laid her hand against his car to catch her breath.

"Jesus," Bobby said as he rolled down the window. "Are you going to vomit?"

"Maybe. If. I. Keep. Looking. At. You," Winter said between gasps for air.

"Nice one," he replied dryly, getting out of the car and flicking the hair from his face. "Are you ready? We need to try to make our goodbyes brief."

Bobby was annoyed Winter wasn't paying attention to him. She was distracted by his parents and Kai, who were walking over from where they parked across the street.

"Uh . . . your parents are here," she said. "We only allotted thirty minutes for parents. Mine. Not yours."

"I didn't anticipate them wanting to come."

Kai was waving at Winter, a goofy smile splashed across his face. He ran up and picked her up off the ground, locking her in a tight hug. He placed her back down, and she was once again a full foot shorter than he was.

"How has your summer been?" Winter asked.

"Good. Can't complain. But I prefer winter."

Winter covered her smile with her hands.

Bobby appreciated the amount of effort Kai put into forming unique relationships with everyone he met. It was part of the reason Bobby loved Kai so much, but it was also one of the main pain points in their relationship because Kai knew absolutely everyone and Bobby often felt anxious every time they had to do a stop-and-chat. This was one such instance, and it was worse because it was Winter.

"How's work? I heard you got a job at the bookstore," Winter said.

"It's dope. I just read all day and draw the people who walk by," Kai replied.

Winter laughed politely. "I'll stop in one day, but please don't draw me."

"She'd sully your collection," Bobby interjected.

He could tell Winter wanted to give him a good smack, but his parents came up the driveway before she could. They took turns giving her hugs, following up with the necessary niceties. Bobby couldn't escape small talk, and it annoyed him how good at it Winter was.

"Diana!" Mrs. Park cried as she came bounding out of the house to hug Bobby's mother.

"Soon-ja! How are you?"

Winter and Bobby rolled their eyes. Every time their mothers saw each other, it was like years had gone by, when actually it hadn't been more than two weeks since their last meeting.

Mr. Park came out to shake Robert Sr.'s hand, and then all four parents broke into the catch-up game. Apparently a lot had gone down in the twelve hours they hadn't spoken.

"Y'all ready for your trip?" Kai asked. "My parents would never let me do shit like this."

"Perks of not having a life, I guess," Winter said.

"Look," Kai said, taking his vape pen from his pocket, "I'm mad I can't come with you guys, but I want you both to take this and think of me, all right?"

Bobby snatched the vape from him, looking back nervously at his parents. He stuffed it in his pocket and said, "Thanks, but way to be discreet."

Winter snorted. "Since when do you smoke?"

"Since you started minding your own business."

"That doesn't even make sense."

Bobby huffed. "Let's get in the car and drive off while they're talking. How long do you think it'd take for them to notice?"

"Probably an hour or so."

Kai looked at both of them and shook his head. "You guys lack imagination."

"Why do people keep saying that to us?" Bobby and Winter asked in unison.

"Probably because y'all do stuff like that," Kai said, and he ran up the lawn and cut into their parents' conversation. "Hey, I'm so sorry to interrupt, but I got a severe weather warning for later this afternoon. Winter and Bobby should really leave now if they're going to do their first tour and make it to their hotel before it hits."

All four of the adults' mouths formed an O, and they followed Kai back over to the two eager teenagers.

"He's a genius," Winter whispered to Bobby. "You're lucky to have a friend like him." She sounded uncharacteristically earnest.

"Where's Emmy?"

Winter shifted her weight from one foot to the other. "She's packing."

Bobby found it odd Emmy would choose packing over seeing her best friend off, but he chose not to press the matter.

Mrs. Park pulled out her phone and demanded the two pose for pictures. They stood next to each other awkwardly, and Bobby smiled with as many teeth as he could manage.

"Get closer, dear," Diana urged. "Pretend you like each other for a minute."

"This isn't prom," he retorted.

"Just do it."

Bobby took a step closer and put his arm around Winter for the briefest of seconds. He changed his mind and let his gangly arms hang loosely at his sides instead.

"Smile, Soon-hee," Mrs. Park said, demonstrating what a smile was with her own face as if Winter had no idea.

"Yeah. *Smile, Soon-hee*," Bobby said.

Winter elbowed him in the side and smiled brightly. "I'm going to throw up on you," she whispered from the corner of her mouth.

"Don't. Then we'll be stuck here longer."

"Do something with your arms. You look like an albatross."

He put his hands on both her shoulders and stooped slightly. "Could you stand on your tiptoes or something? I feel like the Giving Tree."

"Shut up and smile."

After a full *Vogue* spread-worth of pictures, their parents were done. Bobby opened the car door on Winter's side and closed it behind her.

"What a gentleman," Winter said in a mocking tone.

"Only while our parents are watching."

He walked around to his side, stopping to load Winter's suitcase on the way. Winter's parents hung at her open window while Bobby's parents and Kai stuck their heads into his.

"Call us every night," Robert Sr. said. "And I made sure you have an extra tire and all the tools you need, just in case."

"Thanks, Dad. I saw. I also added some flashlights, blankets, and a couple of road flares."

"Good thinking, son," Robert Sr. said, slapping Bobby on the shoulder. "You take care, okay? And take care of Winter too."

"We trust you, but not everyone you meet out there will be you, sweetheart," Diana added, putting her hand on his cheek. "Drop us a pin every time you reach one of your stops. I have your itinerary stuck to the fridge."

"I will, Mom. But we have to go now if we're going to beat that storm," Bobby said, winking at Kai.

Diana took one last look at her son. She and Robert Sr. left Bobby and Kai to say their goodbyes.

"Put that vape to good use, Bae," Kai said. "Put something in the air for me."

"We'll see about that. I'll text you, okay?"

"All right, bet. And if you guys want to go out, my cousin Omari goes to Boston University. I already told him you're coming." He gave the car a few taps, then backed away to wave.

Bobby was astounded they were getting out of there ahead of schedule. Winter smiled at him, no doubt thinking the same thing. He started the car and off they went. Winter was turned around, watching their families for as long as she could before Bobby turned the corner. She turned back around and sat quietly. Bobby didn't know what to say.

They hit the highway quickly, and it was pretty much a straight shot from there. It would be four hours and thirty-two minutes until their first stop: George Washington University.

"Should we listen to an audiobook or a podcast or something?" Winter asked, clutching her dead AirPods in her hands. "I have a bunch on my phone."

"No, I need to concentrate while I'm driving," Bobby replied.

"What sociopath drives in silence?"

"Alive ones."

Winter folded her arms and looked out the window as they put North Carolina in the rearview mirror. Bobby thought to himself, *Only four hours and thirty-one minutes to go.*

♡

Winter Park

9. WE WILL NOT SMILE WITHIN A FIFTY-FOOT RADIUS OF EACH OTHER

They hadn't even made it out of North Carolina yet and Winter was already losing her mind. It was too quiet, and she was beyond bored. Reading in cars made her nauseated, so she couldn't pick up a book or play with her phone. She also couldn't think of a single thing to talk to Bobby about. They had never been alone before. Not really. Their parents were usually in the next room. They typically talked about whatever relevant thing they were doing at that moment, snarked and bantered a little, then parted ways. Winter was starting to seriously doubt her decision. She could have gone on Google Maps and done a street view tour if she was so pressed to see the campuses. She just *had* to go in person.

To make matters worse, she was starving. She hadn't eaten before she went to her grandmother's apartment, and she didn't want to eat the hard-boiled eggs her mother packed, so the only thing in her stomach was a Yakult.

Winter rolled the window down and stuck her hand outside, feeling the wind whip between her fingers as the other cars zipped by. Bobby refused to go even a mile over the speed limit. According to him, it was dangerous and unnecessary since they were a little bit ahead of schedule thanks to Kai. She felt more at ease with the warm wind blowing her hair all over the car, but then Bobby hit an uneven patch in the road and her stomach let out an ungodly *glop* as she was jostled around.

"You didn't eat this morning?" Bobby asked, more of an accusation than a question.

Winter refrained from hurling an insult back. She promised Halmeoni she'd try to be nice. And now that they were officially on the road, it was time to start.

"I went to visit Halmeoni this morning and I didn't get a chance," she replied.

"Well, we're not supposed to stop anywhere before we get to George Washington."

Winter held her stomach. "Can't we get breakfast? We're ahead of schedule anyway. And then instead of eating while we're at George Washington, maybe we can do something else, like go to one of the Smithsonians."

Winter could tell Bobby didn't hate the idea. She knew rearranging his meticulously planned itinerary would give him major anxiety, but one thing he did love was museums. They had gone on a school-wide field trip to the Museum of Life and Science when Bobby was in fifth grade and Winter was in fourth, and everyone else was interested in running around outside and not having to do actual schoolwork for an entire day. Bobby went around to each exhibit, making notes in one of his notebooks, giving each and every plaque of information individual appreciation. It was endearing until he got freaked out in the butterfly exhibit when a "million-eyed beast" landed on his nose. He spent the rest of the trip sitting on the school bus listening to soft rock with the bus driver.

A search for nearby pancake houses revealed there was one called Jim's right off the highway and rated four stars. Honestly, Winter didn't know how someone could mess up a pancake. So if it had good reviews, that must have meant they were really good.

Bobby redirected the GPS, and they drove along a winding road until they arrived at an unassuming building with a parking lot desperately in need of repaving and a letter board sign displaying the day's special (lemon blueberry pancakes) with a few letters either missing or hanging off.

They pulled into a spot, and it already smelled like syrup and bacon. They went inside and were greeted by a hostess with tired eyes in a red-striped uniform and white apron. She told them they could sit anywhere they wanted, so Winter chose a booth in the corner. She slid into it and positioned her paper place mat and rolled-up silverware in front of her. Bobby followed suit and awkwardly smiled at the hostess before she went back to her station at the front of the diner.

"Do you feel like everyone is staring at us?" Winter asked, looking around at the other patrons, who all seemed to all be at least fifty years old.

"We're probably the first Asian people they've ever seen. Don't pay attention to them," Bobby said. "As long as they're microaggression racist and not macroaggression racist, we'll survive."

"You think that's why?" Winter replied. "I think it's just because we're young."

"Maybe. Why don't you ask them?"

Winter gave him a look as she unwrapped her silverware and placed it on top of her napkin. "Let's ask for chopsticks and see what happens."

Bobby let out a begrudging laugh.

They looked over at the booth next to them. There were two men Winter assumed were a father and son because they had the same blue eyes and lack of a neck. They seemed to work at some kind of construction business. They wore plaid shirts, and their pants and boots were covered in flecks of different-colored paint. The younger one looked back at Bobby Bae and whispered something to his father. They both then drained the last few drops of their coffee and went to the front to pay.

"Well, I guess we have our answer," Bobby said.

A waitress with about four inches of silver roots and blue eye shadow came to take their order.

"You both ready to order?" she asked in a thick regional accent Winter wasn't used to hearing.

Winter ordered a stack of lemon blueberry pancakes with bacon and scrambled eggs on the side. Bobby ordered waffles with eggs over medium and turkey sausage. The waitress jotted down their order on her pad and then disappeared behind the breakfast bar to fetch their drinks, an orange juice for Bobby and an iced coffee for Winter.

"Did you order waffles at a pancake house?" Winter asked, trying to hide the judgment in her voice.

"I like waffles better than pancakes."

"Yeah, but we're at a *pancake* house. That's like going to Harvard to study art."

"Harvard actually has a wonderful visual arts program, so the joke's on you." Bobby let out a slow breath. "Waffles are the same as pancakes. They're just cooked differently. They have little pockets specifically designed to allow for even syrup and butter distribution. That combines two things I love: breakfast and innovation. With pancakes, your syrup runs all over your plate, touching all your other food. It's chaos."

"Delicious, sugary, buttery chaos."

"Avoidable chaos."

With the well of insults having momentarily run dry, the two sat in uncomfortable silence, awaiting fresh material.

They were relieved when the waitress came to drop off their plates, and Winter made a show of dousing her entire plate in syrup. Her young arteries quivered looking at it, but it was worth it to see the disgusted expression on Bobby's face.

"Let's adjust the itinerary," Bobby said, taking his notebook from his back pocket and opening it to a page. "We can move everything except our tour appointment." Bobby handed Winter a pen.

"I'm surprised you even wanted to see GW. Doesn't seem like your thing."

"My *thing*?"

"It's not an Ivy."

"People grow."

Winter shrugged, considering Bobby's extremely low standard for growth.

They both looked over the itinerary, to make sure the pancake break wouldn't disrupt Bobby's schedule. He still had to drop location pins every time they made a stop. If it was too far off, their parents, who had printed copies of the itinerary, would be concerned.

The original itinerary for day one was as follows:

0530: Shower and get dressed.

0550: Have coffee. Start oatmeal.

0600: Wake-up text Winter. Eat oatmeal. Review itinerary.

0615: Call Winter if no response to text. Fill water. Load car and drive to Winter's house.

0630: Arrive at Winter's house. Review driving routes while Winter is late 15 mins. If 30 mins. late, review brochures again. If later than that, leave.

0700–0715: Get on the road.

0830: Stop for Winter's tiny baby bladder.

1030: Stop again for Winter's microscopic bladder and for gas.

1230: George Washington campus tour. Procure meal vouchers and study campus map.

1430: Have lunch at the campus dining hall. Tell Winter to pee before we leave.

1530: Head back to car. (Note to self: Take out cash in case parking garage does not accept cards or machine is down.)

1545–1600: Depart for hotel whether Winter has to pee or not.

1630: Hotel check-in, unpack, wash up, and independent leisure time.

1800: Dinner at the hotel restaurant.

1900: Winter-free leisure time. Call parents, light reading, and wind-down time before bed.

2100: Skincare and nighttime routine.

2130: Sleep.

Winter's first bathroom stop would have to be sacrificed if breakfast ran long, but the rest of the day would go as expected as long as there were no more deviations.

"You have the handwriting of a serial killer. Look how narrow your letters are," Winter taunted. "And what are your *i*'s dotted with?"

Bobby glared at Winter over the brim of his juice cup. "Dots."

"And why'd you schedule dinner?" Winter asked, licking homemade whipped cream off her knife. "We have nothing to do after we leave George Washington. We can eat when we want."

"It's habit. I've had dinner at six o'clock every night for basically my whole life."

"If we don't eat at exactly six, will you live, or are you going to have a Pavlovian fit and salivate to death?"

Bobby's fist was clenched. "I'll live. Unfortunately."

He took to spreading his butter evenly over his top waffle, making sure each nook was equally filled with syrup before cutting off a perfectly square piece using the pockets as a grid. "Anyway," he said, placing the square of squares into his mouth. "We never discussed the whole rule-breaking thing any further. Is that still something you wanted to do?"

Winter swallowed her pancakes down with a big gulp of iced coffee and blinked away a brain freeze. "I don't think we should roundtable our rebellion."

"I'm pretty sure every rebellion in history was roundtabled."

"Touché, but I think we should try to be spontaneous about it if we're going to do it at all."

The corners of Bobby's lips curled upward into a cocky smile. "Have you done anything bad since we talked about this the first time?"

Winter raised an eyebrow. There was no way Bobby was winning at having a rebellious phase. She didn't know what that face was all about.

"I stole flowers this morning," Winter blurted.

"Stole flowers?" Bobby repeated with a laugh.

"Yes. I dug them up from the community garden and replanted them on my grandmother's patio."

Bobby put down his knife and fork. "So you're telling me you took flowers from the community property and moved them to another part of the community property?"

"Yeah, so what?" Winter flicked some of the condensation from her coffee at him. "Whatever. We weren't supposed to start without each other. What did *you* do?"

"I smoked with Kai yesterday."

That explained the vape Kai had passed Bobby that morning. That was more in the direction she was thinking for their rebellion, but she didn't want to give Bobby the point.

"That's legal in some places, so it doesn't count. Destruction of property and theft are illegal in every state, so *boom*," she said, miming a bomb explosion with her hand.

They quieted when the waitress came to give them their check and some to-go containers for Winter's extra fruit salad. Bobby was probably afraid the waitress was a nark.

"Do something now, then," Bobby said once the waitress had gone, and pushed Winter the check. "Don't pay for this meal."

"You mean dine and dash? That's a little immature, don't you think?" she asked, pushing the check back.

Bobby put his finger on it and slid it back to Winter. "You just don't want to do it. It's up to you."

And with that, Bobby Bae got up and walked toward the door, tipping his nonexistent hat at the hostess and waitress as he weaved through the tightly packed tables.

Winter looked down at the bill and panicked. It wasn't that much money, and there were so many people in the diner. The waitress probably wouldn't go into financial ruin if she missed the tip on this one check. But maybe she'd have to cover the check with her own money. Winter didn't know if that was a myth or if restaurants actually did that. What if she got arrested? It was technically theft. Would Halmeoni be proud or upset? It would be breaking a rule. But were lemon blueberry pancakes the hill she wanted to die on?

Winter made a snap decision and ran outside to meet Bobby.

"Run!" Winter shouted as she power walked to the car.

"You actually did it?" Bobby asked, eyes wide.

"Get in the car. Let's go."

They both hopped into the SUV, slammed the doors, and secured their seat belts. Just then, the waitress came running out of the diner, waving at them. Her blue eye shadow caught the light, and she looked ten years older.

"You weren't supposed to actually do it!" Bobby yelled, throwing his arm behind Winter's headrest as he reversed. "What do I do?"

"I don't know. Drive!"

"I'll run her over!"

Winter smacked her palm to her forehead as Bobby braked and rolled down the window for the waitress.

"Is everything okay, ma'am?" Bobby asked, panicked.

"Your sister forgot her leftovers, darlin'," she said, handing Bobby the Styrofoam containers Winter had left on the table.

Bobby deflated. "She's not— I mean thank you," he said, tossing them into Winter's lap.

"Enjoy your day, and thanks for the generous tip, dear," she said to Winter, and ran back inside.

"Enjoy your day too!" Bobby said, matching the waitress's perkiness. He turned to Winter, biting back a laugh.

She held up a finger. "Don't."

Bobby held his laughter until they were on the highway. Winter shrank down and leaned her head against the window in defeat.

"I knew you didn't have it in you. This entire thing is just a fantasy," Bobby teased. "You could never do anything wrong, much less break the law."

"As if you could," she said. Bobby was still going exactly the speed limit, still refusing to turn up the radio.

They drove by the WELCOME TO VIRGINIA sign stating that it was a state for lovers. Bobby smiled broadly.

"Why are you smiling, weirdo?" Winter asked.

He didn't answer. Instead, he reached down, took off his left sneaker, and threw it in the back seat. Then he freed himself of the other, and it joined its life partner in the back. Winter looked on in horror. "What the hell are you doing?"

"It's illegal to drive barefoot in Virginia," he said.

Winter couldn't handle the self-assured look on his face. She burst out laughing. "Why do you even know that? Of course you would find the most mundane law to break. The only offense here is the one to my olfactory system!" Winter fanned in front of her nose, but it was only a charade. Bobby always smelled good. It was probably the most Korean thing about him.

"It was a trivia question I had once," Bobby said. "There are weird laws in every single state. Did you know back home you're not allowed to plow a field with elephants?"

Winter could not stop laughing. She whipped out her phone and searched more silly laws in Virginia. "Hey, did you know you have to honk every time you pass a car in Virginia?" she asked as her eyes scanned the page.

"That's so random. That was never mentioned in driver's ed."

Bobby was passing a red Civic, so Winter reached over and pressed the horn. The driver in the Civic flipped them off, and Bobby pushed Winter back into her seat. "Not on the highway, you psycho!"

"My bad. And what the hell? According to this article, it's illegal to tickle women here."

Without missing a beat, Bobby poked Winter in the side, causing her to jump and smack her head on the roof. Bobby laughed so hard he snorted, nearly swerving into the next lane. Winter went in for retaliation, but he pointed to the wheel.

"You're lucky you're driving," Winter warned. "But remember: I know where you'll be sleeping tonight."

"I did nothing wrong," Bobby Bae said dramatically. "You don't even count. You're not even a woman."

Winter feigned offense. "I am so. I'm sixteen! If this was one hundred years ago, I'd already have, like, four kids and a husband named Judd."

"I meant you're not human. You're some kind of flightless bird."

"Says the barely sentient TI-84."

"Cute."

Winter defiantly took the opportunity to play her favorite podcast, *Constellations*. Bobby went to shut it off but appeared to change his mind last minute and put his hand back on the wheel.

♥

Bobby Bae

Bobby had it in his head that touring college campuses would be like being sold a time-share. He thought there would be fast-talking school administrators trying to lure him in with gifts and candy, grooming him so that he would choose them and not some other institution. What he was presented with instead was a hoodie-wearing sophomore with a handful of brochures and maps.

"Welcome to GW. My name is Dante. I'll be your guide today," the tour guide said, handing Winter and Bobby a map and brochure each. "Now if you'll follow me, we can take a walk around the campus, and I can answer any questions you may have."

Bobby thought there would be other people in their group, but Dante made no indication that anyone else would be joining.

He led them into the main courtyard. There were a series of buildings surrounding a grassy patch with a statue in the center: a large metal hoop with a pin through it. Students sat around it, scribbling away in sketch pads. Dante explained the students were most likely from the art school, working on still lifes. They walked past them farther into the courtyard, where there sat even more buildings and blue George Washington flags. A few kids were playing Frisbee, and some others were lounging on the grass, but for the most part, it was empty, which Dante assured them was unusual. School hadn't started yet, and the move-in date wasn't for another few weeks.

"So what programs are you guys interested in?" Dante asked, stopping for a break in front of the library.

Bobby opened his mouth to reply, but Winter beat him to the chase.

"I'm only here for moral support," she said, betraying only the slightest bit of mockery. "But Robert here is interested in . . . actually, what *are* you interested in?"

Dante and Winter were staring at him, making him uncomfortable. He felt like he was on trial, and he knew—at least with Winter—that whatever answer he gave would be the wrong one.

"I'm interested in majoring in mathematics." He let out a breath when Winter didn't immediately jump on his answer.

"We have a great mathematics program here," Dante said. "We can check out the department building if you'd like."

Bobby didn't see how looking at a stack of bricks would affect his interest in the program, but he agreed anyway, and Dante gestured for them to follow.

"I didn't know you wanted to major in math," Winter said as they walked. "What do you even do with a mathematics degree?"

And there it was.

Bobby was not in the mood for Winter's ribbing. He was quickly realizing he had no interest in seeing the math building or attending school at GW at all for that matter. He'd only scheduled the visit because George Washington was Jacqueline Charlotte Turner's top-choice school. And now he was in a four-hundred-thousand-square-foot reminder of her, which soured his mood considerably.

"I don't know what I'm going to do with my math degree yet," Bobby replied. He sounded curt, but he couldn't help it. "I can figure it out later. People with math degrees are always paid no matter what."

Winter snorted. "Is that what you care about? Money?"

Bobby stiffened. "Of course. It's a measurable gauge of success."

"Wow. You *are* a sociopath. Do you even yawn when other people yawn?"

Winter made a show of yawning as dramatically as she could, which made Bobby yawn, which made her yawn again. They were stuck in an Ouroboros of yawns until Bobby finally clenched his jaw and ignored the impulse.

"Stop that," he commanded, and Winter giggled.

"You guys are funny," Dante said with an airy laugh. "Are you siblings?"

Bobby stifled a groan. Didn't anyone see how different they looked? Their skin tones were different; their hair textures were different. Plus Winter had epicanthal folds, and he didn't. Why did everyone always insist they were brother and sister?

"No, we're not related," he said flatly.

"Boyfriend and girlfriend?"

"No, we're just friends. Sort of."

Dante gave them a look that Bobby had become very accustomed to. The "why aren't you dating?" look. Almost every time they were together, they were subjected to a very similar line of questioning, followed by that look. It made no sense. If he was out in public with other girls, no one ever gave that look, but with Winter it was almost a guarantee. He could think of no other reason than the fact they were both Korean.

Bobby scowled once Dante turned back around. He folded his arms and fell behind as Winter and Dante chatted about the architectural style of the school.

Bobby couldn't figure out what had gone wrong between him and Jaqueline. It couldn't have been as cliché as growing apart or not fighting enough, as she claimed. *Who wants to fight?* Bobby thought to himself. He and Winter fought constantly, and they didn't even consider themselves friends, much less partners. He and Jacqueline were together all the time until school ended. They studied for the SAT together, they went on hikes, they shared endless memes, and he took her out on dates as often as he could. Real dates. He'd signed them up for a cooking class once, where they made a croquembouche. It had a dangerous lean, and when it finally fell, Bobby caught it and was absolutely covered in sugary glaze. Bobby sitting amidst the puff-pastry carnage was Jacqueline's most liked picture on Instagram.

He opened his text thread with her and considered sending her a message with a selfie of himself on the campus, but he decided against it. She probably wouldn't receive it well, and there was no way he could conjure up a convincing-enough smile. Instead, he scrolled up past their breakup texts to the last pleasant conversation they'd had.

Chin up, Bae. You may have come in second this year, but you'll always be first to me, she had said.

Bobby wondered what had happened to that girl. The girl who used to text him while they were sitting next to each other, who would buy him a brand-new Japanese pen every year for his birthday, who would laugh at his jokes even though he knew he wasn't funny. What changed? It couldn't have been him. He was a static creature. But now that he thought about it, maybe that was exactly it. Consistency was for porridge. No one wanted to date porridge. The calls stopped, and then the texts slowed, and after a while, days would go by where they wouldn't speak, and he either didn't notice or didn't care. She'd been leaving him in slow motion for months, and he hadn't even realized. Bobby's eyes started to sting, and he resisted the urge to find a bathroom to hide in and watch season four of *Riverdale* on his phone.

Dante went to ask permission to enter a residence hall, and Winter hung back.

"This campus is cool, but you don't look interested at all. Want to head out?" she asked.

"And leave Dante hanging?" He was irritated looking at the girl who'd dethroned him from the top spot in their class. Where was all this concern for his interest when she was eating steak with the governor without him?

"We can make something up. I'm sure he doesn't want to be here either."

"I know this isn't as thrilling as stealing flowers, but this is important," he heard himself say.

Winter stepped back. "Okay, I'm sorry. Chill."

"You never take anything seriously," he snapped. He didn't know where this was coming from, but he couldn't seem to close his mouth.

"Well, you take everything too seriously, Mr. Syrup-and-Butter Pockets. You're going to pop a blood vessel one day. Is this how you treated Jacqueline? Because the breakup is starting to make a whole lot more sense now."

Bobby blinked hard a few times. "What would you know about my relationship or any relationship for that matter? You've never dated anyone. You barely even have any friends."

"At least I'm not desperate for everyone to love me."

Bobby clenched a fist. "I honestly don't know why I agreed to let you come."

"I don't know why I actually came. I knew it would be like this."

Dante was coming back, so Bobby relented. Winter quieted and followed behind the two of them with her arms folded as they continued their tour. Bobby hadn't meant to snap, but Winter took life too lightly for someone who'd beaten him out of number one. She gave off number-four vibes at best with her endless jokes and affinity for trash entertainment. Winter was just there. She was always there, like a thorn in his side, a constant reminder that he was lesser in every way that meant something to him.

They entered the dorms, and Bobby was nonplussed by the modular twin beds and smell of stale beer.

"What kind of grades do you need to get in here?" Bobby asked.

"You're second in our class," Winter said as more of an admonishment than a fact. "You'll get in."

Jacqueline's GPA was a 3.9.

"I know. I'm only asking," Bobby shot back.

Dante cleared his throat. "Well, generally, you have to be a pretty good student, but if you're second in your class, I wouldn't worry." He turned to Winter. "Let me guess, you're number one?"

"Guilty."

Bobby nearly injured himself rolling his eyes so hard.

They continued their tour in silence, letting Dante do all the talking. Although he had lost interest in the tour, Bobby did have to admit that Dante was very thorough and knowledgeable. He wondered if Dante and Jacqueline would have classes together. He was probably her type. Bobby wasn't sure what her type was anymore. Dante certainly seemed to be Winter's type, though. She smiled, and her sarcasm seemed to take a vacation every time he spoke.

Winter was refusing to look at Bobby as they reached the last wing of their tour. He'd upset her, and he knew he'd be hearing about it later when they were alone, even though there was no way Dante didn't already sense the tension. He was talking faster and stopping for fewer questions than before. He all but ran as he led them to the last stop, which was a statue of George Washington standing tall on his pedestal with a cane and cloak in hand.

"That concludes our tour," Dante said, clapping his hands. "Do either of you have any questions for me?"

Bobby wanted to ask if GW had a morality clause and, if so, would breaking up with someone over text be a violation. But he kept his mouth shut. Winter didn't have any questions either, but she kept talking to Dante anyway. Bobby ran his hand through his hair. Small talk again. He couldn't escape it.

Dante and Winter had said "all right" and "anyway" about ten times each already. It was time to wrap it up.

"We've got to go," Bobby interrupted.

Winter shot him a death glare.

"I'm sorry to keep you," Dante said. "I can walk you to the student center. There's a presentation with some snacks and refreshments. The admissions advisors will answer any questions I missed."

"No, it's fine. We'll find our way," Bobby replied.

"You sure?"

"Yes, I'm sure."

"Okay. But listen, let me know if you need anything or if you have any questions." He wrote down his number on Winter's brochure. "And I hope you'll consider GW too."

"Maybe," Winter said with her Dante-reserved smile. "You'll be the first to know."

Bobby fixed his face before Dante looked in his direction. He gave a bro nod and then left. He was a nice guy, but Bobby was glad to be free of him. Winter wasn't as glad. As soon as Dante was gone, she put some distance between herself and Bobby and stood with her arms folded, staring up at the George Washington statue.

The last time he'd seen her legitimately angry with him was when he'd adjusted the thermostat at her house and she got in trouble for it. She seemed much angrier this time. Her nostrils were flaring, and her lips were pinched, like there was a bad smell under her nose. He'd acted untoward. That was unlike him. He hadn't raised himself that way.

Bobby closed the distance between them and assumed her stance. "He was kind of problematic, don't you think?" he said, pointing up at George Washington.

Winter didn't look at him. "If you're referring to all the people he enslaved, then yeah, I would say so," she replied, her voice flat.

Great, he thought. Now they were talking about slavery and Winter still looked like she was going to kill him.

"Have you seen *Hamilton* yet?" he asked, trying to gauge how mad she was.

She pursed her lips. "No."

"George Washington is being played by a Korean actor."

"Is he any good?"

"Uh . . . I don't know. I didn't see it either."

Winter suddenly whirled around to face him. "Let's stop this charade right here," she said, sticking a finger in his face. "You're doing that thing that I can't stand."

"What thing?"

"The Korean-parent thing where you don't apologize, you just start acting nicer."

Bobby was taken aback. He wasn't around many other Koreans enough to know that that was a *thing*. He thought it was only his parents. "I'm sorry. I didn't realize—"

"We were doing okay all morning, then as soon as we stepped

foot on this campus, you went all moody and broody. You better tell me what happened because I'm calling a moratorium."

The air was sucked out of his lungs.

The two of them could call a moratorium on their rules if they needed to say or do something that might cross into friend territory. They'd called it several times over the years. It could be for favors, such as the time Winter ripped her jeans at school and needed to borrow Bobby's hoodie to tie around her waist, or when Bobby locked himself out of his house while his parents were away and needed Winter to rescue him with her spare key. It could be used when one of them had to say something personal. Or sometimes it operated as a sort of safe word for when one of them needed the other to lay off.

"I reject the moratorium. I don't want to talk about it," Bobby said.

"Well, I can't spend an entire week with you if it's going to be like this."

"It's private, and we aren't exactly friends."

"Hence the moratorium. I called it, so you have to honor it."

It was true. It was an addendum to their original document that they'd decided upon freshman year after Bobby found Winter crying at school. It was the first and only time he'd ever seen her cry. She had found out her friend's grandmother, Mrs. Lin, was sick. He had only recently found out she passed, which saddened him deeply. Mrs. Lin was a sweet woman with a kind face, although Bobby had never been able to successfully communicate with her. He'd given Winter a tissue, walked her home, and covered for her at school. They were both such good students, none of the teachers questioned him. The two hadn't spoken of it since.

Bobby conceded. He'd signed a document, and he wasn't going to go against his word. He slumped his shoulders in defeat and said, "This was Jacqueline's top-choice school."

Winter's face immediately dropped. "Oh . . . shit."

"Yeah . . ." He sighed. "And I thought that if it was love at first sight with GW, it'd be a sign that I should try to get back together with her. But clearly that didn't happen."

"Because you didn't let it," Winter said under her breath.

Bobby flicked his hair back. "Could you try to be sympathetic to my situation for a minute?"

"How could I? I've never been in a relationship, remember?"

"I'm sorry. That was a low blow. Even for us."

"Yeah, it was." Winter looked at her feet. "But I guess I shouldn't have pried."

"Yeah, you shouldn't have."

Winter rotated the campus map she was holding, studying it intently. "Well, we don't have to give up yet. We can go to the admissions presentation if you want. And apparently there's a hippo statue or something around here."

Bobby put his hand up in a dismissive gesture. "I appreciate what you're trying to do, but you can stop. I'm ending the moratorium now."

"Should we head over to the Smithsonians, then? That might raise your spirits."

"I'm not a little kid," he snapped. "Can we just go?"

"Yes, but let the record reflect that I tried to be nice."

Bobby knew she probably wanted to see the Air and Space Museum. He regretted telling her anything. He should have done a better job of concealing his mood. Now she kept looking at him with pity in her eyes, which was far worse than her usual disdain.

They walked back to the car together in silence. Bobby dropped a location pin for his mom before they headed over to the hotel.

♡

Winter Park

11. WE WILL NOT SHARE SPACE

Bobby and Winter arrived at the hotel an hour early, which meant they were back on their original schedule. Typically this would have pleased Bobby greatly, but he didn't mention it. He walked straight into his bedroom and slammed the door.

Winter watched his shut door for a while before giving herself the grand tour of their living quarters. The two-bedroom suite Mr. and Mrs. Bae had booked for them was very impersonal but extremely clean. The furniture was a series of moderately comfortable geometric shapes, and there was a kitchenette with a laminate countertop and minifridge. Winter and Bobby's rooms were on either side of the main area, and Winter groaned when she realized there was only one bathroom they'd have to share.

Winter went over to the sliding door that led to a sliver of a balcony and opened the floor-length curtains. The bright red sun was preparing to disappear behind the trees. The air smelled earthy, tinged with car exhaust and weed wafting in from some of the neighboring rooms. Washington, DC, was a city, probably the best city in the world, but even in all the hustle and bustle, there was always a sense of calm and purpose.

A buzzing in Winter's pocket drew her attention for a moment. She hoped it was Emmy, but it was an email from her eye doctor reminding her to schedule an appointment. Winter scrolled down in her recent calls list to find Emmy. Her finger hovered over her name for a while before she finally decided to press it. Emmy's smiling photo popped up on her phone as it rang before ultimately going to voicemail.

Is this what it's going to be like? Winter thought to herself. She had expected things to change and for Emmy to be different after Năi Nai died, but she'd never felt so disconnected from her before. Even when they were together, Emmy was somber and distracted, only in her typical bright mood in short bursts. But Winter couldn't very well be upset with someone who was in mourning.

With a sigh, Winter headed to her room, which was slightly bigger than Bobby's. She laid her things out on the bed for the shower. She had been in the car all day, and Washington, DC, was unbearably humid in the summertime. There was no way she smelled anything even close to good.

Stepping into the glass box the hotel called a shower, Winter closed her eyes under the stream, letting the water wash away the filth of the day. The smell of maple syrup had been following her around, so she wasn't confident she hadn't gotten some in her hair earlier.

As the smell of breakfast disappeared down the drain, she couldn't help but think of dinner. She was covered in fresh mosquito bites from the swamp that is Washington, DC, and all she wanted was some good old-fashioned Korean comfort food—jjajangmyeon. She dreamed of diving headfirst into a bowl of the freshly hand-pulled noodles slathered in sweet and savory black-bean sauce. Thinking about it made her salivate, but it also made her think of Emmy. She'd brought it up to Emmy once and was shocked when she knew exactly what she was talking about. In fact, it was originally a Chinese dish that had been adapted to Korean tastes. Winter couldn't imagine eating it with anyone else. It wasn't that she was embarrassed, but it was messy, and Korean food didn't always smell as nice as maple syrup.

Maybe Bobby would want to get jjajangmyeon for dinner. His mother made it the best, but perhaps they could find a suitable takeout spot nearby. She would ask him later.

Winter pressed her forehead against the shower wall and closed her eyes again with a loud sigh. All her instincts told her to hold on to Emmy with everything she had, but she wasn't sure how they were going to fit into each other's lives anymore. She didn't know many models and aerospace engineers who mingled in the same social circles.

When Winter got out of the shower, she wrapped herself in a towel and lay in bed, letting her hair soak the pillow. She opened Instagram, went to Emmy's profile, and watched a video of Emmy dancing that autoplayed. She was in black spandex, using a sheer white scarf as a prop. Emmy had moved around often, sometimes to countries where she couldn't appropriately communicate. But Emmy always said that in dance, she was unfettered by anything as provincial as a language barrier.

In the video, Emmy lay on the ground, her back arched and arms splayed, exposing the peaks of her rib cage, before rolling and using the strength of her core to lift her body skyward, her toes pointed and chest open, with long clean lines down to her fingertips. Winter was transfixed, watching the muscles in Emmy's legs and arms lengthen and protrude as she shifted her center of gravity seamlessly and sensuously, making use of the entire room and the entire world as her showcase.

The choreography ended with her folded over as if in a traditional bow. Each vertebra in her spine was articulated as she heaved with breath.

"How was that?" Emmy said with a smile as her head popped up.

As Winter scrolled up to Emmy's modeling headshots, she mentally punished herself for being so dense. When they met, Emmy had the biggest ears Winter had ever seen. She wore her hair in a black drape to cover them. Over time she grew into them, and eventually, through the approval of her peers, she learned her best angles and started posting daily. This was the natural progression of things. Emmy had lived all over the world and had to learn to make friends in an instant, knowing the friendships probably wouldn't last. Winter knew all along that Emmy could eventually leave her behind too. College was supposed to be their chance to solidify their friendship for good. Now it could all slip away, along with her childhood.

Everything was happening too quickly.

Winter lost the grip on her phone, and it fell with an unceremonious smack on her face. She threw it to the side and drew the covers over her head.

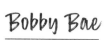

Bobby Bae

12. WE WILL NOT BE COMPLETELY MISERABLE TO BE AROUND

Bobby lay on the couch in his room, trying to ignore his own stench. He wanted desperately to shower, but Winter had beaten him to it.

He decided to pass the time by texting Kai.

> **Bobby:** Hey. Miss me yet?

Bobby sat with his legs crossed at the edge of the couch as he waited for Kai to text him back. It didn't take very long. He was probably working his shift at the bookstore, and there wasn't really much to do in the evenings.

> **Kai:** Let me guess. You and Winter are best friends now and need help picking out matching necklaces?

> **Bobby:** How did you know?

Winter had despised Bobby from the moment they met. He never entirely understood why, but after knowing her for almost a decade, it was clear a friendship between them would have never worked.

They were way too different. And now, after today, she'd probably never speak to him again.

> **Kai:** So I guess you haven't told Winter you're trying to learn Korean yet.

> **Bobby:** No. And I'm not going to. We talked about this.

> **Kai:** 😡

> **Kai:** wE TaLkEd AbOuT tHiS.

> **Bobby:** Please don't mock me. I've had kind of a shit day.

> **Kai:** Lmao, it's all love here, bro. You went to Jacqueline's school, right? How you holding up?

Bobby's lower lip quivered without his permission.

> **Bobby:** I'm fine.

He knew Kai wouldn't buy it. *I'm fine* was in the language of the unfine.

Kai chose to let it go, much to Bobby's relief, and changed the subject. They continued texting back and forth about a graphic novel Kai had written and was in the process of illustrating. He based a character on Bobby, which Bobby took issue with because he would never authorize the use of his likeness on a character named Milquetoast. At least he was a superhero, but his Kryptonite was debilitating lactose intolerance.

Eventually, they had to stick a pin in their negotiations because Kai had to get back to work. Bobby was left to his own thoughts again. He heard Winter vacate the bathroom, and he tried to will himself to get up but failed. Instead, he leaned back and turned on the TV.

♡

Winter Park

13. WE WILL STAY OUT OF EACH OTHER'S BUSINESS

Winter went out onto the balcony with a cup of tea and some cookies she'd bought from a vending machine down the hall. The sun had not completely set, so the sky was a deep purple and orange. Normally she would wait for nighttime to sit outside with her tea so she could watch the stars, but she needed some peace and quiet now. Bobby was locked in his room, watching some soapy teen drama. She was going to suggest they get dinner early, but before she knocked, she heard the unmistakable sound of a whimper. The walls in the hotel were like paper, albeit not Bobby's fancy sugarcane paper.

Winter dipped one of the hard tea biscuits into her mug and wiggled it around until it was the perfect softness. She was a tea aficionado, and under any other circumstance, the black tea that's offered for free in a hotel would be beneath her, as would a vending machine cookie, but she was willing to make concessions. Desperate times called for desperate measures. Still, the one thing she was not willing to compromise on was the density of her cookie.

Despite being in her element, Winter found it hard to focus on anything but her phone. It was weighing on her as though she had a pocket full of lead. She took a few deep breaths, swallowed her pride, and tried calling Emmy again.

"Hey, you called me two times in a row. Everything okay?" Emmy asked.

In all the time Winter had known Emmy, it had never been this difficult to talk to her about anything.

"Yeah, I'm fine," Winter replied. "I just missed you."

Emmy let out a relieved sigh. "I miss you too. Sorry I've been MIA. There are a million things to do before I leave."

"Yeah, I saw your headshots. You look amazing."

"You sound down. Are you sure you're okay?" Emmy asked. "Is it Bobby? What did that little shit do now?"

Despite the secret she revealed last time they spoke, Emmy was one of the rare few who was not #TeamBobby. Being Chinese, she understood why Winter didn't go out of her way to be his friend. People always assumed they were dating, and they couldn't be the only two Asian kids in school and be dating. That would be, like . . . a thing. And Winter didn't want it to be a thing. She wanted to go through high school thing-less and Bobby Bae-less. Winter couldn't help but feel betrayed that Emmy had been harboring a secret crush on him. Regardless, she still told Emmy everything: that she'd started the road trip, about the waffles and George Washington, and how bent out of shape Bobby was over Jacqueline. She talked quickly, not wanting to waste whatever time she had on the phone with Emmy on Bobby Bae.

"Are you guys sharing a room?" Emmy asked.

"Don't be weird. He's literally in his own room crying. He needs to get up and shower so we can go eat."

Emmy snorted. "He seems like the type to take really long showers. He probably gives himself intense scalp massages and thinks about life. Poor guy. What was his girlfriend even like? Does she suck?"

"I don't know anymore. She's a little bossy, but she's gorgeous and probably third in our class after Bobby."

Emmy laughed. "Figures. Bobby is so superficial. Remember

he wouldn't eat the fish your dad made because it had a head? He wanted it to be, like, perfectly filleted and cleaned. Like, bitch, you're Asian. Get over it."

"Do you remember you also wouldn't eat it?"

"Its eyes were following me like the *Mona Lisa*. Sue me."

Winter snorted. She could always count on Emmy for a good laugh. And not just a *ha-ha*, but a "tears streaming down the face, praying to God because it hurts so good" kind of laugh. It was part of the reason she enjoyed talking to Emmy. It was nice to share a joke with her again.

"Have you been by to see Halmeoni, by the way?" Winter asked.

"Not recently. How has she been doing?"

"She's okay, I guess. But did you know all the flowers in her flower box are stolen?"

"Yeah, Năi Nai is the one who put her on."

Winter clasped her hands over her heart. "Aw, Năi Nai. I don't feel so bad anymore. That woman was a saint."

"You're only saying that because she never smacked the mother-land out of you with a wooden spoon."

"True. But still."

There was a pause. Winter could hear Emmy taking in breaths to speak but then changing her mind, surrendering to the dead air instead.

Winter heard Bobby's door open. She looked back, and he was standing in the frame, his eyes red-lined and his face puffy.

"Is that Bae?" Emmy asked, sounding grateful for the distraction.

"Please don't call him that," Winter replied through gritted teeth. "But I should probably go now. Bobby turns into a pumpkin if we don't eat dinner by six." Also, she had run out of things to say.

"I have to go too," Emmy said. "Send my regards to Bobby."

"I will. I love you."

"I love you too."

Emmy was gone with a click, and Winter let out a long breath. Bobby came toward Winter and slid open the balcony door to join her on the terrace. He gripped the railing and looked out over the city. "Was that Emmy?" he asked.

"Uh . . . yeah. Do you even remember her?"

"Of course. Remember when our parents went to that concert in New York and they left us both with Halmeoni? Halmeoni was so tired of our shit, she sent us over to Năi Nai's while Emmy was there for the summer, and we made, like, a billion dumplings."

A sad smile washed over Winter's face. "You mean Emmy and I made a billion dumplings. You made, like, four."

Bobby glared. "I wanted them to be perfect."

"Ours were as perfect as yours when they were in our stomachs," she said, and it was then she caught Bobby's gaze. "Did you hear any of that phone call?"

Bobby shook his head. "No, but my mom told me you were upset about Emmy not going to school with you in Boston. Do you want to talk about it?"

Winter put her head down. "I overheard you in your room. Do *you* want to talk about it?"

"No, we're not supposed to anyway," he replied, stiffening his jaw. "But before we don't talk about anything, can I make an observation?"

Curiosity got the best of Winter. She gestured for him to continue.

"Since I've known Emmy," Bobby began, "she's always been the one who has had to come to North Carolina to see you. But have you ever tried meeting her halfway?"

Halfway to Germany was probably somewhere in Atlantis.

Winter's face scrunched. "What are you going on about?"

"Our relationship has always been defined by our rules, rules that you suggested," Bobby said, pointing an accusatory finger. "Do you think it's possible you do the same thing with her? With . . . everyone, maybe? I get that you guys will be apart, and that sucks. I'm going to be miserable without Kai, but we're going to be off on our own for the first time, so it'll be up to both of us to put in equal effort if we're going to stay friends. For you, it might just mean that you have to start pulling your weight a little more if you want to keep Emmy in your life."

Pulling my weight? Winter thought. Her friendship with Emmy was nothing like her relationship with Bobby. Her first impulse was to get defensive, but maybe he had a point. It had never occurred to her she could have visited Emmy when she lived in Texas or when she briefly lived in Kansas. Winter was flummoxed. She was so flummoxed she was using words like *flummoxed*. Was Bobby right? Now that Winter thought about it, she always chose the books for book club, they always met at Winter's house, and Emmy always spent time with Halmeoni, but Winter never made as much effort with Nǎi Nai because of the language barrier. Emmy existed entirely in her world, but Winter had never even tried to venture into Emmy's.

"You okay?" Bobby asked.

"Sorry, I'm fine," Winter replied. "I'm just thinking about what you said."

"Ignore me. I overstepped."

"Yeah, let's not do that again."

"Say no more," Bobby said with a nod. "Are you hungry? We can have dinner after I shower."

"And go against the itinerary? It'll be after six by the time you're done," Winter said sarcastically, trying to lighten the tone of their conversation. She gestured to her mug and tea biscuits. "I'm good for now. I have a snack, and I'm waiting for the stars to come out."

"You'll get eaten by mosquitoes."

"I know. My blood brings all the boys to the yard."

"The ones that bite are female."

Winter mentally facepalmed. She was trying her best not to call him any of the hundreds of names that popped into her head. Why did he make it so hard to be nice to him?

"Wait here," Bobby said, leaving her on the balcony alone.

"Welp," she said to herself, popping her lips. She should have known better than to tell a joke. Bobby had a very selective sense of humor.

He returned holding a bottle of mouthwash. "Here. Put this on and the mosquitoes won't bite you as much."

"Is this a prank so I'll go to dinner smelling like a minty Christmas tree?"

Bobby rolled his eyes. "It's an old lifeguard trick. Remember Kai used to work at the pool?"

Winter remembered Kai being high at the pool all last summer and getting fired. She took the mouthwash and put a couple dabs of it on her arms and legs. She doubted the efficacy of the repellent, but she was willing to try almost anything.

"Thanks," Winter said, trying to find the least awkward spot to place her gaze.

"So . . ." Bobby said as he rubbed the back of his neck. "Did you know it's illegal to identify and then kill a Sasquatch in Washington, DC?"

"So if I point at someone and yell, 'Sasquatch,' I just have to kill them, and it's a crime?"

"I don't think homicide becomes more illegal if you call your victim a Sasquatch first."

"Whatever, Bigfoot."

They were silent for a moment. The air around them was uncertain. Winter didn't quite know what uncharted territory they were in, but it felt a lot like he was trying to cheer her up after her disaster of a phone call with Emmy.

A few seconds later, Bobby took in a sharp breath. "I guess I'll go take that shower now," he said, bringing his hands together.

"Wait!" Winter said, grabbing Bobby's arm with no plan as to what she would do next. She glanced down at Bobby's watch, and it turned to six right before her eyes.

"What's wrong?" Bobby asked.

Winter took one of her cookies and crammed it into Bobby's mouth without warning. She laughed madly until she felt something wet against her palm. "You licked me!" she yelled, bouncing up and down and holding her infected hand as far away from her body as she could manage. A giggle bubbled out of her.

Bobby struggled to swallow. "What's wrong with you?" he choked.

"It's six o'clock. I didn't want you to miss dinner," she said with a half shrug.

Bobby busted out laughing, spraying Winter with crumbs.

"Oh my God!" she squealed.

Bobby confiscated Winter's tea and washed down the rest of the dry biscuit. He made a sound that was halfway between a choke and a laugh. "I know you don't like me, but I didn't think you'd actually try to kill me!"

"But did you die?" she asked, dusting herself off. "And you drank my tea!"

"It tastes like hot garbage. I saved you."

"My hero."

Bobby tried to give it back, but Winter refused, chucking the rest of it over the balcony instead. The liquid fell into the empty parking lot below with an unceremonious *splat*.

"I needed that laugh," Bobby said with a bemused smile on his face. "Thanks." And with that, he slid open the balcony door and left Winter on the terrace alone.

"Thanks?" Winter mouthed to herself.

She watched him walk to his room, trying to see what apparently everyone else seemed to. He was tall, like Emmy said, and his hair was thick and healthy-looking, though he could use a cut. He turned to look at her, pausing at the bedroom door. His face was relatively symmetrical, and he had that great nose her mother always talked about. *Was* Bobby Bae hot? He stepped into his room to gather his things for a shower. She turned back to the sunset and took a deep breath. Her findings were inconclusive.

As she looked out over the city, a pit formed in her stomach. She couldn't help but feel she had stepped into an alternate dimension, the darkest timeline, where she was getting along with Bobby better than she was with her best friend. There was no science to explain what was happening. And what even was that observation he gave? She took one last look at the sky before texting Bobby.

Winter: Let's just order takeout to our rooms. I want Thai, and I know it's not your favorite.

Bobby: K.

♡

Winter Park

14. WE WILL NOT ABUSE MORATORIUMS

In the morning, Bobby stormed into Winter's room and demanded she get dressed, packed, and in the car. Within thirty minutes of her opening her eyes, they were on the beltway nearing Baltimore County. Winter could almost smell the Old Bay in the air. She leaned her head against the car window and nearly dreamed before Bobby hit a bump and she was startled awake. She groaned.

"Are we really going to UPenn early, or is this the part where you kill me?" Winter asked. "I don't really care, but I don't want to die in this outfit."

"We were seen on at least ten cameras together in the hotel and at least three traffic cameras. Plus we both have location services activated on our phones, and no less than ten people know exactly where we are," he replied. "If I were to kill you, it'd likely be second-degree murder, which carries a sentence of forty years or more. I don't think they'll let me go to Harvard from prison."

"It's creepy you know all that."

"You're not the only one who likes mysteries."

"You watch straight-up murder documentaries and cold cases. I watch reimaginings on *Lifetime*. We are not the same."

Bobby cut his eyes at her. "Just be patient and act surprised when it's time."

The pit that had formed in Winter's stomach the night before returned. She leaned back against the headrest in defeat. The trees hung over the road, trying to high-five in the middle. She watched them go by as they got closer to Baltimore. She'd hoped they'd find some time to pick blue crabs and devour crab dip pretzels, but it seemed unlikely now. It more than likely wasn't Bobby's thing either. If he couldn't even eat fish with a head, he definitely couldn't contend with the knobby black eyes of a crab.

They were barely on the beltway for any time at all when they turned off at an exit. Bobby probably had to go find a charging port to plug himself into. She closed her eyes and tried to go back to sleep. It was about ten a.m., but had she known that they were going to leave two hours earlier than planned, she wouldn't have stayed up late the night before pacing around the balcony on her stargazing app, looking for Polaris. She decided to call it quits around three a.m. when she almost dropped her phone over the railing and nearly went over trying to catch it.

"We're here," Bobby said as Winter started to doze off.

A snore escaped her throat, which startled her completely awake. She was disoriented, with floaters dancing in front of her eyes. "We're where?"

"Are you not seeing this? Open your eyes."

"First of all, racist. And second of all, there's no way we're in Philly yet."

"Would you just look, please?"

She rubbed her eyes, and when her vision cleared, she saw the Goddard Space Flight Center, one of NASA's major research facilities. She looked at Bobby as if to ask if she was actually seeing what she was seeing, and he nodded. Her heartbeat jumped into her ears, and she started flapping her arms wildly like a flightless bird. The pit in her stomach moved to her throat. She was having trouble putting together the hodgepodge of scattered thoughts in her brain so she could say something, anything, coherent.

Bobby was looking at her, trying to gauge her reaction. Her first impulse was to pull him into a hug, which was strange because one, they were in a car, and two, it was Bobby. She reddened and put as much distance between them as she could. "I'm so sorry. That was weird, right?" she asked.

Bobby had no discernible expression. "It was a little weird."

He threw the car in park and hopped out.

"Why am I so awkward?" Winter whispered to herself as Bobby walked around to open her door. "Our parents aren't here. You don't have to do that," she said to him as he gestured for her to step out.

"Force of habit," he replied. He shut the door behind her.

"Right." She pushed her hair back behind her ears and took a deep breath. "So, uh . . . what are we doing here?" she asked, trying to pretend she hadn't had a mini freak-out.

"I'm not proud of how I acted yesterday," he said plainly and resolutely, as though he'd rehearsed it. "I violated our rule about discussing my girlfriend, among others, so I was hoping you'd accept this as a reset button."

Winter almost felt like he should get down on one knee. He was already being so dramatic about it; she squirmed under Bobby's pleading gaze.

"I accept," she said, not knowing what else to say.

"Good. Should we go inside?"

They started walking to the door like they were marching in a funeral procession. This was one of the nicest things anyone had ever done for her, and she didn't know how to act.

"Race you to the front door!" Winter said suddenly as she shoved Bobby down and took off like a dart toward the entrance.

They always used to race when they were kids. They'd be dragged along on church retreats, and it was the only way they could entertain themselves while their parents "caught up" for hours upon hours. Winter always won because, admittedly, she cheated.

"Not this time!" she heard Bobby yell from behind.

Winter glanced back and saw Bobby scramble to his feet. She squealed as he gained on her, keys jangling, a youthful, pleased look on his face. She didn't even care if people were watching them running around, giggling like kids.

"On your left!" Bobby yelled as he passed her and touched the door before she did.

"How the hell did you beat me?" Winter asked. They both were bent over, trying to catch their breaths. "You don't exercise. And trolling people on the internet does not count." She held her burning chest.

"I'm a trombone player. I have superior lung capacity," he replied with a smirk.

"Weird flex, but okay."

"Whatever, you're just mad you lost."

Winter rolled her eyes and then looked around. There was absolutely no one there to watch her embarrassing herself, and no cars in the parking lot either. "Where is everyone?" she asked breathlessly.

Bobby went to check the hours on a sign in the window. "They're closed!" he exclaimed. Winter looked at the sign for herself. They were closed one day a week, and that happened to be it. "You have got to be kidding me," Bobby said, throwing his hair out of his eyes. "I can't get a single thing right."

He was so hard on himself. It wasn't that big of a deal. She wasn't the dermatologist in her family, but if this is how he reacted to everything, she was pretty certain his eczema was stress-induced rather than a side effect of his shower cries.

Winter took him by both shoulders. "Relax, Robert. It's fine."

"Really?" Bobby asked with a pout.

"Yes! I mean, this place has a rocket garden. Meaning there's a garden full of rockets. You can even see some of them from here." She stood on her tiptoes and tried to look behind the building. "You seriously didn't have to do this."

Bobby wrung his hands. "You seemed sad after your call with Emmy, and there's no use in us both being sad."

Winter was going to have to put him in rice like a waterlogged iPhone and restart him later. It was likely he had some love left over from his breakup and nowhere to put it, but that love was reserved for his parents and all the people at school who liked him. None of that was meant for her, especially not Jacqueline Charlotte Turner's portion.

"You're doing fine, Robert." She gave him a few pats on the chest.

"Good." He got down in the middle of the concrete entranceway and lounged, propped up on his elbows, like he was getting a tan at the beach.

"What the hell are you doing?"

"If we can't go in, we can at least sit here and enjoy the energy a little bit. Plus I'm out of shape. No more racing, okay?"

Winter shrugged and joined him, cross-legged. The sun wasn't at its hottest, so the ground was still cool. Her heart felt like it'd explode as she looked at the NASA logo plastered on the building with the Delta rocket behind it, aimed at the cosmos. She followed where it pointed, and her eyes rested on the fluffiest white clouds she'd ever seen. Everything was elevated. The sun was brighter, the air was fresher, the birds were even singing better melodies.

She felt eyes on her suddenly.

"Why are you looking at me like that?" she asked.

He raised an eyebrow. "Moratorium?"

"Moratorium."

"I'm trying to understand your obsession with space. I feel like it doesn't really fit your whole . . . thing." He waved his hands over her like he was searching for a barcode to scan.

Winter snorted. "My *thing*? What thing?"

"You know, your . . . thing. With the sweaters and the tea and the Hallmark movies."

"I wouldn't call it a thing. I just like to be comfortable."

She lay down on the concrete with her ankles crossed and her hands clasped over her stomach. Bobby stared.

"I don't see how you do it," he said. He put his hand on the back of his neck. "You seem like nothing bothers you. Absolutely everything bothers me. Any little thing, and I crumble."

She didn't know if she understood what he meant. If she wanted a warm beverage and cookies, she got them. If her hair was in her face, she put it up. If she wanted an extra pillow and a blanket on her bed, she requested them. There was no great mystery. It was easy to be comfortable. Space was the hard thing to figure out.

Winter did what she did when she didn't know what to say; she said nothing at all.

"You don't have to tell me about your space thing if you don't want to," Bobby said. "It probably stretches beyond the limits of a moratorium."

"No, it's not that. It just feels obvious to me," she replied with a shrug. "Everything has been done before in some form or another. Exploring the entirety of our infinite universe is one thing we know that hasn't. It's there, above us all the time, untouched, waiting to be understood." She reached up and grabbed at the air.

Bobby made a steeple of his fingers under his chin. "Space is so big and empty. It seems really lonely."

"It isn't empty, though. It's full of dust and gas and raw energy. And so are we. We're full of the same stuff as the stars. So when we look up, we're actually looking at ourselves and all of creation. It's not lonely to me. And yeah, it's big, but everything is a smaller version of something else. Like the irises of your eyes are oceans and galaxies, and our Earth is a speck of sand on a cosmic beach, right? So everything is huge and unfathomable if you really think about it because we're all made of the same material."

He scratched his head. "And that's comforting to you?"

"I like feeling small." She hugged her arms closer. "I know that scares a lot of people, but to me it's comforting. When your own world inside of your head feels too big, you tend to focus on things that don't really matter."

"You mean like girls breaking up with you because you're too boring?"

Winter wilted. "Carl Sagan said that 'we are like butterflies who flutter for a day and think it is forever.' So in a grand sense, we are the last letter of the last word of the last page in the book of time. In your case, Jacqueline is maybe a sentence in the *Book of Bobby Bae*."

Bobby lay down too and looked up at the sky with her. "But you don't actually want to go to space, right?"

Winter wrinkled her nose. "No. Never. Have you ever eaten dehydrated space food? That's a level of discomfort I'm not willing to contend with."

Bobby laughed. "I think it's starting to make sense now."

"But things aren't always as they seem. I just take comfort where I can get it."

Narrowing his eyes, Bobby opened his mouth as if to say something else but then closed it.

They lay on the ground in silence, watching the clouds chase one another across the sky for what seemed like at least an hour. Winter felt like a gooey, melty chocolate chip cookie on a baking sheet. She felt that if she stayed there any longer, she'd become melded to the concrete.

"Let's get out of here," Bobby said at last. "We don't want to be late for UPenn, and I won't tolerate any more itinerary deviations."

Winter sat up slowly. She had little pebbles sticking to her elbows and the imprint of the sidewalk on the backs of her legs. "Do you really want to go to UPenn?" she asked.

"I mean, yeah. It's on the itinerary."

"But can you picture yourself going to school there? I can't see you in Philly. And if I hear you say 'jawn,' I'll steal all your pens and dump them in the Schuylkill River."

Bobby got up as well and dusted himself off. "Are you trying to unsubtly hint that you don't want to visit UPenn?"

"I feel like it was pretty subtle."

"As subtle as a blitzkrieg. What do you want to do instead?"

She played with her hands. "Well, did you know it's illegal in Maryland to eat while swimming in the ocean?"

Bobby frowned. "You want to go to the beach?"

"The beach doesn't sound better to you than UPenn? You and I both know neither of us are going there, and it's impossible to be sad at the beach."

All she'd done all summer was sit around her house eating carbs and getting nearsighted, and she presumed Bobby hadn't been doing much better. It was time to seize an opportunity as it presented itself, as Halmeoni had advised.

Bobby rested his thumbnail between his teeth. "We have to drop my parents a pin. They'll know we're not in Philly."

"You lack imagination."

"You know I hate when people say that."

Winter pushed her hair behind her ears. "Which is why we should do something fun today. We can put a VPN on your phone and be anywhere in the world. What do you say?"

"Yes," Bobby said in a flash, apparently without even thinking.

Winter's chin jutted back. "Seriously?"

"Yeah, why not? Let's go before I change my mind."

Winter giggled and prepared to stand.

"Actually, wait," he said.

Well, that was short-lived, Winter thought to herself. "You changed your mind that fast?"

"I need to call one more moratorium."

Winter groaned from deep in her throat. "You've got to be kidding me. What is it now?"

"Answer me one thing. Would you consider this a park?" he asked, motioning all around him.

"Please don't be weird."

Bobby bopped Winter on the forehead with his palm. "Just answer the question."

She looked around and noted the bench and grass. Her jaw firmed. "I guess it's sort of parklike."

"Good," he said, opening up a chess app on his phone. "Care for a game, Erik?"

Winter's eyes crinkled at the corners. "Prepare to get your ass beat, Charles."

♥

Bobby Bae

15. WE WILL NOT LAUGH AT EACH OTHER'S JOKES

Bobby looked up the closest beach, and they ended up in Annapolis with a view of the Bay Bridge stretching across the horizon. There were children giggling as they chased one another around the picnic tables and collapsed in the grass. There were families with matching T-shirts, out-of-towners slathered in sunscreen, and more than one ice-cream cone melting on the beach. The sand was warm, and Bobby could smell its earthiness mixing with the salty ocean. Winter was seemingly enjoying it, tilting her chin up so she could lavish in its aroma while drinking up the sun. But Bobby found the smell appalling as the water circled around his ankles.

"We didn't think this through," Bobby said, hiking up his pants so the water wouldn't soak them. "We didn't bring swimsuits."

"I did," Winter said, to which Bobby raised an eyebrow.

"Why aren't you wearing it, then?"

"Solidarity?" Winter offered.

"You can wear a swimsuit in front of me, you know," Bobby said, to which Winter shook her head. "Why do you have one anyway? Did you always know you'd be suckering me into going to the beach?"

"Of course not. My mother packed my bag."

"You can stay dressed, but this is ridiculous. I feel like a wet dog."

"Please keep your clothes on."

Bobby ran back onto the sand and wiggled out of his jeans. Winter covered her eyes even though there was no way anyone could tell his boxer shorts weren't a swimsuit. She pretended to gag as he removed his shirt as well, but her pleased expression was hard to hide. He smirked at her discomfort.

Although the sun was beating on his back and he didn't typically enjoy the beach, he couldn't help but feel at ease. It was still early, so not many people were surrounding them, and the blue-green ocean was calm. The waves were more so swirling around rather than crashing, and the seagulls were loudly contributing to the sounds of the ocean. Winter was walking around in the shallows, scooping up sand with the tops of her feet and then shaking it off. Maybe she was right: It was impossible to be sad at the beach.

Bobby opened up Winter's bag, took out a package of gummy bears, and called to her.

"I'm not looking at you until you put on some clothes!" she yelled back, keeping her eyes firmly planted on the ocean.

"Okay, fine. I'm covered up," he lied.

She looked over. "What the hell? Did you go into my bag?"

"Yeah . . . Catch!" Bobby threw a gummy bear right at Winter's forehead. It fell into the water with a satisfying *bloop*.

"What was that for?" She laughed, seemingly in earnest. Did this mean Winter Soon-hee Park enjoyed his company? Alert the presses.

"We're supposed to be eating in the ocean. You can't break the law if you don't catch it."

"Then why don't you actually aim for my mouth this time?"

She parted her lips and waited. Bobby took a handful and threw them all, pelting her in the face.

"Hey!" Winter kicked water at him, but it didn't go far. She ended up throwing herself off-balance and landing on her butt, completely soaking herself.

Bobby snorted. "Good job!"

Winter said nothing as she charged past him to the car. She returned moments later in a yellow one-piece, and Bobby felt the immediate urge to look away. But he didn't want to make it weird. Not knowing what to do or where to look, he got up and went back to the water.

Winter assumed his previous post and grabbed the bag of gummies. "Your turn!"

She spiked one right into his mouth, and they both whistled and cheered. Bobby stuck his hands up in the air and started chanting, "USA! USA! USA!"

"Wait, I can do better. Let me try again."

"You got it into my mouth. How could you do better?"

"Just open your mouth!"

This was the neurotically competitive girl he knew—the one who came to school with strep throat because she couldn't stand to let him be the Republic of Equatorial Guinea's sole delegate at their ninth-grade Model UN conference. Now she was chasing him around the water, trying to jam gummy bears into his mouth. She got him on his back, and he writhed around like a beached whale. Bobby's shorts were sticking to his legs.

"Mercy!" he cried as he struggled to stand.

"That's what you get for going through my bag."

"Oh, relax. The gummy bears were sitting on top."

Bobby splashed her, and she splashed him back with a wave that'd make Poseidon blush. He brandished a mimed white flag, and she helped him up. They walked along the water's edge together as Winter collected sea glass.

"Any other dumb laws in Maryland we can . . . circumvent?" Bobby asked.

"There are some really wild ones here," Winter replied as she counted her findings in her hand.

Bobby walked backward so that he and Winter could talk face-to-face. His feet squished into the wet sand and left perfect molds. "Like what?"

"Well, in the entire state of Maryland, oral sex is illegal."

Bobby stopped in his tracks, and Winter crashed right into him, causing her to drop all her sea glass.

"You okay?" he asked, trying to pick up her fallen sea glass.

"Yeah, amazing," she said, straightening out her swimsuit. She took out her hair elastic and flipped her hair over her head before piling it on top again. It always fascinated Bobby how quickly girls could do that. Bobby Bae enjoyed an orderly life, but he was a sucker for a messy bun.

"What was that?" Winter asked, pulling out the sides of her bun so she had hair sticking out in every direction.

"Huh? Oh . . ." Bobby bowed his head. "It was nothing. I tripped."

"Did you think I was offering to . . ." Winter said slowly. "Bobby Bae," she continued, with scandal in her voice, her lips curling into a dark smile. "Keep your hands and Freudian slips to yourself." She laughed hard at his expense.

His face got hot. "Come on, stop it. You promised to be nice to me."

"How nice were you expecting?"

"I yield. You win this one," Bobby said, throwing his hands up in surrender.

"But, Bobby—"

"I'm calling a moratorium!"

Winter hung her head to the side. "You can't be serious. You're getting moratorium-happy."

"Doesn't matter. I called it. You have to honor it," he said, marching ahead.

"Ugh, fine!" she yelled after him.

Bobby shook his head and continued walking. Maybe if he walked fast enough, he could escape his own embarrassment.

"*You can wear a swimsuit in front of me, you know,*" Winter mocked his words from earlier as she caught up.

He glared at her. "You're not honoring the moratorium."

"We're calling them every five minutes now. I'm not even sure what the original purpose of moratoriums was to begin with."

Bobby was tight-lipped. "They were to maintain a level of peace and civility between us."

"Well, we've been civil . . . mostly. I mean, until you tried to get me to blow you," she said, her mouth splitting into a devious smile.

Bobby's face got hot. "That is not what happened!"

"That's exactly what happened!"

Bobby put up a finger. "Moratorium!"

Winter deflated. "Fine. Whatever."

He sighed. "Should we go for a swim?"

"I can't swim."

"Me neither. Should we get food?"

"You're buying."

♡

Winter Park

16. WE WILL NOT DISCUSS PERSONAL MATTERS

Winter was filthy in the way that she liked. She had sand in every crevice, and the seawater in which she'd been drenched evaporated, taking all her scented moisturizer and antiperspirant with it. Her complexion seemed to glow in the light of the sun, her newly tanned skin reflecting its warmth.

Bobby and Winter were sitting at a table made of uneven wooden planks, right on the water. They already had a smorgasbord in front of them and hadn't even gotten their crabs yet. The smell of briny sea breeze made Winter's stomach rumble, so she went in for a soft pretzel rod and ripped off a piece. Hot steam billowed out of the pillowy pretzel. She dunked it into the creamy crab dip and danced as she shoved it into her mouth along with some salty Old Bay fries. Bobby, who was fully clothed again, was eating his fries with a fork and had a napkin in his lap.

"Describe your perfect day," Winter said. Between the beach, the space center, and this feast, she was having hers despite Bobby Bae's presence.

"You want to talk?" he replied, raising an eyebrow.

"I'm in a good mood, and I've never had lunch with a supercomputer before. Indulge me."

He put his finger to his chin. "My perfect day would probably include chillin' in my boxers, irony-playing *Fortnite* with Kai but actually kind of enjoying it, with a giant sweet tea next to me—on a coaster of course—and the promise of a sandwich."

"The *promise* of a sandwich? Not the actual sandwich?"

"Well, no. I'm playing video games. It'd be a mess. But knowing I was going to get one later would be nice."

She threw a fry at his head. "Thanks for reminding me why I hate you."

The waiter came, and they lifted their plates so he could roll out some brown craft paper over the table. He then disappeared and returned with a plastic tray of a dozen blue crabs crusted in Old Bay seasoning, waiting to be cracked open. Winter took a slow-motion video of the waiter dumping them out onto the table.

She rubbed her hands together and chose her first victim. She ripped the claws off and sucked out what she could, then broke it in half. The juices ran down her arms as she happily stuffed the bright white meat into her mouth. Bobby was cracking his and forming a neat pile of crabmeat before he even thought about eating it. Winter shook her head but said nothing about it.

The saltiness was giving her that pinched kiwi feeling in her cheeks. She raised her glass of fresh-squeezed lemonade to Bobby, and he raised his in return. "Jjan!" she said as they clinked glasses, then took a drink.

"Is that Korean for 'cheers'?" Bobby asked, wiping the bottom of his cup before placing it back on the table.

"Sort of. It's the sound glasses make when they touch." She knocked her fork against her cup. "See? *Clink. Clink. Jjan. Jjan.* It's the same thing."

He raised his napkin from his lap and dabbed his mouth. "It's not the same thing."

"Well, you can take it up with Korea."

"I should. I hear the north part is particularly open to suggestions."

"Bobby Bae, did you just make a joke?" Winter asked, hiding a smile behind her cup.

"You could be normal and laugh."

"You're not that funny."

He shrugged and went back to surgically removing the insides of his crabs. Winter watched him until he caught her looking. He didn't seem as tightly strung as usual. If he were one of her violin strings, he'd be only moderately sharp.

Winter readjusted in her seat. "Why didn't you ever learn Korean anyway?"

Bobby's smile faded. "I appreciate you trying to be nice, but don't feel obligated to make conversation."

Winter was taken aback, but he was right. Just because they'd been getting along for the last few hours didn't mean they were friends. She had no right to pry. "I wasn't aware I was being nice."

Bobby leaned back, folded his arms, and looked out over the water. "I don't like to talk about it. My parents never taught me, and it's embarrassing."

Winter put everything down so she could give him her full attention. "Why is it embarrassing? It's not like there are a lot of Koreans around."

"My parents never shared much of the culture with me, but I feel like the language is the one thing they could have. It's, like, the key to the rest of it."

"I mean, I only use it to speak to my grandmother, and my vocabulary is like a child's."

He turned to look at her. "I wouldn't expect you to understand."

Winter felt she should back off, but she was genuinely curious. She had never heard Bobby express any dissatisfaction about how he was raised or mention wanting to know about their culture or language. Her parents would have been more than happy to help, or even Halmeoni. Bobby volunteered at her senior center enough. All he'd have to do was sit with her and have a cup of tea. She would enjoy the company.

"Why didn't your parents teach you?" she asked. She suspected it was the same reason her own parents didn't put great effort into teaching her either. Halmeoni raised her children with English as their primary language in order to better her own language skills, and Umma carried on that pattern with Winter. If not for Halmeoni's fear of losing the language after Harabeoji died, Winter would probably be in the same situation as Bobby.

"I don't know for sure," Bobby replied, pushing his hair back. "But they no longer speak to either of their families, and I think it has something to do with that."

Winter stopped her mouth from falling open. As well as she thought she knew the Baes, she was clearly missing a lot of details. This explained why they held on so closely to the Parks. "Can I ask what happened?"

"They never really told me. This is just what I've gathered throughout the years," he continued. Winter snorted. She knew what that was like. Her parents never volunteered much personal information. There could be an elephant the size of the universe in the room, and they'd never address it. "From what I understand, my dad's parents owned a farmer's market, and after they died, my dad inherited the store over his brother because of his business degree. My dad wasn't able to keep up the store, and it caused a rift after he sold it. And since my grandparents had been very active in the church community, the church took my uncle's side after the fallout. He was a big churchgoer at the time. Last I heard, Uncle Eugene bought the place back. But our families aren't speaking."

123

"So that's why you moved from New Jersey," Winter said.

"Yeah, I think so. I think it got pretty bad for them, handling my grandparents' debts and everything."

"And your mom's family?" Winter asked.

"They still live in Korea. My mom was supposed to go back after college, but she never did. I'm not really sure what happened there either, but she doesn't talk about them, so it's like they don't exist. Sometimes I wonder if they didn't teach me anything because all this is so painful for them."

Halmeoni had raised her family with plenty of hugs and affection, and they always made a point of having weekly calls with the cousins in Korea or on the West Coast, and visits whenever they got a chance. Even if Halmeoni and Appa were having a battle of wills at the moment, Winter considered her family exceptionally close. But she knew that wasn't the case with every family. She'd asked Halmeoni once why that was, and the answer she got surprised her. She mostly talked about the Korean War. Halmeoni said it'd produced a culture of brokenness. But Koreans were very prideful, so they grinned and bore it, except without the grinning because happiness as Winter knew it was never the goal. Happiness to them was having a full stomach. That's why the Korean way of saying *I love you* was to ask if you'd eaten. To feed someone was to literally give them life. Halmeoni said that generational pain was bound to produce a group of people who only wanted to avoid conflict, so they didn't talk about things and never hashed things out if they felt slighted by a loved one. They punished them quietly by holding a grudge and pushing them out of their lives. And when you've held on to something for so long, it amplifies in the mind, and the distance only grows wider. Maybe that's what it was like for Bobby's family.

"Why didn't you ever tell me you wanted to learn Korean?" Winter asked. "I would have helped you."

"We both know that's a lie."

"Okay, fine. You're right. But still . . . I can help you now," she said. "I have a word for you."

"You're being serious?"

Winter put her hand over her heart. "We're still under moratorium. I promise."

Bobby reached into his back pocket and took out his leatherbound notebook. He flipped through it, and she got a look at a few of the pages. It was like he'd written his own English-to-Korean dictionary. He clicked his pen and looked at her expectantly.

"Gochu," Winter said.

Bobby repeated it, and she snorted.

"What did you make me say?" he asked, his jaw tightening.

Winter flashed her teeth. "Nothing. It means 'pepper.'"

"Then why are you laughing?" he demanded. "What does it actually mean?"

She held her sides. "'Pepper'! I told you."

"Winter."

"Bobby."

"Soon-hee."

"Okay, fine." Winter motioned for him to get closer. He leaned over the table, and she whispered, "It's slang for 'penis.'"

"Penis!" Bobby yelled. Some people looked over, and he smiled and waved at them like he was Miss America. He swiveled his head back around. "You had me write 'penis' in my notebook?" he hissed. "*Ugh.* I can't erase it, and if I cross it out, it'll look ugly."

Winter was beside herself with laughter. "I'm sorry. We were getting so serious," she said, regaining her calm. "I'll actually teach you something." She motioned for his notebook.

Bobby narrowed his eyes at her. "If you draw dicks all over it, I swear I'll drive off and leave you here."

"Calm down. I'm not going to draw dicks."

Bobby handed the book over the table, and a paper fell out. Winter wiped her hands and reached under the table to get it. When she picked it up, she recognized her own handwriting.

"What is this?" she asked, pinching it between two fingers.

Bobby looked down. "You don't remember the letter you wrote me when you were in in fifth grade?"

Winter's breath quickened. "What letter? What are you talking about?"

"Our parents made us go to the Spring Fling dance together. You wrote me a letter to invite me, and you laid out exactly how that night was going to go—what we could and couldn't do, what we could and couldn't talk about."

Winter's cheeks were hot. "You kept it?"

"Of course I kept it. It's rare that you know exactly where you stand with someone."

Winter had completely forgotten about that dance, but she did remember the dress. She went shopping for it with her mother and Mrs. Bae. It was a peach-colored sundress that fanned out when she twirled. She rarely enjoyed wearing dresses, but that one had pockets.

She bit her lip. "Can I read it?"

"I mean, you wrote it. Go ahead."

Winter slowly unfolded the letter. It had been tucked between the pages and seemed not to have been opened in several years. It was typed out, perfectly formatted according to *The Chicago Manual of Style, 17th Edition*.

"Oh God," Winter said. "This is so embarrassing."

"But very well written for a ten-year-old."

"Still mortifying, though," she said, her voice softening. "I was really horrible back then, wasn't I?"

"Probably no worse than I deserved."

She read over each word. Each maliciously written word. "Why did you really keep this?"

Bobby exhaled deeply. "It's in there with our original rules and all the many amendments. I figured we'd laugh about them one day."

It felt like a string snapped in her chest. She was having a hard time reconciling who this person in front of her was, this person who apparently girls loved; who had an interest in his culture; who was thoughtful, intelligent, loyal, dutiful, and sensitive almost to a fault. She knew so much about him, but she didn't actually *know* him. She wasn't sure that she even wanted to know him. They had been getting dangerously close to friend territory all day, and the realization wasn't agreeing with all the seafood in her stomach. The letter didn't help her sick feeling—it was like a mirror reflecting back all the bad parts of herself.

"Maybe we should end the moratorium now," Winter said, and Bobby silently agreed.

Winter folded the letter carefully, put it in her bag, and spent the rest of lunch not drawing dicks in Bobby's notebook.

Bobby,

As you know, the Spring Fling dance is in two weeks. Normally this is something I would go to alone, but our mothers would like for us to go together because they think it's safer that way. I didn't want to disappoint them, so I agreed to ask you.

Obviously we will have to abandon some of the rules currently in place for the night. Here are some additions so that we can enjoy this dance as best we can:

1. We will promptly shut down any questions about us liking each other.

2. We will not dance together.

If you are to refuse, you'll be the one to tell our parents this, and that I did my part by asking. But if you accept, please sign below.

Winter Soon-hee Park

♥

Bobby Bae

After spending a few quiet, uncomfortable hours on the road in his filth, Bobby was anxious to get to the next hotel and shower.

They kept their reservation in Philadelphia since their next stop was Princeton. This time they had two adjoining rooms, so he didn't have to share a bathroom with Winter, which was nice.

An entire beach fell out of Bobby's shorts onto the white-tiled floor as he peeled his clothes off. He set the shower to *dracarys* and stayed under the water until he was sure his eczema would bother him, and then stayed some more to wash the day away. He had promised himself never to tell Winter about his desire to connect with his culture. She had beaten him by a fraction of a point for the top of their class last year, and now this. She had all the ammo she needed to make his life a living hell if she wanted to.

Kai was calling, so he dried his hands and answered it on speaker.

"Dude, what's that noise?" Kai asked. "You hear that? You think the government is listening?"

"I'm in the shower."

Kai giggled. "Oh. Word. What's up, Bae?"

Bobby held back a laugh. "You called me, man. What's up with you?"

"Right. I have to tell you something." *I have to tell you something* was right there with *We need to talk*. He sighed. "Jacqueline came into the store today."

Bobby's chest hollowed out. It wasn't until that moment that he realized he hadn't thought about Jacqueline all day. "Did you talk to her?" he asked.

"For, like, two seconds. She asked how you were doing, and I told her you were on a trip with Win—"

"Why'd you tell her that!"

"I didn't know it was a secret! I didn't expect to see her. I panicked."

Bobby took a deep breath. "What did she want?"

"She literally bought the first book she saw and left. It was a copy of Malcolm X's biography."

"She came in just to ask how I was doing?"

"Either that or she's joining the movement."

Bobby beat his fist against the shower wall. It was all he could do not to return to where he was last week, curled up in his bed, wondering why Archie and Betty wouldn't just get together already. Bobby ran both hands through his wet hair. He watched the water droplets fall from the tip of his nose onto the floor. "It's fine. I've got a lot on my mind. Things are getting weird with Winter, and I don't know . . . I think I'm losing it a little."

Bobby could hear Kai smiling. "Weird how?"

"She was nice to me today, and I just got broken up with. That's all I'm saying."

"You two need to smoke that vape I gave you and chill. You guys are always doing the most when you're together."

"Can we not talk about me anymore? Tell me about that guy who keeps coming into the store. You get his number yet?"

Kai laughed his signature laugh. "Yeah. We're hanging out in a little, so I actually have to go."

130

"Kai, teach me your ways."

"I gave you my ways. Go smoke it."

"I love you, man."

"Love you too, Bae."

They hung up, and Bobby felt Kai's absence immediately. He was jealous, in fact, that Kai was going on a first date with someone. Bobby remembered his first date with Jacqueline. They were fifteen, so they went to the movies while his parents had dinner nearby. He'd been friends with her for years, but he was still so nervous. He barely spoke to her during the movie, but they kissed during the entire ending credits.

He missed that feeling. That nervousness. The performance involved with a new crush. He sighed and turned the water hotter.

♡

Winter Park

18. WE WILL BE DECENT

Winter was getting dressed after her shower when her phone rang. It was Halmeoni. She wrapped her hair in a towel on top of her head and picked up the phone.

"How are you, Soon-hee?" Halmeoni asked in Korean, without even waiting for Winter to say hello first.

"I'm great. Bobby and I ditched UPenn and went to the beach instead," Winter said. She didn't see the point of lying.

"Did you have fun?"

"Surprisingly, yes. How are Umma and Appa?"

"I'm sure they'd appreciate a call."

"Noted."

Winter lay down on her stomach on the bed. It'd been in knots since lunch. She didn't know if it had to do with the exorbitant amount of food she consumed or because she realized Bobby might actually be made up of something other than ones and zeros.

"Halmeoni?" Winter asked, staring at the door leading to Bobby's room. "Am I a bad person?"

Halmeoni let out a breath. "Of course not, Soon-hee. You are a miracle. What happened?"

"I think I'm losing Emmy, and it's all my fault. I've been trying to control our whole friendship, and I'm probably pushing her away.

And I think I've been doing the same thing with Bobby, only I started eight years ago. Why am I like this?" Winter whined.

Halmeoni clicked her tongue. "Have you eaten?"

"I'm trying to ask you a question!"

"Answers come to you when your belly is full and your mouth is shut."

Truthfully, Winter was getting hungry again.

She rolled over and looked up at the ceiling. As much as she wanted to speak with Halmeoni, she didn't feel well. Every time she thought about Bobby, the pit in her stomach got bigger. It wasn't the seafood; it was guilt.

"Can I ask you something else, Halmeoni? Do you think Bobby is good-looking?" she asked, not waiting for the permission.

Halmeoni clicked her tongue. "You and your dramatics, Winter. Bobby Bae is a very handsome boy."

Winter scoffed. "I don't mean handsome like he cleans up nice on Sundays. I mean, is he, like, really attractive? Like, do people want to date him?"

"Do you?"

Winter wrinkled her nose. "Ew. No."

"He's intelligent, and for some that's enough. You are as smart as he is, if not smarter, so maybe it's not enough for you. I called to ask you about your college visits, Soon-hee," Halmeoni snapped.

Her reasoning made sense. As a matter of fact, it might have been the only thing that made sense.

"What's really wrong?" Halmeoni asked.

"Nothing. My stomach is all in knots."

"Go get Bobby and get something to eat. No trash."

"Fine, Halmeoni. I'll eat. But there are some things that food can't fix."

133

That was a lie.

Winter took her hair out of the towel and threw it on the bed. Halmeoni was in her ear talking about her bingo game, which had been the night before. Mrs. Landau ended up winning and taking the $4,600 pot. Winter nodded to signal that she was paying attention, forgetting that her grandmother couldn't see her.

The adjoining door wasn't locked, so she opened it and found herself face-to-face with Bobby, who had just stepped out of the bathroom with only a towel around his waist. A gasp escaped her.

"Winter, what are you doing?" Halmeoni asked. "You sound strange."

"I'm getting Bobby for dinner," she whispered.

"Why are you whispering? Are you antagonizing that boy? You promised you would be nice."

"If I whisper, maybe he can't see me."

Bobby waited a moment, probably for Winter to explain herself. But when she didn't, he asked, "Are you okay?" sounding more annoyed than concerned. "Why are you here?"

"I came to get you for dinner. Want to say hi to Halmeoni?" she asked, extending the phone to him.

"Um . . . no. Not right now."

Winter was wide-eyed and so very caught. Her phone slipped out of her hand onto the floor, drawing her attention away from Bobby for the first time since she opened the door. She scooped up her phone, ran back to her room, and threw herself on the bed. Her head dropped against the pillows, and she looked up at the ceiling.

"You still there, Halmeoni?" she asked, putting the phone back up to her ear. "Tell me more about bingo night."

♥

Bobby Bae

Bobby leaned on the jamb of Winter's open door. She was sitting on her bed, reading a book, with a pencil between her teeth, which she then used to secure her hair into a messy bun.

Winter finally noticed him and jumped about a mile into the air. Her hand shot to her heart. "You're like the basement person from *Parasite*. You scared the shit out of me."

Bobby smirked. "What are you doing?"

She gestured to her book. "I'm trying to salvage my friendship with Emmy. You?"

He had no idea what she was talking about, but he stopped there. Her mind was always on another plane of existence, and he didn't want to bring her down to his level. In fact, he wanted to elevate himself to hers.

"We're supposed to be breaking rules, and I remembered we have a vape. Want to get high?" Bobby asked. He hoped she'd say yes. He didn't want to go on the adventure alone. Last time he'd ended up crying into a meatless burrito.

Winter placed her book on the nightstand. "We haven't been following any of our Geneva Conventions. Maybe it's not such a good idea to do something like this together."

"We don't have to talk."

"You must be really lonely if you're asking me to hang out," Winter joked.

Bobby auditioned a few smiles in his head before deciding which one looked indifferent enough. "You're the one waiting outside my shower." He was satisfied when Winter's mouth dropped open in horror. "Come on, then," he said, nodding in the direction of his room.

Bobby found the vape in his things, and he sat on the bed while Winter plopped down on the floor, a blank expression on her face. He let her fumble around with the vape until she figured it out because he knew he wouldn't hear the end of it if he tried to tell her what to do. She took one long pull and then he took one himself.

Within a few moments, although Bobby purposefully did not inhale all the way, he felt warm, and everything was hazy. His nerves had been doing somersaults since he'd decided to surprise Winter with the Goddard Space Flight Center that morning. He never liked surprises—giving or receiving—but Winter was the type to appreciate such chicanery. He feared another anxiety attack might come on as it had the first time he had smoked, but he was far too distracted by Winter. He lay on his bed and watched her as she dug around in his luggage. He had no idea what she was looking for, but he didn't have enough muscle function to care.

"Bobby, you can't seriously tell me you plan to use every single thing you packed in here."

"It's better to have something and not need it than to need it and not have it."

Winter pulled his extra pair of shoelaces out of his bag's side pocket. "Do you plan to have a shoelace emergency?"

"You don't plan for an emergency. That's why it's an emergency. It's emergent."

"And you have an extra toothbrush. Why would you need an extra toothbrush?"

Bobby looked over at her completely rearranging everything in his immaculately organized bag. "What if something happened to my first toothbrush? It would be stupid not to have a second one."

"Then you brush your teeth with your finger like anyone else who's ever had a toothbrush emergency."

"But why would I brush my teeth with my finger if I have an extra toothbrush?"

"Are you sure you're human? Humans like their lives with a little drama. You ever turn an assignment in, like, a minute before it was due?"

"Um . . . yeah."

"Then you're messy just like the rest of us, and you're pretending to be better by having this extra toothbrush."

Bobby threw one of his pillows at her. "What happened to not talking?"

"Bobby, why do you have so many sheet masks?"

"How is the vape having the opposite intended effect on you? Could you please sit down and shut up?"

All he could hear was the ripping of plastic as Winter tore open a package and unfolded one of his face masks. It was the one he'd saved for Tuesday. If she was going to cause so much chaos, she could have at least gone in order of the days of the week.

"The serums won't do anything for you if you drip them all over the floor," Bobby said flatly. His skin always misbehaved when he traveled, so he was annoyed the carpet was going to be more moisturized than he was come Tuesday.

"You should do one too. You're looking a little dull," Winter replied as she tried to position the mask on her face.

"I'm dead inside. I wouldn't want to misrepresent myself."

Winter grabbed another mask and jumped on the bed. Bobby felt like he was being thrashed around in a boat for a moment. Winter really had no sense of calm. She flattened out the citrus-scented mask and reached over him.

Bobby put up his hand. "We have a rule against this."

"I feel really restless all of a sudden, and you're boring me."

He sighed in defeat and nestled his head into the pillow, closing his eyes in preparation. He barely breathed as Winter hovered over him. He winced when the cold cotton touched his skin. Winter's hands were even colder. "Do you have any iron in your blood at all?" Bobby asked, flinching under her touch.

"You're making fun of somebody with anemia," she said, putting her cold hands on his neck. "Are you proud of yourself? Remind me not to stand up too fast in front of you."

With all his senses heightened, Winter's hands were the only thing he could focus on. He sat up abruptly and came face-to-face with her. This put Winter in a better position to apply the mask. She concentrated hard, her lips slightly parted like some people did when they were putting mascara on in the mirror. For a split second, he thought he might kiss her. She was so close—it would only be practical.

"There, don't we look pretty?" she asked lazily, giving his cheek a few sharp taps, which he felt in his entire body.

Throwing his legs over the edge of the bed, Bobby turned away from Winter. He tried to blink the intrusive thoughts away, but he had serum running into his eyes. He ripped the mask off and rubbed his eyes with the back of his arm. He then leaned his elbows on his knees and held his face in his hands, taking slow, deep breaths as he tried to calm the tingling feeling in his palms and soles.

He suddenly felt Winter's hand on his back. She drummed lightly against him with her thumb. In perfect silence, he allowed her the minimal physical contact. He counted each tap to thirty, and then she removed her hand abruptly.

"How did you know to do that?" Bobby asked in a low, tired voice.

"We've known each other a long time, Robert. I've observed a few of your deactivation codes throughout the years."

Bobby pouted. "I'm not the Winter Soldier."

"Is that why you're never ready to comply?"

"Why are you like this?" he asked, throwing a pillow at her head.

She threw it back at him, then lay down with her ankles politely crossed and her hands folded over her stomach. She was quiet, but Bobby could feel her wanting to speak. There were so many unsaid words in the air, and it seemed like she wanted to say them all. "We're allowed to talk if we're actively breaking a rule. You still high?" Winter asked.

"Very," Bobby lied.

♡

Winter Park

20. WE WILL NOT HANG OUT AT NIGHT

Ann Druyan once said, "The greatest thing that science teaches you is the law of unintended consequences." Those unintended consequences were why Winter loved science so much. The history of the universe was basically a series of mistakes. A bacteria floated into a cell nearly two billion years ago and became the powerhouse of that cell. If not for that, humans wouldn't have come into existence. If asteroids hadn't wiped out nearly every living thing on Earth, humans wouldn't have made it. They'd have been eaten by a Spinosaurus, and history books would have been very short. There were so many things that were the result of unintended consequences, without which amazing things couldn't have happened. If not for someone picking a plant with pointed leaves and burning it a few thousand years ago, this moment wouldn't have been possible.

The sinking feeling had left Winter. She felt relaxed. Her eyes were shutting on her without permission. The only thing that woke her was the rumbling of her empty stomach.

"Bobby, I'm dying," she said, clutching her sides.

"It'll pass."

"No, Bobby. You need to feed me."

"I can't move."

She did her best pout, which she usually saved for her dad. "Bobby, please. Can we get something to eat?"

"You're incorrigible."

Winter dragged Bobby out of bed and out of the hotel. Everything was hazy, and she was having trouble focusing on more than one thing at a time. She had tunnel vision on food, so everything she did was in service of that desire. The only bodily functions she needed for that were walking and breathing. Everything else was thrown to the wayside. Bobby was quiet too.

On the street, Winter felt small. The buildings were standing over her, looking down at her with judgmental faces and darkened windows. They knew. Everyone must have known how far up in the stars she was. She had to learn to walk and use her limbs and even how to breathe again. This was the first time she had ever been altered by any substance. It was something of which she had always been afraid. Winter had an uncle who suffered from alcoholism, and Halmeoni had once said that he wasn't sick—he was only looking for God in the wrong places. She wondered if he'd ever found Him. He still drank, so maybe not.

The sidewalk was covered in dark spots of chewed gum, and it smelled of car exhaust and city filth. The air seemed to dirty her skin in a way only a city could. Philly was the City of Brotherly Love. It was blue-collar through and through. It felt heartier than Washington, DC, and less assuming. It was your job to find its charms; Philly didn't want to just hand you all the magic it had to offer.

Bobby was ahead of her, doing his best not to step on the cracks in the sidewalk, like they used to do when they were kids. He won every time because Winter would get impatient and start stomping on them. But Bobby had always been more patient. He found his God in order and patience. His life was like the Container Store, while hers was like the sales rack at Forever 21. She was really starting to feel it now. She caught up to Bobby, and everything slowed down enough so she didn't mind skipping over the cracks next to him.

"Hey, did you know you can't be governor in Pennsylvania if you've participated in a duel?" she asked. She wasn't sure if she was yelling or whispering.

Bobby's lips curled into an amused smile. "Shall we have a duel, then? My honor has been besmirched, and I demand satisfaction."

They drew finger guns and held them at their hips. Standing back-to-back, they walked ten paces. Winter stuck her arms out like she was balancing on a tightrope. Gravity was misbehaving, and she giggled every time she teetered. The two called out their tenth step before turning on each other and firing. Bobby's nonexistent pistol jammed, and Winter had the aim of a Stormtrooper. They both lived to tell the tale.

"Now neither of us can run for office in Pennsylvania," Winter said, chewing on the inside of her mouth, trying to stifle a laugh.

"There you go, ruining my political ambitions again."

"It's been three years. You need to let that governor's dinner *for women* go."

"Never."

The elastic in Winter's hair had slipped almost entirely down the length of her ponytail. Bobby snatched it before it fell and handed it to her. She stopped to throw her hair back up into a bun as he watched her with a lazy smile and dead-behind-the-eyes look.

"What's your problem?" she asked.

"Nothing. We're here."

They stopped at a crossroads, and her eyes fell upon Pat's and Geno's, the two most well-known Philly cheesesteak spots in the city. Their retro multicolored lights illuminated the entire street. Winter could smell the hot grease sizzling on the industrial stove tops intermingling with caramelized onions and fresh bread rolls. She was drawn to them like a moth to flame.

"Which one should we go to?" Bobby asked.

"Both?"

He stepped forward, and Winter stopped him. "Wait. There's a special way to order them. Do you know it? I don't want to embarrass myself in front of a bunch of Philadelphians. Did you see what happened after they won the Super Bowl?"

"I don't know how to order. I don't speak cheesesteak."

"I don't have any dietary restrictions. You order."

Bobby folded his arms. "No, you. You were the one who was hungry."

Winter stomped her foot. "Bobby, just go. Pleeeeease. You'll have to carry my body back to my parents if I don't eat soon."

"Chivalry has died, Winter. I may open doors for you sometimes, but you're perfectly capable of opening them yourself."

"Well, don't stop being a gentleman on my account. Order away, sir."

"I can't. I'm way too high. And it's too bright over there."

"Come on, Bobby. We know who's going to win this argument."

They stared each other down for what felt like forever but realistically was only about five seconds. Bobby was the first to look away. He sighed and ran his fingers through his hair.

"Fine, I'll handle this," he said.

♥

Bobby Bae

21. WE WILL NOT GIVE EACH OTHER ADVICE

Bobby and Winter, under the light outside of Pat's and Geno's, waved down their delivery boy. Bobby had never seen anyone look so confused. He had red hair and freckles, and was not much older than they were, probably a college kid trying to make some honest pocket money, not deliver food a block over to red-eyed teenagers with social anxiety.

They started walking back to the hotel with their greasy bags. Bobby didn't typically eat like that, but his stomach was turning inside out and eating itself. He went to take a big bite, but Winter stopped him.

"That one has cheese on it," she said, opening up all the foil wrappers to check the others. "They all have cheese. Our order was wrong."

Bobby didn't care. He was starving. "I can pick it off."

"You can't pick off Cheez Whiz. It chemically binds to things."

He took a giant defiant bite. "Relax. It's basically orange plastic."

"Your funeral, Milquetoast."

Bobby whirled around. "How'd you know about Kai's graphic novel?"

"He posted a few panels online. They're good. They really capture your struggles as a lactose intolerance sufferer."

Bobby shook his head. "Please don't tell me he posted the one of

Milquetoast missing an entire alien invasion because he was on the toilet."

Winter laughed. "He did."

Bobby's shoulders sagged. "I keep telling him that character makes no sense. If milk hurts him so badly, why doesn't he stop drinking it?"

"Are you serious?" Winter broke into a fit of giggles that almost got the better of her. "It's so obvious."

"What's obvious?"

"Milquetoast is a coward. That's why he eats a gallon of Chunky Monkey before every single fight."

Bobby's face got hot. "He's not a coward. He's a flawed hero. He could even be a pacifist."

Winter giggled out of control. He'd never heard her laugh like that. She must have still been high. "Or maybe dairy is delicious, and he's willing to sacrifice the greater good for a Chobani. I would do the same. A world without milk is a world not worth saving."

She was like his dad. Mr. Bae was the only one in the house who could have dairy, and he had no experience buying food for only one person. Everything he bought always went bad. This bothered Bobby so much he developed an app called Uyu, which was a milk tracker that sent reminders when the milk was nearing its expiration date. You'd input the date you purchased it and the kind (because skim spoiled faster than whole), and then it sent reminders and dairy-based recipes so you had no reason to let your milk spoil ever again.

Bobby told Winter about the app, and she nearly choked on her cheesesteak. "You're just like Milquetoast. You're completely obsessed with milk!" she said, wiping tears from her eyes. "Oh my God, I'm dying. Kai is a genius."

Bobby pulled the app up on his phone. "You laugh, but this app has saved my parents a lot of money, and I'm currently programming it to include cheese and yogurt as well. The Baes run a tight ship, and my dad was ruining it until Uyu came along."

Winter wiped off her hands and took the phone. She paused in the middle of the sidewalk. "Bobby, this is really cool. It looks so professional. No lie. Have you released this in the app store?"

"No, it's just for my dad to use."

She was scrolling through the app with the phone held closely to her face, slowly, not blinking. "This interface is so clean. I can't believe you designed this."

"I only coded it. Kai designed the interface."

"Seriously? I didn't know he was into tech."

"Yeah, he wants to go to Berkeley next year to study UX design."

"I can totally see him on the West Coast. That's perfect," she said as she checked out each menu option. She gave his phone back and took a monster bite of her sandwich. "I'm surprised Kai knows what he wants to do and you don't. It seems so unlike you."

Bobby bit his lip. "I just want to—"

"Make money, I know. But I thought you'd have some specific goal."

Truthfully, he didn't. He only knew he wanted to be successful. He wanted a comfortable life for him and his family, just like the one he grew up having. With a mathematics degree, he could be an actuary or a statistician or something else for which he'd have to look up the job description.

"I want to do right by my parents. I don't want my parents to be disappointed in another family member," he said.

"Forget about them for a second. What would you do if it was only you?" she asked, taking another large bite. "You're annoyingly smart. There has to be something you like that you could monetize."

He thought for a moment. "Nothing that would bring me security."

"Forget about that too. Imagine whatever it was gave you infinite heaps of money. Would you maybe consider studying computer science and creating apps for a living? I could totally see you as one of those elitist types in Silicon Valley."

"I don't know. I made the app because I was getting tired of spoiled milk," he said, looking at Winter under the moonlight.

"Well, isn't that what tech is all about? Identifying a pain point and then creating something to fix it?"

He hadn't considered it as a career. It wasn't something he'd want to do unless he was the CEO of his own company. It was a very up-and-down, ever-changing industry. Things became obsolete in seconds. It was also for people who could charm investors and grease palms. That wasn't him. But maybe it was Kai. Bobby had to admit he enjoyed developing the app, and it felt good every time his parents actually used it. He and Kai also had so much fun putting it together.

"I guess I'll look into computer science programs. It couldn't hurt," Bobby said.

Winter had stopped paying attention to him. She'd unwrapped her second cheesesteak and appeared to be thanking it for its service. He couldn't help but smile as he opened the door to the hotel for her and she walked in, not realizing that the doors weren't automatic.

Never in a million years did he think he'd get advice that could potentially alter the trajectory of his life from someone who was using her sleeve as a napkin. And never in a trillion years did he think that person would be Winter Park.

♡

Winter Park

22. WE WILL RESPECT EACH OTHER'S PERSONAL SPACE

Winter was in that lovely space between being asleep and awake. The warmth of the sun was on her face and the chirping of morning birds filled her ears, but her mind was still dreaming. She smiled and snuggled her pillow tighter, wanting to stay like that for as long as she could. Through the haze, she felt something prick the skin just above her elbow, followed by the most terrible itch. She smacked at it and only managed to smack herself awake.

A mosquito was buzzing around her head. She screamed and buried herself in the blankets.

"What happened?" It was Bobby. His voice came from the other side of the bed.

"Bobby, what the hell are you doing in my room?" she barked.

Sleep was thick in his voice. "You're in *my* room."

She wrinkled her nose. "*Your* room?"

"Yeah, *my* room."

Winter was still disoriented from sleep, so she had no memory of how she'd gotten there. She remembered little after they'd gotten cheesesteaks. Her intention had been to figure out which one was the better of the two, but she'd fallen into a food coma before she could make deliberations.

"Why'd you scream?" Bobby asked.

"There's a mosquito in here. I told you they're after me!" she squawked.

"Relax, it'll die soon."

"It's not a bee, Robert! If it was a bee, I wouldn't mind taking a couple for the team!" Winter couldn't stop scratching. "*Ugh*, I'm going to kill it. I've had enough of them."

"Calm down, Bill Gates. It's early."

She didn't listen. She whipped off the blankets and tried to clap the mosquito between her hands but kept missing. It got her a few more times, so she ran around to the other side of the room and hid behind a chair.

"I think it can see you, Winter," Bobby said lazily, pulling the blankets back up over himself.

"Do something, Robert! I could go into anaphylactic shock!"

"I'm not a mosquito slayer. Stop freaking out."

"Robert!"

"Okay, fine! One second. I have to . . . check something." He lifted the blankets and looked underneath.

"What are you doing?" Winter snapped.

"It's the morning—"

Winter put up her hand. "Oh my God. Don't explain. Just help me."

Bobby groaned and came to her rescue with the first thing he could find—the customary hotel Bible.

"Are you going to use the power of Christ to compel it away?" Winter asked hotly.

"It's only a mosquito. Stop singing your swan song."

"They're the number-one killer in the world! I will not calm down!"

"Well, they're attracted to CO_2, so could you at least shut your mouth?"

Winter threw him a look.

Bobby tried to slam the mosquito onto the table using the Bible, but it was too quick for Bobby's sloth-like reflexes. It ended up biting Bobby in the neck.

"God damn it!" he yelled.

"Don't say that with the Bible in your hand, Robert!"

He threw the Bible down, and the mosquito landed on his arm. "Now it's after me!"

Winter threw one of the chair cushions, and it hit Bobby square in the face. "I'm sorry!"

"What were you aiming for?"

"The mosquito, obviously!"

"That was not obvious."

The mosquito flew back over to her. "What kind of mutant mosquito is this? It's after me again!"

"I told you to shut up," he said, swinging at it with the cushion she'd thrown at him.

Winter screamed and ran to hide behind Bobby. She crouched down, her hands clasped around his shoulders as she used him as a human shield. It was then that she noticed he was shirtless.

"Why are your hands always so cold?" he asked, flipping around.

Winter's face became hot, and she jumped back, tripping onto the bed and pulling Bobby down with her. The wind was completely knocked from her lungs. Bobby struggled to get up, pinning Winter against the bed. She was wide-eyed, and her breath had completely stopped as he covered her entire body with his own.

"Bobby, you can get off me now," she said, tucking her arms into her sides.

"Don't be coy now. You slept next to me all night."

The blood was pumping hard through her ears. "Bobby—"

"Just shut up for a second and don't move. It's on your arm."

Winter stayed perfectly still, and Bobby paused for a few moments before swatting the pesky mosquito with a resounding *smack*.

"Ow, Bobby!" she said, rubbing her arm where he'd smacked her.

"I'm not going to lie, that was really satisfying."

"Well, could you kindly get off me now?"

"Could you thank me nicely?"

"Thank you, Robert Dae-seong Bae Jr."

Bobby smiled and rolled over next to her. When she looked at Bobby, he was grinning. He was so strange. Most of the time he had something up his ass, but other times he was almost . . . charming. When you're not actively flirting but come off as flirty anyway, that's charm. Unless he was, in fact, flirting. That would be a different story. Winter scooted away a few inches so he wouldn't notice her discomfort.

"How'd you sleep?" he asked.

"Fine, I guess."

She was being modest. That was the best she'd slept in a long while. That is, until she was attacked by a prehistoric beast and realized she was in Bobby's bed.

"You talk in your sleep, you know," he said, smirking.

"I do not."

"You do too."

"What was I talking about?"

"About how much you love me and how sorry you are for torturing me for the better part of a decade."

Winter pushed his arm. "You're such a dick. I was not. How did I end up here anyway?"

He pushed her back. "We got back from getting food, smoked some more, and watched a couple episodes of *Cosmos*. I think it was

151

a bit of a system overload for our brains, so we knocked out early."

"Right. And your shirt?"

"You turned the thermostat up to, like, a billion. I was boiling."

"I like to be warm while I'm sleeping."

"You set it on hell."

"Well, you could have turned it down."

"I don't touch thermostats around you after that one time."

She remembered how mad she'd gotten when he'd turned the air conditioner up at her house and her parents blamed her for it. She let all the air out of her lungs.

"I'm sorry," she said.

"For what?"

"I don't know. I'm just sorry."

Bobby kept looking at the ceiling. "Since we're technically breaking a rule right now, I want to tell you something." The way he was looking at her made her nervous, but Winter nodded. "I had fun last night."

The pit in Winter's stomach returned. "It had its moments."

Bobby rolled over to face her, so she did the same. "I've always tried to imagine what it would look like if we were friends. I think it would look a lot like last night."

Winter laughed without meaning to. "Why would you imagine that?"

"Because you're the only person who doesn't like me, and it's infuriating."

Winter rolled back over and looked at the ceiling. She bit her lip and glanced at Bobby from the corner of her eye. "You've seen how shitty of a friend I am. Trust me, you're not missing out."

"Emmy doesn't—"

He stopped abruptly, midsentence.

"Bobby?" Winter asked. "What happened? Is it anaphylactic shock?"

His face dropped color, and his stomach made the most terrible noise. He got up and ran into the bathroom, slamming the door behind him. She heard him retch and immediately realized what had happened.

It was the cheese.

♡

Winter Park

23. WE WILL NOT FRATERNIZE OUTSIDE OF RULE BREAKING

The UPenn campus didn't look unlike the GW campus. There were students in pajamas and loose ponytails, with vats of iced coffee in their hands, laughing and smiling together in groups. Trees shaded the walkways that wound through the quads like ruddy rivers made of brick.

Winter lavished in the feeling of being alone again. Bobby was back in the hotel resting. He was no longer sick, but Winter had a sneaking suspicion he was trying to avoid telling her she'd been right about him overestimating the fortitude of his stomach. She still couldn't believe that she fell asleep in Bobby's room, in his bed. She remembered that they started to binge-watch *Jeopardy!* They competed, answering the questions themselves, but after a six-episode tie, they got bored and switched to *Cosmos*. Neil deGrasse Tyson started explaining the multiverse, and it was so much for their impaired minds to comprehend that they went into system failure. It wasn't sleep; it was more like low-power mode.

She walked by the library, which had large windows like a cathedral. UPenn wasn't one of her preferred schools, but it occurred to her as she watched kids studying despite school not being in session that she wasn't guaranteed a spot at MIT. It was easy to feel smart in high school. Most people didn't even want to be there. In college she'd have far more competition than only Bobby Bae.

An uneasy feeling turned her stomach.

Making her way through the buildings she was able to sneak into, she felt small as she passed room after room filled with computers and books that had endured so many generations of hands that their original color was indiscernible. She exited a building and made her way to the football stadium.

Taking a seat in the center of the field, she looked up at the thousands of empty seats and imagined they were stars.

With warm grass tickling the backs of her legs and the coppery smell of dirt filling her nose, she thought of Năi Nai and Halmeoni unearthing petunias together. Then she thought about Emmy. Winter was completely ready to become a broccoli-headed ajumma with a visor, floral housecoat, and hands as hard as the dolsot she cooked in. She had always imagined Emmy would be there with her, her smiling eyes collecting lines like trophies awarded for each year they got to be friends.

It wasn't easy to accept that Emmy was well on her way to having the life she deserved. A life that didn't necessarily include Winter.

It was like everything that made Winter *Winter* was being dismantled before her eyes, and there was nothing she could do. It started with Năi Nai, a woman she had known her entire life. Now it was Emmy planning her future in Europe. Next it would be her home, her parents, and Halmeoni when Winter eventually left for college. And did Boston even have good barbecue? Too much was changing all at once, and she wasn't allowed to be sad about any of it. Năi Nai wasn't exactly hers to mourn, and she was supposed to be happy for Emmy and herself for starting their lives. Excited, even.

Winter emptied her hands of the blades of grass she'd been ripping to shreds and shook her head at her own stupidity. She'd always liked space because it made everything seem small, but it seemed that she had shrunk her world so much that she left no room for anything or anyone else.

♥

Bobby Bae

Bobby was lying in the bathtub, using a towel as a pillow. Everything hurt. Everything. His stomach, his throat, his legs, even his eyelids. That was the first bit of dairy he'd had in years, and it did not agree with him. However, he felt some food poisoning might have been at play as well. Of course Winter was impervious to greasy street meat. An iron stomach was another thing she could lord over him.

A bout of nausea came on, so he crawled up the side of the toilet, leaned over it, and threw up what he hoped was the last of the cheesesteak. He'd only eaten one, unlike Winter, who had wolfed down two without even taking a breath.

His body sweat profusely as he emptied his stomach, but then he shivered as soon as he was done. He wiped his mouth and crawled back into the bathtub. Winter had left him a cup of tea, but even drinking that in his current state had him praying to gods he didn't believe in. It was a kind gesture, though. If he'd learned one thing on this trip, it was that Winter could be nice when she wanted to be. Actually, he'd always known it, but he'd never been on the receiving end. She told her parents she loved them every time they spoke, she picked up litter and threw it in the trash if she saw it, and she smiled at everyone. Sometimes it seemed like he was the only person not worthy of her kindness. All it took was being forced into a road trip together, taking her to a space research center and the beach, sharing some drugs, keeping her fed, and poisoning himself. No big deal.

He was thankful for a moment of rest. He thought that it might be over, but it still meant they'd missed their tour at Princeton, which he had scheduled months ago. Those were two schools in a row that he'd be missing. He didn't mind that Winter went to visit UPenn alone, but Princeton was a distinct possibility for him.

With everything going on, Bobby had completely forgotten to stress over what Kai told him about Jacqueline coming into the bookstore. He couldn't figure it out. Pathetic information-seeking visits were more on-brand for Bobby Bae than Jacqueline Charlotte Turner, the future political analyst and broadcast journalist, the leader of the debate team and listener of NPR. All her moves were calculated. Showing her hand like that was unlike her. She had to have known Kai would tell him. It was a trap he was willing to walk into.

Bobby had his phone in his hand and had dialed Jacqueline before he even knew what he was doing. She answered after three rings.

"Bae?" she asked, her voice low and uncertain.

"Why did you go to Kai's bookstore? You could have just called me."

Jacqueline didn't answer immediately. He could hear her breathing on the other side of the line. "I was checking on you. I stopped by your house first, and your parents told me you were gone but didn't tell me where," she said in her martyr tone, as if he'd done something to her by not being available for her unannounced check-ins.

"I'm visiting colleges. You knew about this trip."

"You told me you were going with your parents, not Winter Park. Isn't that correct?"

"It's none of your business, Jack. You broke up with me, remember?" he snapped. "And the worst part is that you never even

158

meant to. You wanted it to fizzle out like we hadn't been together for a year and a half. Do you know how long it takes for a fire that's been burning for a year and a half to fizzle out?"

Jacqueline's sigh crackled in his ear. "Nothing about your reaction suggested you even cared. You thanked me for letting you know like it was some kind of work memo."

"You caught me off guard! I wasn't going to beg you to be with me if that's not what you wanted to do."

"Maybe I wished you would," Jacqueline replied, her voice uncharacteristically soft.

Bobby put the phone on speaker and rested it on his chest. "I'm not the bad guy here, Jack."

"Don't belabor the point," she hissed. "I know you aren't the bad guy. I just wish you would be sometimes. It's always me. You make me feel ridiculous."

Bobby turned his palms up as if to ask the universe what the hell she was talking about. "How?"

"Bobby. We're seventeen. You take me to cooking classes and silent films and trivia nights. Sometimes I just want to play beer pong at Carly Bishop's house, but I feel like I can't tell you about it because it's beneath you," she said quickly, as if she were trying to chase the words out of her mouth. Bobby wished she wouldn't cry because then he would probably start, and he was already dehydrated.

"So you did break up with me because I'm too boring," he said as more of a declarative statement than a question. He wiped his face. This felt more to him like a breakup than their actual breakup had. He called to be broken up with a second time by a girl he wasn't even dating anymore. His stomach was turning again. "Is it cliché to say that I think we grew apart?" Bobby asked.

"No, because that's exactly what happened. You've always been my best friend before anything else," Jacqueline said. "After our friend group disbanded, it was only me and you. I guess I thought that if we broke up, I would lose my only true friend."

Jacqueline was a bit of a loner like he was, and that's part of the reason they clung to each other. She always had strong opinions on everything, which would one day make her a very effective political analyst, but it didn't help her make friends in high school.

"We haven't been friends in a while, though, Bobby," Jacqueline continued. "I tried so hard to get you to be present, but you're always in your head. You never let yourself have fun, and it was miserable to watch."

"Do you think you would ever want to get back together with me?" Bobby asked, and immediately slapped himself internally. He was winning this breakup. Why did he say that?

Jacqueline cleared her throat. "Aren't you dating Winter Park now? Why are you on a trip with her?"

"It's . . . complicated. My parents forced me to bring her, but I promise we're not dating."

"I don't know if I believe you. You've always been suspiciously preoccupied with her."

"We're not even friends. As soon as we're home, we're going to go right back to ignoring each other."

The word vomit was pouring out of his mouth worse than the real vomit.

"I don't know. This conversation is outside the scope of what I wanted to discuss. I only wanted to see how you were doing, and I guess I've done it. Goodbye, Bobby." She hung up without another word.

Bobby's head flopped against the edge of the tub. He gave himself exactly two minutes to wallow before he dragged himself out of the bathroom. Winter was standing in the doorway of their adjoining rooms when he walked out.

"Hey, what are you doing here?" he asked.

"I came to check on you," she said, tight-lipped.

"Oh. Did you hear me . . . on the phone?"

Winter was stone-faced. She didn't have to reply. He crawled into bed and put a pillow over his face.

♡

Winter Park

25. WE WILL NOT DESTROY EACH OTHER'S PROPERTY

Winter hated to admit it, but Bobby had hurt her feelings. Only hours before, he'd told her that he had always wanted to be her friend and he was glad that they were getting along. What he said to Jacqueline was a completely different story. They would go back to ignoring each other once they got home? Maybe they weren't meant to be friends. Not that she believed in fate. She only believed in the stars, and they apparently didn't want to align for the two of them.

She ripped the covers off Bobby and opened up the blackout curtains. He winced and hissed like a vampire being exposed to the sun.

"We have to go, Bobby," she said. "You must be better already. If we leave now, we can even walk around the Princeton campus ourselves without the tour and still make it to Boston by nightfall."

"I feel like garbage," he replied, shielding his eyes with his arm. "You'll have to drive us."

Winter froze. "I don't have a license, remember?"

Bobby scoffed. "You must have your permit. You've driven before, right?"

"Yeah . . ."

"Well, you were the one who wanted to do all this rule breaking. So here's the rule. Break it."

Winter gulped.

Driving was the one thing that made her extremely nervous.

There were too many variables. She could go the exact speed limit, use her signals, and observe all traffic laws, but all it would take would be one asshole in a rush running her off the road, and all of a sudden, she'd have killed a family of five and she'd be in jail for vehicular manslaughter. It was way too much pressure.

"I don't— Don't make me tell you that I'm bad at driving," Winter said, clenching her fist.

Bobby took the keys off of the nightstand and threw them into Winter's hands. "It's a straight shot from here to Princeton. I trust you."

"You shouldn't."

"But I do."

"You're just trying to get in my good graces," she said, throwing the keys back. "This isn't the way."

"Then what is?"

Winter sighed. "We should go back to how things were. Why wait until we get home?"

"I didn't mean that."

"But you said it, and you're getting back together with Jacqueline, right?" she asked, tapping her foot. Bobby didn't answer, so Winter snatched the keys from him. "Whatever. I need to get the hell out of here."

The keys felt heavy in her hands. He trusted her, but he probably shouldn't. He was probably only saying that he did to get out of the doghouse. If he was willing to risk his car to make amends with her, she should at least be slightly willing to crash it. If he continued to piss her off, there were probably many beautiful ditches in New Jersey they could tour instead.

They packed their things into the car, and it was Winter's time to overcome her fear. She hopped into the driver's seat and took a deep breath. It was strange viewing the world how Bobby saw it. The seat was way too far back, and she couldn't see a single thing in any of the mirrors. She adjusted everything and said a silent prayer.

Bobby was slumped in the passenger seat as she started the engine and gingerly drove off. She was going exactly the speed limit, and she braked for every little thing. Every time she did that, Bobby lurched forward, so she did it more.

She went through an intersection, and another car zipped behind her, nearly swiping their bumper. They laid on the horn and Winter's heart beat fast as the sound swelled and disappeared with the Doppler effect.

"Be careful of the lights!" Bobby snapped. "They're on the sides."

"How was I supposed to know that? I don't drive. Ever. Especially in big cities."

Bobby's tone softened. "I'm sorry. You're doing fine. Just mind the lights."

"Can you be quiet? I can't concentrate."

That was the last time they spoke until they got to New Jersey. Bobby was right about it being a short and pleasant ride. The roads were empty enough, and the part she hated about driving most was other people. In engineering and robotics, trial and error were par for the course, but in driving, if you made a mistake, you literally died.

After arriving in New Jersey and several mansplain sessions from Bobby about jug handles, they were there. All she had to do was park. *I can do this. It's literally my last name*, Winter thought to herself.

Princeton was greener than she expected. But she supposed that made sense since New Jersey was the Garden State. The trees made the campus feel cozy. There was also a long lake with lanes set up and people with strong-looking arms using their paddles to chop through the water and glide under the bridge she was driving on.

They passed by the library with its large open windows and hanging lights and past a fountain with a statue made of crushed metal in the center. There were couples walking around it and children splashing in the water.

"Park on this street," Bobby said, pointing at the next street over.

Winter got nervous and missed the turn. Because she missed that side street, she ended up on the main street. It was a lot more crowded than the highway. She was starting to sweat, and Bobby's phone ringing loudly through Bluetooth was making her nervous.

"Can you answer that?" she asked. She looked at the caller ID, which told her it was Jacqueline.

Bobby sent the call to voicemail and put his phone back into the cup holder. It rang again.

"Just answer it, Bobby," she demanded. "I can't concentrate."

"Keep your eyes on the road."

"If you want to drive, then drive. Otherwise shut up so I can concentrate."

Winter let out a long breath and hoped all her frustration would come out with it. She was cruising along a street with several consignment stores and ice-cream shops and places to get bubble tea when Bobby's phone rang again through the speakers.

"Jacqueline clearly needs to talk to you about something important," she said.

"I don't want to talk to her."

"Why? Because I'm here? You can only talk to her about me if it's behind my back, right?" Winter retorted.

Bobby was quiet. He was trying to appear calm, but he had a death grip on the door that gave him away. "Please pay attention to the road."

"Stop telling me what to do!"

"You're going to miss the turn, Winter. Shut up and drive."

"Stop telling me to shut up!"

The phone ringing through the car was distracting her, and her heart was pounding. Bobby yelling at her wasn't helping.

"You're going to take the turn too fast. Slow down," Bobby said, gripping the dashboard.

"I swear, Bobby. You need to back off."

"Slow down!"

Winter did end up taking the turn too fast. She neglected to see the curb—she felt it, though. The car went up and down, shaking them around inside like a pair of dice. Several bystanders clapped their hands over their mouths and others went, "Ohhhhhhh," as the back of the car followed and dropped down onto the street.

The car was shaking violently as Winter pulled into the nearest parking lot. She shut off the engine and got as far away as she could. She hadn't even driven a full hour and she'd already wrecked Bobby's car. She was only joking when she said she wanted to ruin it. Had she subconsciously done this on purpose?

Bobby jumped out of the car and had both hands on his head. He looked like her dad when he was watching a particularly disappointing basketball game.

"Is it bad?" she asked.

"There's a giant hole in the tire and the rim is bent."

"And . . . that's bad?"

"Well, it's definitely not good!"

♥

Bobby Bae

Bobby tried to replace the damaged wheel with a doughnut to no avail. He had hands made for Dove commercials and couldn't loosen the bolts. He called a tow truck, which took hours to arrive.

After the tow truck left, Bobby sat near the fountain they'd driven by earlier, trying to come up with a new plan. He and Winter hadn't exchanged two words between them since she tried to lay waste to all of New Jersey's curbs. He was seated on a stone bench, watching her at the reflecting pool with her feet in water. She sat on the edge, using a handful of pebbles she'd collected to play a solo game of gonggi like Mr. Park had taught them when they were kids. The pebbles clacked together as she shook them up and spilled them onto the concrete.

At least I got to use my road flares, Bobby thought.

The mechanic said that the car wouldn't be done until the next day, so they were utterly stuck with very little money because what he had in his debit card went toward the tow truck and fixing the rim. He wouldn't be able to use his credit card without his parents knowing about it, and he couldn't very well tell them he allowed Winter to drive. If he told them he had done it, they would never trust him to drive alone again. "A car is a privilege," his mother always said.

He looked at his reflection in his phone screen and saw someone familiar looking back. His breath was steady. *Your car isn't a vase, and you're not a kid anymore,* he muttered to himself. He'd impulsively asked Winter to drive when he felt like Death was around the corner. When your insides are desperately petitioning to become outsides and you're too weak to get not only your toothbrush but your emergency toothbrush is when you are your most honest. His truest self is the one who handed over the keys, and his body didn't supply the panic attack to alert him he'd done anything wrong.

Bobby shook his head at his own stupidity.

He knew what he wanted to do, but he didn't know if he should. He had always imagined reconnecting with his uncle Eugene after he'd moved away to college and had his own life. He never thought that it would be under these circumstances. His finger hovered over the call button as he watched Winter splashing around. She was by far the oldest one doing so. The kids were pushing one another under the jets, and Winter smiled every time they screamed.

A group of skateboarders flew in front of his face and broke his trance. He clicked the green button, and his phone rang. The call couldn't have lasted more than three minutes, and Bobby barely remembered what he said. His only physical reminders that it had occurred were the tense grin from ear to ear on his face like Uncle Eugene could somehow see him through the receiver and the sinking feeling in his stomach from knowing that his estranged uncle would soon be arriving to save him and Winter.

Bobby sat transfixed to the spot, focusing on the sound of Winter's gonggi stones hitting the pavement.

Bobby remembered very little of his uncle. He knew he was very religious and used to say something to his father every time they skipped church. He also remembered that he used to smoke, and his car always smelled like cigarettes. Bobby used to hate getting rides from him. Anything else he knew about Uncle Eugene was constructed from little bits and pieces that his parents would let slip occasionally, like the fact that he didn't go to college, and he had never married and appeared like he never would. The way his parents painted him, he expected to see Uncle Eugene in all leather, flicking a coin while leaning against a dim streetlight. But the man he saw marching toward him couldn't have been more different. He was in jeans and a polo, with his hair slicked back and a watch on his wrist. He didn't look unlike Robert Sr.

Winter slipped her sandals back on and joined Bobby at his side.

"Don't start," Bobby said.

"I wasn't going to say anything."

"I can't right now. I haven't seen Uncle Eugene in ten years," he said, tensing up. "Maybe this was a mistake. It was a mistake. We should go."

"Calm down. He's your family."

"My family isn't like yours. You don't understand."

Uncle Eugene's mouth split into a wide smile when he noticed Bobby. He made his way over and slapped him on the back, much like Robert Sr. often did.

"I'm so happy you called me. You're just like your father. Smart. Of course he would raise a boy smart enough to go to Princeton. But you're handsome like me."

Bobby smiled shyly. "Thank you, Uncle. I'm sorry to call you like this. I was going to call you anyway, even if something hadn't happened to my car, I swear."

"No worries. We're family," he said, locking Bobby into a firm handshake. Then he looked at Winter. "Your father ran away from his heritage and moved you to that town. I didn't think he'd ever raise a son who'd date a nice Korean girl."

Bobby's face was hot. He didn't want to slander his father in front of his little brother, but Robert Sr. hadn't raised a son who was dating a Korean girl.

"Hello, Ajusshi. I'm Soon-hee," she said, bowing her head slightly.

"It's nice to meet you. How long have you two been together?" he asked.

"We've known each other practically our whole lives."

"I'm really surprised how you turned out, Bobby. But I'm really proud of you. Now come, both of you. I want to show you the farmer's market. I fixed her up a little after I bought the place back."

Bobby found Winter's eyes, and they exchanged a glance while Uncle Eugene was turned around. Winter shrugged, and they both followed behind Uncle Eugene.

♡

Winter Park

27. WE WILL NOT ENTERTAIN DATING RUMORS

Uncle Eugene walked ahead of Winter and Bobby with his chest puffed out, proudly smiling at passersby. Winter supposed Bobby was the kind of son or nephew someone would be proud of. He was well-mannered, didn't slouch, and looked like someone who'd read at least one academic paper in his life and understood it.

The three of them walked in V formation like birds flying home for the winter and ended up at an unassuming farmer's market with black awnings whipping in the breeze and sun-bleached ads for fresh fruits and vegetables. Uncle Eugene saw Bobby admiring a table of rainbow-colored fruits separated into individual cardboard cartons. Winter laughed. She knew he was trying not to fanboy over how organized it was. Each fruit was waxed and glistening in the sun, with the stems all pointing toward the sky. Uncle Eugene grabbed a bright orange persimmon and gave it a shine on his pant leg before presenting it to Bobby, who smiled like a little boy and took it in both hands.

"I'll be right back. Have a look around," Uncle Eugene said before heading to the back of the store, where one of his employees was flagging him down.

Winter bit her lip and looked out the corner of her eye at Bobby. "So this is the farmer's market. There are a lot more jars of assorted artisanal jams than I anticipated."

Bobby busied himself with turning some jostled pears stem-side up.

"Why didn't you correct Eugene when he called you my girl-friend?"

Winter froze. "I've never been anyone's girlfriend. I didn't think it was that big of a deal." Truthfully, she had always wondered what it would be like. So far it wasn't so bad. She had been Bobby's pretend girlfriend for only about twenty minutes, and they were already shopping for organic fruits.

"I take who I call my girlfriend very seriously."

"You take *everything* seriously," Winter fired back, but then softened. "I'll tell Eugene the truth."

"It's okay. Let's not make things awkward for no reason."

Winter pursed her lips. It wasn't lost on her that Bobby didn't correct Eugene either.

"I feel like I should apologize."

Bobby lifted an eyebrow. "For getting jealous of Jack and wreck-ing my car?"

"Don't flatter yourself, Robert."

"Whatever." Winter could have sworn she saw Bobby smirk before he tossed his hair away from his eyes. "Peace offering?" he asked, handing her the persimmon.

"Ew, I don't want your uncle's pants persimmon." She wrinkled her nose but took it anyway and marveled at how perfect it was—a blazing orange, as if plucked from the sky and placed in her hands. She took a bite, and juice ran down her arm.

"Remember how your mom would bring a box of persimmons every time she came over?" Bobby mused. "I always liked that. I thought it was really classy. My mom would try to one-up her by bringing Korean grapes to your house."

"I liked *that*," Winter said. "Those things are like candy."

Bobby shook his head. "They're too messy."

Winter scanned the aisles for the grapes and snatched one off the vine. She squeezed it between her fingers, and the sweet insides burst out of the leathery purple skin into her mouth. She took another and held it to Bobby's lips. He spun around to avoid her, but Winter had it at his lips again.

"Open your mouth, Robert!" Winter demanded.

He pawed at her. "Cut it out!"

"Robert!"

"No!"

Winter brought her hand across Bobby's face, and she popped the grape into his mouth when he gasped.

"Ugh, it's like eating an eyeball!" he said, laugh-choking.

"Excuse me for trying to immerse you in our culture."

"By literally jamming it down my throat." He coughed dramatically, and Winter rolled her eyes. "Are these even Korean, or did we just claim them as our own?"

"Who cares? They're ours now."

Winter was going to launch a few grapes at Bobby's head, but Uncle Eugene shot them a look, so she decided against it. He turned back around and went about his business. He was talking to a man who appeared to be a delivery driver, and based on their body language, there was some sort of issue with the shipment. She couldn't tell exactly what was going on because Uncle Eugene and the driver were speaking to each other in an English-Spanish hybrid.

"Your uncle isn't what I thought he'd be like," Winter said.

"My parents always made it seem like he was a loser college dropout," Bobby said. "But look at him. He speaks at least three languages. This store looks amazing, and he seems to do okay."

"I don't think parents are always right."

Bobby let out a deep breath, which sent his bangs flying upward. "I'm starting to see that."

Uncle Eugene made his way back over, and the same cheesy smile was splashed across his face. "How are you liking the store? I recently had it remodeled, and my stepdaughter helped me with some updates."

"The store is really lovely," Winter said, debating whether it was rude to spit out the grape seeds she had tucked in her cheek or if she should swallow them. Her father always told her grapevines would grow in her belly.

"You're married, Uncle Eugene?" Bobby asked.

Uncle Eugene's smile faded. "My wife passed away a few years ago."

Bobby fell silent.

Winter took a gulp and quickly said, "I'm sorry for your loss." Bobby wasn't good in situations like this. He largely avoided heavy conversations, probably because of his desire to control absolutely everything. However, this time, he wasn't overreacting. His uncle had lived an entire life away from the rest of the family, and so much time had gone by that he'd become a husband, a father, and then a widower.

"No matter. It's good to remember people sometimes," Uncle Eugene said. He then took a faded black-and-white photo off the wall behind him and showed it to the two teenagers. "This is your grandmother and grandfather right outside the store the day they bought the place. This picture has been hanging in here since 1976."

Bobby's grandfather was in a pin-striped suit with a skinny tie and his hair slicked back. He looked like Bobby, but he had more stories etched into his face and unspoken ones tightening his jaw. He was a hard-looking man, impeccably dressed for the time. Bobby's grandmother was wearing something Winter's halmeoni would wear. She had on a black dress, a boutonniere on her wrist, and a brooch pinning both sides of her long coat together.

"Your grandfather lived in this store," Uncle Eugene said. "He was brilliant. He came here not speaking a word of English, but he got a good education and worked as an accountant for a decade before he quit one day and bought this place."

"Could you tell me more about them?" Bobby asked.

Uncle Eugene was thoughtful for a moment. "They were odd but good people. I remember your grandfather never slept. Maybe only a few hours a night. Then he'd wake up at four a.m. and shave his face in complete darkness. I remember I tried it once and cut my entire chin." He chuckled. "And I remember Mom would cry if she got a run in her pantyhose, and every day when she heard Dad pull into the driveway, she'd run into the bathroom and put on lipstick. She was raised on a farm, but you'd never know it until she was in this store." Uncle Eugene placed the picture back on the wall, then gave Bobby a sharp tap on the cheek. "They'd be so proud of you. You're smart like your dad."

Winter sensed a hint of disdain in Uncle Eugene's voice at the mention of Bobby's father.

"I'm getting a little tired," she said.

"Right. Let's head back to the house. You can meet my stepdaughter, Simone."

Simone came in while the three were sharing a pot of tea in Uncle Eugene's kitchen. Winter was in her element, swirling cookies in her mug, so she didn't budge, but Bobby stood up as soon as he heard the door unlock. Simone threw her purse down on the counter and headed upstairs without saying a word, leaving Bobby standing in the middle of the kitchen, his napkin having fallen from his lap to the floor.

"She'll be back," Uncle Eugene said. "She went down to the shore with her friends and probably needed a shower."

"Of course, Uncle," Bobby said, taking his seat again.

"She's in the nursing school at Rutgers. She stops by now and then. Otherwise this house can feel so empty."

"Ajusshi, what happened to your wife?" Winter asked.

Bobby elbowed her in the side.

"It's okay. She was sick, but we didn't know until it was too late," Uncle Eugene said.

"I'm sorry we didn't get the chance to meet her," Bobby said.

"You're here now. How is my big brother anyway?"

The air was instantly sucked out of the room, and a humongous elephant gleefully perched itself in the corner and prepared to be ignored.

Bobby shifted nervously. "He's . . . fine, I guess."

"Still working in risk management? And your mother, is she still working in arbitration?"

Winter snapped her head around to see Bobby's face. She hid a giggle in her teacup when he looked completely baffled. Arbitration fit Mrs. Bae; she could neutralize any situation with ease. But risk management for Mr. Bae? She didn't see that coming.

"Yes, Uncle," Winter said, seeing that Bobby clearly was not going to answer. "Business is good, and everyone is in good health."

"What are you both going to school for?"

"I'm studying aerospace engineering, and Bobby is studying—"

"I'm considering computer science and app development," Bobby interrupted.

Winter tried to hide her surprise in front of Uncle Eugene.

"Very impressive. Both of you," Uncle Eugene said.

Simone came bounding down the stairs, hair wet, in a new outfit. She gave Eugene a kiss on the cheek and then said, "Hi, I'm Simone. You two must be Robert Jr. and Winter." Simone flipped her red sheet of hair over her shoulder. The light caught it, and it sparkled like a Christmas ornament. Winter was envious.

"I've always wanted a cousin," Bobby said, giving Simone a kiss on both cheeks. "It's truly a pleasure to meet you."

Winter extended her hand to shake Simone's, but Simone grabbed hold of Winter's arm and pulled her into the kitchen. "Let's get dinner started and let these two catch up."

Winter tried to eavesdrop on Bobby and Eugene. Since the house was new, the walls were thin and she would have been able to make out what they were talking about if not for Simone rummaging loudly through the refrigerator. Winter finally gave up. She would have to get the meeting minutes from Bobby later.

"So how do you like Rutgers?" she asked Simone, trying to make polite conversation.

Simone pushed the fridge closed with one manicured finger. She drummed her red nails on the marble counter. Her eyes became dead and empty. "Is Rutgers one of the schools you're considering?"

"No, I was only making conversation."

"Let me guess. You're only visiting Ivy Leagues?"

Winter wrung her hands. "MIT and GW aren't Ivy Leagues."

Simone's naturally red lips turned up into a humorless smile. "Right. Why are you even here?"

Winter wasn't sure if she meant in the country, in this town, or in her house. It wouldn't have been the first time she'd been asked any of those questions. She went the safe route and assumed she meant in Princeton.

"We were going to do a short visit at Princeton on the way to Boston when we had some car trouble," Winter replied.

"I meant why are you *here*? In my father's house. In his life again."

She'd chosen wrong.

"Eugene is Bobby's uncle." She didn't believe any further explanation was needed.

Simone gave Winter a moment's reprieve as she washed her selection of vegetables. She then handed them to Winter along with a knife and heavily marred cutting board. All the ingredients were so vibrant and colorful, as though a rainbow had thrown up in the sieve. They must have been from the farmer's market. She'd never marveled at how gorgeous a carrot could be before. Emmy suddenly came to mind. If Uncle Eugene could live in this big house, surrounded by these stunning carrots, with a stepdaughter who was clearly ready to skin her along with the sweet potatoes for him, then maybe Emmy could make her own way too.

"Is Robert Jr. your boyfriend?" Simone asked, her expression still vacant.

Winter wasn't sure if this was a trick question and whether she should tell the truth or the *truth* truth.

"He prefers Bobby."

"Help me understand," Simone said, putting the peeler down for a moment. "Eugene told me so many times that his brother hated him and that he moved away so we couldn't corrupt their perfect son, Bobby. But somehow here you both are. What could you possibly want from us?"

"We don't want anything. Bobby missed his uncle. He doesn't have a lot of family."

Simone threw the cubed sweet potatoes into a black Dutch oven and leaned her back against the counter. She scanned Winter up and down with her bright green eyes. "Did you come here to gloat? To see how poorly he was doing? Because the store is doing really well. Eugene is even paying for me to go to nursing school. And I've taken good care of him since my mom died."

Winter bristled. "No . . . he does seem to be doing fine."

Simone's voice dropped into a flat, mocking tone. "No thanks to you all," she said, and Winter's spine went cold. "Eugene bought back the market after Robert Sr. sold it. He wouldn't let that stupid store go because he had something to prove to his brother, even though Robert probably doesn't know he owns it. It's like he's obsessed or something. I don't get it. Is it, like, a cultural thing?"

A cultural thing. That was Winter's answer every time someone asked her something about her culture that she didn't feel like explaining. Why do Koreans make noises when they eat? *It's a cultural thing.* Why do Koreans care so much about age? *It's a cultural thing.* Why do Koreans sit on the floor? *It's a cultural thing.* She didn't like hearing how Simone said it, as though culture could be blamed for every little confusing thing Eugene did. What if Winter said that how Eugene acted was cultural? Would that satisfy Simone, or would her answer only go against something she'd already decided long ago? That everything she didn't understand about her stepfather was because of the country he came from?

Winter stood up straighter. "I'm sorry if our being here is bringing up old feelings, but I promise you, we really had the best of intentions."

"He's the only dad I've ever known, but sometimes I just don't know what he's thinking—whether it's a cultural thing or a Eugene thing."

"I can't really speak to the culture," Winter said. "I was born here, and my family is nothing like Bobby's. I'm sorry."

Simone closed the lid on the pot. "Forget it," she said. "Let's just have a nice evening."

Feeling like she should have the last word, Winter said, "I know this means absolutely nothing to you, but you kind of remind me of my best friend."

The hardness in Simone's eyes diminished somewhat.

Winter settled in next to Bobby at the dining room table. Wiggling her eyebrows as if to ask, *Is everything okay?* she waited for his signal as to how he wanted to proceed. She was fine with leaving and sleeping on a park bench somewhere or calling her parents and admitting what happened. Whatever he decided, she was willing to do. However, Bobby gave an "I can't complain" shrug and then nodded slightly as if to ask, *How about you?* The way Uncle Eugene was gazing adoringly at his estranged nephew made it obvious that they were having a good time together. She smiled, and Bobby smiled back. It appeared they would be staying.

Simone leaned down and placed the Dutch oven on top of the trivet in the center of the table. The hearty stew bubbled within. She'd made some kind of vegetarian dish with lentils. Winter felt healthier just looking at it.

"My Simone makes sure I eat right when she's home," Uncle Eugene said, rubbing his tummy and tucking a napkin into his shirt collar. "This old heart isn't what it used to be."

"We had to cook healthy meals for Mom. Low sugar, low dairy, and no processed foods. I guess we just never broke the habit."

"I guess I had more than one reason to buy the market back."

Bobby attempted to avoid bringing up his father again by commenting on the feast in front of him. "Well, this looks amazing," he said. "Your mother was fortunate to have someone to take such good care of her, and I'm glad you have someone to look after you too, Uncle Eugene."

"It seems that you have someone too," Uncle Eugene replied with a chuckle. "I hope my nephew isn't too much of a handful, Miss Winter."

Winter reddened when her and Bobby's eyes met. "No," she said, averting her gaze. "He's . . . all right."

Uncle Eugene threw his hands up in delight. "Well, with that glowing review, meokja! Let's eat!"

The dinner went surprisingly well, despite the weirdness with Simone in the kitchen. They joked and laughed in a way Winter did with her own family at the dinner table every night, though she still felt the undercurrent of unspoken words. She also couldn't help but notice how Bobby was different when he was happy—his usual scowl was replaced with a smile full of teeth. She felt a sense of joy and warmth in her chest seeing him like this. She never observed him without at least a modicum of anxiety, though. Discreetly, she lifted the edge of the tablecloth, and as expected, his leg was bouncing nervously underneath. She paused, a gentle smile on her face, before resting her hand on his knee. The movement stopped, and he looked up at her and mouthed, "Thanks."

After dinner, Eugene led Bobby and Winter upstairs to show them where they would be sleeping. Winter walked past what she assumed to be Simone's bedroom. It was empty for the most part but still had remnants of a childhood. She had wooden shelves that went up to the ceiling. Only about two shelves were full of books, and the others had stuffed animals and objects made poorly out of clay, probably from a grade-school art class. She also had a few pictures of herself with a woman whom Winter believed to be her mother. She and Simone looked a lot alike. They had the same fiery red hair and clear pale skin. It was odd to see a bedroom that looked similar to hers that belonged to a girl only a few years older, who had seemingly outgrown it already. Is this what she would feel like when she returned from college?

Eugene gave Winter a towel and left her to fend for herself. He then showed Bobby to the guest room next door. She should have known Eugene wouldn't put them together in the same room. Not that she wanted to share a room with Bobby.

Winter plunked down on the bed and closed her eyes. Her body was so tired that it wasn't long before she fell asleep.

♥

Bobby Bae

28. WE WILL NOT INSERT OURSELVES INTO SITUATIONS WHERE WE DO NOT BELONG

It was well past five a.m., and Bobby was still awake. He couldn't sleep in strange places, and the streetlights were blasting through the window. He finally dozed off until a noise from downstairs startled him.

Bobby tiptoed to the top of the stairs and peered down. Uncle Eugene was sitting at the dining room table with his head in his hand and a rocks glass filled halfway with amber liquid in the other. Bobby recognized that look; it was the same one his mother had when she'd knit in the dark or when his father would absent-mindedly drown the garden. Faraway, thinking about the past. Something clicked seeing him like that. It was like hearing both sides of a phone call, not having to guess anymore what was being said on the other side.

The step under Bobby's foot creaked, and Uncle Eugene looked over.

"Sorry, Uncle Eugene, I didn't mean to disturb you," Bobby said.

"No, no, I'm sorry if I woke you," Uncle Eugene replied, pulling the glass toward him in a poor attempt to hide it. "Come, sit."

Bobby reluctantly agreed.

Eugene was quiet for a long while. He swirled his drink around, and when it sloshed over the brim onto his hand, he seemed to snap out of his trance and said, "I'm glad you're here. You probably don't remember, but I used to watch you when your mom and dad were at work."

Bobby tried to think back as far as he could, and he vaguely remembered going to the park with Eugene almost every day before he started school. They'd feed the ducks, and one time he approached a mother duck and was on the receiving end of her wrath when he tried to give her babies a grape. When his father read him *The Ugly Duckling* as a bedtime story a few weeks later, he bawled.

"I was really young, but I have flashes of memories sometimes," Bobby replied. "I should have reached out to you sooner."

"There are always sacrifices you have to make when you're trying to do right by your parents. I didn't go to college because I had to take care of your grandparents, as you know."

Bobby's eyebrows raised. "I actually didn't know that."

Eugene's eyes flashed with anger. "Your father didn't tell you? Your grandmother had Parkinson's, and your grandfather and I took care of her while Robert was in school. I always figured he'd come back and help with the business at least, but he ended up getting married and starting a job and never did." The elephant that had been in the corner finally took a giant dump in the middle of the room.

"Uncle, you don't have to—"

"You should know what kind of man your father is," Uncle Eugene said. "Our parents opened that store when they came to this country, and he sold it like it was nothing. I took care of Umma and Appa, and I ran the store when they couldn't anymore, yet they gave it to him because of his degree. It should have been mine." His eyes were bloodshot, and a vein pulsed in his head.

Simone and Winter came down the stairs in their pajamas as

Bobby was picking the skin around his nails, which eventually started bleeding. Winter took a few steps forward to join him, but Bobby held up his hand, indicating that she should not get any closer. Simone, however, slid past her and squeezed Uncle Eugene's shoulder.

"Does Robert know that you're here?" Eugene asked.

"No, he doesn't," Bobby answered calmly.

"I'm sorry, Bobby," Eugene said. "It's late, and it's been a long time since I've thought about my brother. You have to understand the pain he's caused."

"The pain *he* caused?" Winter blurted. She had a hand over her mouth when Bobby turned to her.

"You're young. You don't know what happened," Eugene replied.

Bobby froze. He was shutting down, and he knew Winter could feel it. There was more to be said, but he was simply too polite to say it.

He felt a whoosh of air past his face when Winter came charging past him, getting between him and Uncle Eugene. "Your parents left Mr. Bae with a pile of debt," she said. "Selling that store was the only thing he could do to break even and keep the whole family from sinking. They tried for years to save it, but they couldn't. Do you not know that, or do you not care?"

Eugene opened and closed his mouth. He gawked for several moments before his jaw firmed and he said, "He had that fancy degree—"

"Which told him that the store wasn't profitable," said Bobby.

Eugene sucked his teeth. "You really are my brother's child, aren't you? He even gave you his name."

"Bobby is better than Mr. Bae. And you," Winter said to Eugene. "And me, if we're being honest. He shows people he cares about them even if they don't show him the same back."

"Why don't you have some water and go to bed, Eugene?" Simone asked gently.

"Don't patronize me!" Eugene barked. His face contorted in rage, and his grip on the glass tightened until it exploded in his hand. Red leaked down Eugene's arm, shards of glittering glass embedded in his palm.

Bobby's stomach churned with a wave of nausea at the sight of blood, but he clamped down on it and forced himself to stand. He stepped in front of Winter, his arms spread wide in a gesture of protection. "I want to get to know you, but if you frighten Winter, I will never speak to you again, and my dad will have been right about you," he said, his voice steely and unfamiliar.

Eugene opened his mouth and shut it. He was still visibly red and covered in a thin layer of sweat. His face immediately calmed at the sight of Bobby's and Winter's fear. A look of shame darted across his face.

"You both go to bed, and I'll handle this," Simone said, just loud enough for Bobby to hear.

Bobby's fists were clenched at his sides, his nails leaving half-moon imprints in his palms. He did an about-face and took Winter up the stairs with him.

"I'm sorry about all this," Bobby said, standing in the doorway of Winter's room as she settled on the bed.

"We're getting out of here as soon as the sun comes up," she said sternly.

Bobby's posture became rigid. "We can't just leave. It would be rude."

Winter let out a heavy breath. "Can't you see what he's doing?"

Bobby pressed his lips together. "He's projecting years of family drama onto you. Some of it happened before you were even born! You ever heard the saying 'the sins of the father'?"

"That's not what's happening."

"Yes, it is. You should have heard the spiel Simone went on earlier," she said, lowering her voice to just above a whisper. "She thinks we're here to rub it in how well we're doing compared to them. According to her, every bad thing that's happened to Eugene is because of your dad."

"Okay . . . so what if he wants me to see what my father has done? Don't I deserve it? My family was awful to him if what he says is true."

"That wasn't you, Bobby!" Winter said in a yell-whisper.

Bobby sighed. "Look, Winter," he said. "I used to think my mom was just this person who chased me around the house with open water bottles, asking if they were mine, and my dad was a dad joke in golf shorts, but they've held some really dark things from me. If Uncle Eugene thinks my parents ruined his life, then maybe they did, and so did I by extension."

"It's not your responsibility to atone for your parents or to put your family back together."

"Then why does it feel like it is?"

Winter was silent for several moments, and Bobby let their words breathe for a minute.

"Bobby, can I ask you something? And I want you to be honest with me," she said.

"I'm always honest with you."

She paused. "Right. I— Err . . . Why do you care so much?" she asked, her voice slipping in and out of a whisper. "If I'm being real, I never got the impression that you were in love with Jacqueline. I feel like the way you've been mourning your relationship doesn't match the relationship. Then you try to get her back, and now this?" She got quiet for a moment. "And . . . with me. You've taken my shit for years, and you could have told me to shut the hell up on day one. You didn't have to keep up this routine we've been perfecting for all these years."

"It's the only way you'd talk to me."

"You see what I mean? I don't know how you got it into your head that people will love you less if you don't act exactly how you think they want you to."

Bobby clenched his fist. "You just . . . I don't know. I stand by what I said before. Despite what you heard me say to Jacqueline on the phone, I've always wanted to be your friend. I still do." Bobby grabbed his hair by the roots. "I don't know why I can't get it together. I don't know what I'm doing."

"You're trying to be what you think you're supposed to be," Winter replied. "What you need to do is what every movie, TV show, and Hallmark card has been advising for basically all time and be yourself. If no one wants to come with you for the ride, then keep looking!"

"But they're my family."

"They'll always love you, even if you're not perfect. You don't have to make everyone happy. Like, do you even want to go to Harvard? Your parents will never love you less no matter what rules you break or what school you go to or if you can't speak Korean," she said, not bothering to whisper anymore.

Bobby's breath caught. "My parents abandoned my uncle because he disappointed them. I guess I always kind of thought my parents would abandon me if I did the same."

"You're their son. That's never going to happen."

"My mother is estranged from her parents and siblings, and Eugene is my father's brother. They've cut people off before. Who's to say they won't do it again?"

"Regardless of what you do, they love you."

"Do *you*?" Bobby crossed his arms and propped himself against the doorway. "Why'd you defend me back there?"

Winter heaved a big sigh. "It's difficult watching you allow yourself to be everyone's punching bag, including mine. I didn't get it before, but I think I see you now."

"I see you too," Bobby said, just above a whisper. "You're kind. You act like you're not, but you can't hide it. Your problem is you shut people out."

"I'm not kind. You are."

"I'm polite. There's a difference. Kindness comes from within. Politeness comes from without," he said, and the two stayed silent for a few moments, allowing the conversation to linger in the air.

"We need to do better. Try harder," Winter said finally.

"How? What am I supposed to do about Jacqueline?"

"She dumped you. Cut your own bangs and burn all her stuff in a trash can."

Bobby laughed despite himself. "I'm not a teenage girl from a movie."

"Halmeoni wanted us, meaning you too, to have fun. Does watching Simone give your uncle stitches seem like fun to you?"

Bobby stood up straighter. A surge of courage and determination took hold of him, and he activated like the Winter Soldier. "You know what? You're fucking right."

"Bobby, you've been back in New Jersey for, like, five minutes and you're already dropping f-bombs?"

"Get your stuff. Let's go."

Winter's eyes grew wide. "Really? Now?"

"Yes! Now! Before I change my mind," he said, running back to his room to grab his things.

Winter took her phone charger out of the wall and stuffed it in her bag. It seemed to be the only thing she had unpacked or was at least the only thing she cared about taking with her. She was in her pajamas, with her hair sticking every which way out of a ponytail holder, and couldn't look less bothered by it. She slid past Bobby, and he followed behind her.

Simone was done patching up Eugene when they got back downstairs. He was quietly sitting at the table, his eyes staring into nothingness, a fresh white bandage on his hand. Simone looked over, and noticing the bags in their hands, she said, "I understand you wanting to leave. He's not usually— Well, things have been hard since Mom died."

"I hope you'll come back," Eugene said, looking up at Bobby. "You can always come here to stay, anytime. You could even live with me if you decide to go to Princeton. I'm so happy that you called."

Winter was having trouble hiding her face. Eugene was going full Scar to Bobby's Simba.

"Do you hate my mom and dad?" Bobby asked simply.

Uncle Eugene lowered his eyes. "Sometimes."

"Do you miss them?"

"All the time."

Bobby slowly turned his head, his eyes meeting Winter's gaze. His jaw tightened at the sight of her, a deluge of memories from their past flooding his mind. But then he breathed in deeply as he let go of the tension in his body, and his shoulders relaxed. It perhaps wasn't unreasonable to hate and miss someone at the same time. He'd always had a burning rage toward Winter but felt her absence in equal measure.

"I'm not my father," Bobby asserted. "This isn't the last time you'll see me. I promise."

Uncle Eugene only nodded.

Simone stepped lightly over the broken pieces of glass that lined the floor, carefully picking up a bottle of liquor from the top of the fridge. She handed it to Bobby, her eyes full of apology as she said, "He doesn't usually drink. It doesn't agree with him. Do you mind getting rid of this for me?"

"Of course," Bobby replied, taking it in his hands. "I'll stay in touch, Cousin."

"Hopefully our families can work things out."

"Thanks for everything, Simone."

Simone touched Winter's arm as a gesture of farewell and then went back to tending to Uncle Eugene.

Bobby urged Winter toward the street, and he considered discarding the bottle as they passed the recycling bins, but he decided to put it in his bag instead.

"What are you doing?" Winter whispered.

"I'm not sure. Just go with it."

"You saw how Uncle Eugene was after drinking this stuff."

"I know, but I'm not him either. My family's problems are their own."

"I like you like this," Winter said. Her eyes creased at the outer corners. She looked otherworldly with the moon staining her skin. Her lips were pink and parted, and her cheeks were flushed from running. He reached to brush some flyaways from her face but changed his mind and grabbed her hand instead. They scurried out of the light and didn't stop running until they were blocks away. Bobby's blood was pumping fast, and his skin was bristling with the feeling of being alive. Winter had a smile splashed across her face, the creases staying firmly in place. An energy coursed through him that he was hesitant to acknowledge.

"Can we make a new rule?" he asked.

"Bobby, don't you think we have enough?"

"Hear me out," he said, noting how precious her hand felt in his and how soft her skin was. "When there's no one else around, you feel like my best friend. So what I'm proposing is we shut out all the background noise, because right now, I could use a best friend."

"What about Kai?" she joked.

"He'll love again. What do you say?"

Winter was looking up at him with the most peculiar expression on her face. Like she had seen someone she thought she knew and was trying to place them. Bobby's heartbeat was loud, and she could probably feel it in his fingertips. She gave his hand a squeeze that he felt in his entire body.

"I'm in," she replied with a bright smile.

They made their way through what Bobby believed to be his old neighborhood, but he couldn't be sure. He'd been too young when he left, and his memories had been convoluted by the passage of time. They raced down the suburban streets littered with colonial houses and manicured lawns. There was nothing to be heard on those quiet blocks but their laughter and the din of cicadas hiding in the trees.

"Where's your lung capacity now, bitch?!" Winter proclaimed as she beat Bobby to the end of the block.

"Will you shut up?" Bobby laughed. "All we need is for someone to call the cops on us."

"Don't tempt me with a good time. In New Jersey, it's illegal to frown at cops."

Bobby pushed Winter. "Nerd. Can you even frown? It's hard."

She tried a few times. The corners of her mouth went downward, but it was still only a straight line across her face. "I feel like my face just doesn't do that." Bobby tried, and Winter snorted with laughter. "Ew! Your mouth goes completely upside down!"

Bobby did it again, and Winter ran away. He grabbed her arm and kept frowning while she giggled madly and tried to break free. Finally, she poked him in the side, and he broke.

They walked through open fields of freshly mown grass where battles of the Revolutionary War had taken place. A police SUV cruised by, the first car they'd seen in an hour. The windows were blacked out, so they couldn't see who was inside, but the car slowed as it passed them. Winter gripped Bobby's arm. The cop car kept going. Winter loosened her grasp. Her nails left little indents on his arm. Bobby turned around and frowned at the back of the cop car until it disappeared.

Winter swatted him in the stomach. "Idiot."

Bobby smiled to himself.

The sky was the color of chai with a teaspoon of milk, with not a single star in sight. The two of them had nowhere to go and no means of getting there.

♡

Winter Park

29. WE WILL NOT ENTERTAIN PEACE NEGOTIATIONS

When the mechanic shop finally opened a few hours later, Winter and Bobby retrieved the car. They were on the road for a short while before they had to stop for gas. Winter waited while Bobby got out and ran inside the station, returning with a brown paper bag and two coffees. Winter opened it and unwrapped a disgusting, gooey cherry Danish.

"I know you get cranky when you don't eat hourly," Bobby said with a satisfied smirk.

Winter bit into the Danish like it was the first food she had seen in months.

Bobby took the plug out of the gas tank and did some fiddling with the gas pump. A man in a uniform came charging out of the convenience store, yelling, "Hey!"

Bobby nearly dropped the nozzle. Winter was going to be pissed if the gas station exploded before she had time to finish her Danish. It was one of the best she had ever had. It was flaky but not too dry, buttery but light; the cherry filling was sweet but not too syrupy. In a word, it was perfection.

"You can't pump your own gas here. It's illegal in New Jersey," the gas station attendant said to Bobby.

Bobby turned bright red. "I'm so sorry. I didn't know."

He got back into the car with his tail planted firmly between his legs, and the gas station attendant picked up where Bobby left off.

"You broke a rule without meaning to. Doesn't count," Winter said, only mildly paying attention. Her focus was on her treat.

Bobby's mouth fell into a flat line on his face. "This isn't a competition."

"Isn't it always with us? Keeps things interesting."

"We're not an old married couple."

"Whatever." Winter was licking the sugar off her fingers. "Didn't you know, anyway? Aren't you from New Jersey?"

"I've never driven here."

"Likely excuse."

Winter was absolutely destroying napkins as she tried in vain to wipe off her hands. Her scrunchie had slipped down her ponytail and was prepared to make its final leap. She kept pushing her hair back with her arm so as not to get sugar in it, but it only went right back to her face, making everything even messier. Her hair ties often walked off the job because of unfair working conditions, so she frequently found things like cherry jam or maple syrup in her hair when she washed it. This was nothing new.

"Why are you looking at me like that?" Winter asked.

Bobby's eyebrows went up. "Nothing. I mean no reason. You're just a sight to behold."

"You're still looking at me."

"Because you're talking to me."

Winter glowered. "Well, I'm going to stop talking now. You're making me nervous." She brushed her hair back with her arm again.

"Do you need help?" Bobby asked. He was gripping the steering wheel tightly.

"Yeah." She leaned toward him. "Can you put my hair up for me?"

Bobby raised his chin and looked down at her. "You want me to do your hair?"

"You don't need to go all Jonathan Van Ness. I just need you to get it out of my eyes."

"I'll do you one better. Turn around."

Winter didn't know what he was going to do, but she was curious to find out, so she turned around and looked through the window. Bobby slipped the hair tie out of her failing ponytail that had started as a messy bun. He grabbed all her hair and jerked her head back playfully. She gasped, and he chuckled. He started braiding, his fingernails grazing against her scalp each time he made a part.

"Overachiever," she said dryly.

"Don't move."

He said it with such force that she immediately fell quiet.

Winter was not alone in admitting that she loved when people played with her hair. She closed her eyes and listened to the gas meter roll. Bobby ran his fingers up the nape of her neck, and she took a sharp intake of air. She didn't know if it was accidental or not, but the sensation made her tense up. She jumped when the gas nozzle clicked, signaling that it was done.

Bobby secured her hair in the elastic and sat back to admire his work. Winter looked in the mirror. Her hair was in the neatest French braid she'd ever seen.

"You're such a show-off," she said. "Why do you even know how to do that?"

"Jacqueline."

"Oh," she said, sinking into her seat.

Winter finished eating in silence. Bobby got his credit card back, gave Winter some hand sanitizer, and they got on the road. They'd taken to negotiating their school activities so they could be more civil when they returned.

"You can have treasurer, and I'll take class historian," Bobby said.

"You want to be historian?"

"I enjoy documenting things. Plus the student council looks good on a college application, but I don't have time for president and neither do you."

Winter shrugged. "You're right. Okay, deal. Now for the science fair—we only use trifolds. If we have any table displays or experiments, we have to let the other know so they can adjust their projects accordingly."

"Deal. And we can't have the same guidance counselor this year. They always end up comparing us, and frankly, it's annoying."

"Oh my God, I know! I'm not convinced Mrs. Sweeney knows we're not related. Isn't there, like, a confidentiality agreement or something?"

Bobby wrinkled his forehead. "One of us will have to take stinky old Ms. McCleary instead."

"I'll do it as long as you don't challenge me for marching band captain. You can be a section leader."

"Done," Bobby said, and they smiled at each other.

She and Bobby settled into a comfortable silence and stayed that way for a long while. They drove with the windows open, letting the hot summer air whip them in the face. It was crisp and earthy, and the clouds drifted across the sky like ducks in a pond with nowhere to go. The highway had steep rock cliffs on either side, with thick forests on top. There were pools of probably toxic waste that'd give you a third limb if you fell into them and aluminum towers that connected the world. The dirt was being kicked up and swirled around before being shot through the car vents, drying out Winter's eyes as she and Bobby cut through like Snowpiercer. It was a freeing feeling—not like she'd been let go, but more like an escape.

Winter and Bobby shared a quick smile before returning their eyes to the highway.

♥

Bobby Bae

30. WE WILL NOT DO ANYTHING EVEN IN THE NEIGHBORHOOD OF FLIRTING

The WELCOME TO NEW YORK sign was underwhelming. It looked like any old sign, and they easily could have missed it had they been talking. They were listening to an oldies radio station. Winter liked to perfectly curate her playlists and podcasts, but against his better judgment, Bobby found something charming about the randomness of the radio. It was one of the only places where a certain amount of controlled frustration seemed fair.

"Did you know that it's illegal to flirt in New York?" Winter asked as they whizzed by the sign. She had her hand out the window, and she was making a wave motion with her arm.

"Illegal?" Bobby said with a smirk. "Couldn't we just round up anybody who's currently in a relationship? We have to assume there was flirting at some point."

"Round up? This isn't a sting operation," Winter said. "You only have to pay a twenty-five-dollar fine."

Bobby was overtaken by a smile. "Okay, then. Hit me with your best pickup line. If I can keep a straight face, you give me twenty-five dollars."

"Are you serious?" Winter was grinning from ear to ear. She was sitting completely sideways, facing him with her legs folded on the seat. "You go first. If I don't laugh, the same deal applies."

Bobby put his finger to his chin as he thought of his best pickup line. He wasn't a master flirter, he did hear one or two cheesy pickup lines that Mr. Bae dropped on Mrs. Bae every now and then. It had always been vomit-inducing. He never thought they'd be useful.

He grinned and took Winter's hand. "You ready?"

"Yeah, don't be dramatic. Just go."

Bobby cleared his throat. "Are you sitting on an F5 key? Because that ass is refreshing," he said, and she immediately ripped her hand away.

Bobby locked eyes with her, daring her to laugh. She was chewing on the insides of her cheeks. Her eyes were misting, and her jaw was quivering. She buried her face in her hands and laughed so hard she snorted.

"Ha!" Bobby shouted, and stuck out his open palm. "Pay up."

"You're such a computer nerd!" Winter yelled. "How was I not supposed to laugh?"

Bobby winked. "You liked it."

"Oh God. Moratorium! You win."

"Your turn."

"Okay, fine." Winter took Bobby's hand and gave a dramatic pout. "If you were a space station, I'd call you Deep Space Fine."

Bobby barely gave any effort. He choked on a laugh so hard it hurt his chest. "And you called *me* a nerd?"

Winter walked her fingers up his arm. She hadn't broken character yet. "Are you mass and space? Because, boy, you matter." She kept going. Her fingertips were tickling his shoulder. "Are you a vacuum in space? Because you take my breath away."

Bobby tried to lean as far away from her as he could, but she was relentless. She walked her fingers up his neck and stroked his cheek with the back of her hand.

"You're so weird," Bobby said, trying to stifle a laugh. "Are you done yet?"

Winter stuck out her bottom lip. "One more?"

"Fine."

"Are you a supernova? Because you're the hottest thing in the universe," she said, and gave his cheek a little smack.

Bobby was speechless for a moment. His hand instinctively went to his cheek. He looked in the rearview mirror and saw that both of his cheeks were red, not just the one she'd slapped.

"That was weak," he said.

She leaned back and folded her arms. "Then do better."

"Fine." Bobby sat up straighter and puffed out his chest. "Do you have any raisins?"

"Uh, no."

"How about a date?"

Winter turned her head away, but Bobby could see her lips curling into a smile in the reflection of the window.

"Okay, that's enough," she muttered.

They settled back into their comfortable silence as they passed through Connecticut. Soon enough, Winter had fallen asleep, and Bobby was left listening to her snoring along to the whir of the passing cars. He shook his head and bit back a smile.

♡

Winter Park

31. THE RULE BREAKING STOPS WHEN WE GET TO MIT AND HARVARD

Winter was sleeping soundly, her head resting against her seat belt. She was dreaming about walking around a stationery store with Bobby as he explained the difference between paper and parchment. He suddenly yelled her name, and the dream ended.

"Have you eaten yet?" Winter murmured as she reentered the waking world. She wiped her mouth and looked around. Bobby was dying laughing. "Where are we?" She rubbed her eyes.

"Cambridge. Harvard is only a few blocks away."

"Great, let's go," she said, opening her door. Bobby reached over her and closed it again. "What gives?"

He had the bottle he'd stolen from Eugene in his lap and a devilish look in his eye. "We already missed the tours I'd scheduled for us, and our parents only allowed us one extra day."

Winter eyed him suspiciously. "So?"

"*So* I'm tired from driving, I've recently been broken up with, I dropped a bomb on my family by visiting Eugene, and I honestly want to see Kai's cousin Omari more than I want to see more buildings and statues of old white men," Bobby said. "Let's turn these tours into a drinking game."

Winter put her hand on his forehead to check for a fever. "Are you feeling okay?"

Bobby slapped her hand down. "I feel great. I want to have fun and enjoy our last day in this road-trip bubble."

She took two water bottles from her bag. "Let's do it, then. We have about an hour before most of the buildings close to visitors."

Bobby poured the jet fuel–smelling alcohol into the water bottles. He took one and held it up to Winter for a toast. "To bad decisions we'll one hundred percent regret later."

"Amen," she said, knocking her bottle to his.

Winter took a sip, and heat seemed to rise in her belly and expel from her mouth as she let out a throaty *ahh*. The warmth settled back down and rested behind her navel. Her entire body then became hot, and she was alert, firing on all cylinders.

They speed-walked down the street toward Harvard. They agreed to pick one thing that they wanted to see at each school, and that's where they'd go. The catch was, they had to find it without a map. Whoever found it first got to count (as slowly or as quickly as they desired) to three while the other drank.

Winter got distracted by the colonial-style row houses with their big bay windows and thick crown molding. Many of them were run-down and crumbling. While she was busy staring, Bobby took the lead.

His choice was a setup anyway. He picked Harvard Yard, which was probably the biggest, most recognizable place there. They had to find an empty Luxembourg chair and take a seat to win.

She walked as fast as she could without running to catch up to Bobby.

"On your left!" she yelled as she sped past.

He held out his arm and scooped her back behind him. She was shocked by how strong he was. It took her off guard, and as soon as she tripped over her own foot, she decided to let Bobby win. Her thighs were burning, and she'd have shin splints later. She stopped near the mouth of Harvard Yard and marveled at the life happening around her. The students looked much more diverse than at her and Bobby's high school. For the first time, she felt like she was looking at a mirror instead of through a window.

She ambled over to Bobby, who was seated in the center of the lush green courtyard in a yellow Luxembourg chair. He was grinning as he soaked up the energy Cambridge was giving off. She pulled up a red chair and did the same.

"What do you think about Harvard? Have you been shot by Cupid's arrow?" Winter asked.

He was slumped over, picking grass and splitting the blades apart. "I hyped it up so much in my mind, and now that we're here, it's just another set of bricks. I don't know what I expected."

He was right in a way, but Harvard did have a certain life about it that she hadn't anticipated. She expected to be rubbing shoulders with trust-fund babies and that she'd see the child of a politician or celebrity walk by and have to pretend to be cool. It wasn't *all* like that from what she could tell. There were clusters of students gathered, deep in conversation. Winter couldn't hear them, but she presumed they were talking about whatever smart people talked about: world politics, philosophy, or religion. Or they could have been talking about the most recent episode of *The Bachelor* for all she knew. It seemed like there was more room to *be* than at their high school. She could see herself fitting in. She could see Bobby fitting in too.

Winter scooted her red chair closer to him. "I think I'm coming to realize that schools are a culture, and you and I both know you can never fully learn a culture even if it's your own."

Bobby shook his head. "You're so smart, it's infuriating."

Winter smirked. "I'm also a loser. I have to drink."

"Your funeral. Drink up. I'm counting to three."

Winter tipped the bottle to her lips, and Bobby started counting like he'd forgotten how. By the time he got to three, her throat was on fire. She gagged but held it together long enough for it to go down. It burned through all the garbage she'd eaten and sloshed around in her stomach, reminding her of how hungry she was.

"That wasn't nice," she said, then burped loudly and unceremoniously. It was probably a psychosomatic reaction, but she felt the alcohol almost immediately.

Bobby was in stitches as he watched her. After he took a solidarity swig, though, he had to bite back his prepared quip. With his face contorted, he said, "I kind of hate this too."

"You know what would make it taste better?" Winter asked. Bobby raised his eyebrows in anticipation. "If we threw it in the trash and got bubble tea instead."

"Agreed. But no tapioca balls. They're just like the grapes."

A few minutes later, with a lychee green tea with aloe vera jelly and a fifty-percent-sweet boba-less taro milk tea with soy in hand, Bobby and Winter were off to find the next thing on their list. The attraction Winter chose was the passenger pigeon exhibit at the Harvard Museum of Natural History.

Bobby had longer legs and a faster gait, so Winter pretended to fall. When Bobby went to help her up, she pulled him onto the grass and took off. She ran into a main plaza with rust-colored buildings and a columned church with a white steeple touching the sky. Winter asked a few passersby where the museum was and raced in that direction. She looked back, and Bobby was gaining on her. He ran by her, so she jumped on his back and hitched a ride.

"Cheater!" he yelled as he tried to shake her off like a wet dog.

"You're so sweaty!" Winter exclaimed, wiping her hand on Bobby's shirt.

He responded by shaking his hair in her face. She leapt off his back and beat him to the door of the museum. She opened it for him this time. When she followed, it was like walking into a freezer. She took a deep breath. She always liked the smell of cold air.

The museum was full of families checking out each of the displays, which were mostly taxidermic animals and dinosaur bones in glass cases. Winter was momentarily distracted by a forty-two-foot-long Kronosaurus, which didn't look unlike a Pokémon.

She glided through several rooms, her eyes scanning each one, looking for the passenger pigeon exhibit. She'd read about Martha, the last passenger pigeon, in an article about endlings once. Passenger pigeons used to be one of the most ubiquitous species of birds in North America, but they were hunted to extinction. Winter liked reading about lonely animals. They'd probably been around for thousands of years and were the product of natural selection, gods in their own right. But they couldn't adapt to the changes humans made, so they simply died off, and most people didn't even know about them to eulogize them. Martha was her favorite because she was the last of her kind, like Superman, only no one cared because she was a pigeon. Winter didn't know what it said about her that she identified so much with a stuffed dead bird.

Winter found the exhibit, and Bobby was already standing in front of it. She'd lost again.

"This dead bird is creepy," Bobby said. "Why did you choose it?"

Winter grasped her bubble tea tighter. "Before the last of them, Martha, died, there was a thousand-dollar reward to find her a mate. That was, like, twenty-five thousand dollars at the time, and even with the world looking, no one found her one, and she died—taking the entire species with her."

"That's profoundly depressing."

"Maybe, or maybe she didn't want a mate."

"You at least know she didn't want to be alone."

"She wasn't. She had thousands of fans who came to see her. More than a hundred years later, she still does."

Bobby raised his tea in Winter's direction. "To Martha."

They touched their plastic cups together and chugged down their three seconds together.

"This is so much better. How does yours taste?" Winter asked, chewing on the jumbo straw.

"Purple," Bobby said with a smile as he wiped his mouth with the back of his hand.

Winter returned the smile.

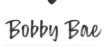

Bobby Bae

32. WE WILL NOT DO ANYTHING ILLEGAL

Winter had chosen the amphitheater outside of the famous Stata Center at MIT. The building looked like it'd been planned as it was being constructed. There were odd colors and shapes jutting out at bizarre angles and shiny chrome-like fixtures. It was one of the messiest building designs he'd ever seen, but that didn't stop him from appreciating it. It was lovely in its own way.

Winter was sitting on the step below him, looking out over the campus.

"Don't you want to try to see more?" Bobby asked.

"I don't know. I think I'm fine here," Winter said. "If I'm being perfectly honest with you, I was always going to go to MIT if I got in, regardless of whether I liked the campus or not."

Bobby laughed. "Then why did you come all this way?"

Winter bit her lip. "I wanted to hang out with you. Hasn't it been obvious all along?"

"Shut up," Bobby said, yanking on her braid. She laughed. He enjoyed making her laugh. "Tell the truth."

"I don't know. I guess I was just anxious about it. I was doubting my decision, but being here now, I feel like I could do this. That is, if they'll have me."

Of all the cities they'd visited, this felt the most comfortable to Bobby. He liked the accents, the wide array of restaurants Winter would no doubt explore, and the sheer number of intellectuals walking around. There were at least thirty colleges in the Boston area alone. He could see her here, but he wasn't sure about himself. He wasn't sure about anything anymore.

"I don't know how you can be so decisive and so sure of everything," Bobby said, leaning back against the step behind him.

"I'm not so sure about everything," Winter said.

Bobby didn't know what she was talking about. She not only knew exactly what she wanted to do; she knew exactly how she wanted to get there. She didn't care about all the background noise— friends, girlfriends, and family drama.

"What do you mean?" he asked. "You're the most driven person I know."

She turned back around and faced away from him. "School isn't as easy for me as you think it is. I try a lot harder than you know. Everything else is even harder."

"Everything else?"

"You know. Everything else." She still didn't look back.

"Are you talking about dating?"

Winter sighed. "Friends too. I've never said this out loud before, but I feel like if Emmy didn't live so far away, we wouldn't still be friends. Am I a bad person? My mother told me I keep everyone at a distance, but I don't know why I'm like this."

Bobby reached out to put his hand on her shoulder, but he changed his mind at the last second. "I didn't know you cared about stuff like this. I thought you were above it."

"I'm a sixteen-year-old girl and a human. How could I not? Emmy has a catalog of potential boyfriends, and even you—" She stopped short. "I'm sorry. Old habits."

"It's okay. But you're smart, and you're ambitious. I'm sure you could date whoever you want."

"People say they like smart girls, but they don't. Ask Jacqueline."

That was true. Jacqueline didn't have many friends because she wasn't afraid to let people know she was the smartest person in the room.

"Well, you're funny too. That has to count for something," Bobby said.

"Everyone likes a funny girl, but no one wants to date one." Winter twirled her braid with her finger. "I think this is the alcohol talking because I would usually never say any of this, but I haven't even had a real kiss yet. Like, one that I actually wanted."

Bobby wracked his brain for something supportive to say, but nothing immediately came to mind. He was yelling at himself internally to think of something, anything at all. Did she tell him that because she wanted him to kiss her? He went for the shoulder again and followed through this time. Winter put her hand over his. He completely froze. He was worried that if he moved even a centimeter, she'd take her hand away.

"What changed?" he asked. "Why do you care now?"

"I feel like I lost Emmy, and I've been blaming the distance and her life choices, but I think it might be me."

Bobby snorted. "This sounds like serious imposter syndrome. Who cares if all the stuff you do doesn't come easy to you? You still do it. Are you afraid that if you let people get close to you, they'll think you're a fraud?" He gave her shoulder a reassuring squeeze. "When people get too close, you push them away. In my case, hard."

Winter dropped his hand and stood up. She covered her face and refused to look even remotely in his direction. "What should we do next?"

Bobby stood up too. "I thought we could walk around MIT for a while, then head over to Kai's cousin's party. What do you think?"

A dark expression passed over Winter's face, and she giggled. "You want to go to a frat party? That's not like you."

"I don't know . . . You're here." He stepped closer, still trying to gauge whether she had wanted him to kiss her.

"What are you doing?" Winter asked, not looking up from her feet.

Bobby tilted her chin up so she'd look at him. He'd never seen her like this, so close, without any hint of a scowl or an impending insult. His breath was labored, and his blood was running hot as he held her face between his hands. She was so beautiful with her nearly black eyes and parted pink lips. The ridiculous, neat braid he'd put in her hair had to go though.

"I want to tell you something," Bobby said.

Winter's pupils were wide. "What is it?"

He moved his lips to her ear. "I don't like your hair like this," he said, and pulled the hair tie out.

"You're so weird," she laughed, pushing him away lightly.

"Wait," he said, and clutched her hand to his chest before she pulled away. "There's something else." His heart was beating hard.

"What is it? You're making me nervous."

He ran a hand through his hair. He was regretting saying anything, but his mouth was already open, so he had to say something before she thought he'd lost his mind.

"When we first met . . . I . . . uh." He cleared his throat. "Well, what I'm trying to say is that I didn't only want to be your friend.

I mean, I was, like, seven, so it wasn't all that deep, but I . . . I don't know. I told my mom I liked you, and she told me you were only mean to me because you liked me too. So do you know what I did?"

"Cried?" she asked with a nervous laugh.

"Well, yes," Bobby said with an eye roll. He swallowed the lump in his throat. "But after the tears dried, I decided to wait you out until the teasing stopped. At some point, I think I forgot to keep waiting, but now I'm thinking maybe I shouldn't have."

Winter tugged on her loosening braid. "I don't know what to say."

"I'm completely misreading this situation, aren't I?" he asked, and took a step back. "Yes, I am. And . . . I'm sorry for making this super weird." Bobby looked around. "Hey, did you know there were other people here?" he said with a nervous laugh.

Winter buried her face in her hands. "I'm sorry I don't know how to act. No one has ever told me they liked me before."

"You don't have to act different. You're perfect as you are."

"I am, aren't I?" she said, and took a gulp of her bubble tea with a satisfied *ahhh*. Her cheeks puffed out as she chewed on the grass jelly. Bobby was deeply charmed and overwhelmed with the sheer cuteness. He didn't know what was wrong with him. It was like a dam had broken inside of his own body, and all the discipline he'd been restraining himself with for years wasn't enough to stop him from grinning like a fool.

They walked through the MIT campus, and he didn't look at anything except for Winter. Her hair had a wave in it from the braid, and it appeared even wilder than usual. Her cheeks were flushed, and her neck and chest were red and splotchy with Asian glow. She kept glancing at him and saying, "What?" and giggling.

Winter massaged her cheeks. They ached from smiling so much. Bobby wanted to keep her smiling, so he ran to a food truck nearby and bought her a shawarma with extra tahini sauce. When he presented her with it, her face lit up like he'd given her a bouquet of roses.

They ate and walked around the rest of the campus, exploring every single nook and cranny they could get into. When it got too dark, they bought gelato and waited for the stars to come out.

♡

Winter Park

33. WE WILL NOT HAVE PHOTO EVIDENCE OF OUR RULE BREAKING

A space nerd and a future tech wunderkind walked into a party. Winter had heard that joke before, but looking at a flushed-face Bobby pretending he wasn't completely out of his element, it was more likely being written before her eyes.

MIT students worked so hard that when they partied, they partied like it was the end-times. Their generation had seen the end-times many times before, so they'd adjusted their partying accordingly. Bigger was not better; quirkier was. There was a homemade Slip 'N Slide running the entire length of the backyard, and some of the brightest students in the world were sliding down it, unable to hide their childlike joy. There were Christmas lights hung around the living room, because why not? And people Winter had never seen before, but who somehow felt familiar, were sitting on mismatched couches with red cups in their hands and delighted laughs in their lungs. She couldn't help but feel that this city—with these people, some of whom looked just like her—was where she was meant to be. She felt up, higher than the clouds, higher than the universe, like she was looking down on herself, wondering what the hell she was doing. At a college party. With Bobby Bae. But at that moment, she didn't care. Bobby was there to hold her hand through it.

Bobby spotted Kai's cousin Omari through the crowd. He had

Kai's same low-key energy with a certain dapperness to him. He had on all black with a pair of browline glasses perched on his nose. Bobby and Winter weaved through the slippery bodies covered in soap and sweat to get to him.

"Bae! You made it!" Omari said, locking him in one of those handshake-hug combinations that men seem to have perfected over generations of bro-dom.

Everything fuzzed out as Bobby and Omari engaged in the obligatory small talk. Winter's body swayed to the beat of the music without her even telling it to do it. She hiccupped and giggled and then found herself posing for a selfie. Omari draped his arm over her, but that didn't stop Bobby from squeezing in between them and putting his hands on her waist as they said cheese. She could feel his chest against her back and his hand pushing her shirt up ever so slightly. Would these pictures be online for everyone back home to see? Would people care she was with the very person she'd always been so careful not to be seen with? And would they notice her leaning farther into his arms? Android users probably wouldn't see it, and it didn't matter anyway. She was happy.

Bobby followed Omari to the card table bar, and Winter was pulled into a conversation with the people on one of the mismatched couches. Everyone there was so intelligent and so drunk. A series of information dumps was only broken up by cheering and hollering every time a soapy body flew across the backyard.

Alissa was a marketing major at BU and an Instagram influencer for a startup company that sold T-shirts with empowering phrases on them. Seth had moved from Egypt to attend MIT so he could major in biology and eventually work in forensics. Last there was Blaise, who Winter couldn't quite figure out because he'd self-medicated into an unintelligible slur. She was charmed by them all. Rarely did

215

she feel she made sense within the context of a group.

The entire time she was talking, she couldn't stop finding Bobby's eyes with her own. He was making a mess of mixing drinks while he struggled through small talk with Omari. He kept looking over at her and smiling, pleading with his eyes for her to rescue him, but she liked to see him squirm.

Bobby eventually broke free and found his way back to her. He sat down next to her on the couch and handed her a drink.

"Jjan," he said, and they crashed their cups together before taking timid sips of what tasted like gasoline mixed with red Gatorade.

"Immediately no," Winter said, handing it back.

"Can't say we didn't try," Bobby replied, placing the cups on a side table.

"You both look dry," Alissa said. "You haven't tried the slide."

Winter poked Bobby in the ribs. "I dare you."

She saw something in his eyes change, a flicker of emotion, an acknowledgment of her challenge and a promise to accept it. "Let's do it."

"You can't be serious."

"I think you've known me long enough to know that I'm always serious." He extended his hand to her, and everyone in the room held up their cups and egged them on.

Winter shrugged. *When in Boston*, she supposed.

Her hand felt good in Bobby's as he pulled her through the house into the yard. There were about a dozen partially dressed people out there, throwing their hands in the air every time another body slid and spun on the bright blue tarps. It was her turn next. She put her phone aside, noticing for the first time she had a million missed calls. Bobby probably forgot to drop the pin. She'd deal with it later.

Winter looked down the barrel of the gun, which was a plastic death trap covered in duct tape and dish soap. Omari was spraying everyone with a garden hose, doing his best impression of Tony Montana. There was dancing and mingling and flirting. The lights were low, and she had her entire universe above her.

She held her breath and prepared for her running start when Bobby grabbed her arm.

"Together?" he asked. He had stars dancing in his eyes.

"Together."

They clasped hands, ran, and jumped. Winter screamed the entire time as water droplets pelted her in the face and the smell of wet grass entered her nose and all the blood in her body rushed around in one big assault on her senses.

When they got to the end, the crowd erupted into indistinct screams, and hands reached out seemingly out of nowhere to help them up.

"What the hell am I doing?" Winter asked the universe, hoping it'd answer, and it did, using Bobby's voice, which simply said, "Making your own rules."

"Take me somewhere else. I want to move around," she replied.

Omari threw his arms over their shoulders. "I've got just the place."

He invited them downstairs. Winter hadn't even realized there was a downstairs. Bobby took her arm and pulled her along. She could feel every atom and molecule in and on their skin bouncing against one another as they descended the stairs to the basement. She could hear the muffled music from below, but she could barely see a thing. She followed Bobby in the darkness, and they found a second door. She turned around and leaned against it, wanting one moment where it was only them.

The bass rattled against her back as she looked up at Bobby, not hating his stupidly long bangs for once. She could hardly breathe as her mind raced, wondering how on earth they'd ended up there. She got her moment, and everything was still. She breathed in deep, ready to find out what was on the other side of the door. Bobby leaned in and pushed it open. Sight and sound immediately filled her up.

The sensory overload was almost unbearable. She was white-knuckling her phone in one hand and Bobby's arm in the other. The entire basement was black except for the strobe lights that wound their way through the crowd. There were sweaty bodies squished together like sardines, moving and swaying as the music swelled and gave reprieve. It was like they were choreographed to move like the waves of the ocean. Bobby motioned for her to join the sea of undulating bodies. They cut through the crowd, found a spot near the middle, and danced. It was like ocean waves crashed against her. She was wet from either sweat or gross hose water, and her skin was hot. She felt amazing.

Bobby shook out his wet hair, and Winter hummed with laughter as the droplets hit her. She could barely see his face to gauge his reaction, only his silhouette against the vape smoke and stray strobe lights.

"This is weird, right?" Bobby yelled over the music.

"It's a little weird," she shouted back.

"Can I make it weirder?"

"You might as well."

"I may be off base here, but it seemed like you wanted to kiss me earlier. Now you look like you definitely do."

"*I* look like I want to kiss *you*?" she said with a smile that she felt in her whole body.

Bobby grinned. "You do."

She pushed his face away. "You're projecting."

"You're right. I am," he said, stepping closer.

Typically, Bobby had something, a microexpression, a twitch, something small that betrayed him when he wasn't being entirely genuine. She couldn't find it. His face was steely, and he was as serious as ever. He really wanted to kiss her. She surprised herself when she said, "Then do it."

"It would violate every single one of our rules."

"That's the point, isn't it?"

Bobby held her face in his hands and tilted her head up, his thumb dragging her lips open to a part. Every time the red strobe light hit him, he was a little bit closer, like he was moving in stop-motion.

♥

Bobby Bae

Bobby felt electrified. He'd gone out on a limb, and that wasn't something he did. He was more of a trunk guy or, better yet, a ground guy. What was he doing? He didn't kiss girls at parties, especially if those girls were Winter. This had to have been some elaborate joke. Though everything on Winter's face told him it wasn't.

He pulled her closer, and she gasped into his mouth. He pressed his lips to hers ever so softly and was surprised she kissed him back. *She told you to do it*, he reminded himself. He was all but supporting her entire weight. Every time the lights flashed, he could see another face screaming at him to just go for it. Really go for it. None of this timid, soulless kissing like it was a kiss between strangers. He saw them telling him he'd wanted to kiss her from the moment he met her. That every time he tried to beat her at something, he was really punishing her for not liking him back. He saw Kai telling him he was stupid for keeping up his feud with her. He saw his parents urging him to go on this trip because they knew it wasn't working with Jacqueline. He saw Jacqueline . . . He saw Jacqueline.

He pulled away suddenly and touched his fingers to his lips.

"Oh my God," Winter said, turning around and putting her hands to her burning cheeks. "Were we wrong?"

"No, I'm sorry. Turn around."

"No, this is so not right. I didn't imagine it like this. Not that I've

imagined this. I just mean we're in a basement and I'm wet and . . .
oh God. Not like that. I mean from the slide."

Bobby laughed. "Relax. I'm sorry. I just want to look at you."

"Well, I'm all red now. I don't want you to look at me like this."

"You've never cared about what you looked like in front of me
before."

"What do you want me to say, Robert? I do now."

Bobby brushed Winter's damp hair aside to expose one of her
shoulders. He leaned down and placed a kiss on her collarbone,
and her breath caught. He placed another on her neck. Her skin
was hot and tasted vaguely of soap, but he could smell her warm
familiar scent beneath it. He placed another kiss along her jaw
and then another rough one on her cheek. Winter turned her head
toward him, and his next kiss caught the side of her mouth. They
let the kiss linger for a moment, and Winter leaned her back against
Bobby's chest, their wet clothes clinging together. Bobby couldn't
take it anymore. He flipped Winter around, and in an instant, her
hands were tangled in his hair and their lips collided. All coherent
thoughts fell out of Bobby's head. He couldn't believe what he was
doing and how right it felt. Every time he inhaled, he peeked at her
to make sure he wasn't imagining it.

Bobby put his hands on Winter's waist, and she folded, a laugh
bubbling out of her into his lips. He pulled away and leaned his forehead against hers.

"What's wrong?" he rasped.

"I'm sorry. I'm ticklish," she whispered, her breath ragged.

"It's okay. Things were getting . . . kind of intense."

"Maybe we should get some air."

Bobby agreed.

Winter led him back into the stairwell, then shut the door behind them and pulled him into another kiss. This one was short and sweet. She leaned against the wall and looked up at him, her lips swollen and cheeks flushed.

"Can I call one last moratorium?" Winter asked, her hands wringing anxiously.

Bobby nodded.

"I really like you."

Bobby craned his neck to kiss her again, but a hand on his shoulder interrupted the moment. It was Omari.

"Didn't you tell me you weren't dating?" he asked, flashing a broad, judging smile.

"We're not. I don't even know him. I met him today," Winter joked.

Omari smirked. "I won't tell Kai. But I did want to tell y'all that you broke the only rule I have in this house."

Bobby's spine turned to ice. "What rule?"

Omari shoved two beers in glass bottles into Bobby's hand. "You're not allowed to be empty-handed. Enjoy, you two," he said with a wink, and disappeared into the crowded basement.

Bobby handed Winter her bottle, then chased her up the stairs, making her laugh wildly until she snorted. She beat him to the top and wrenched open the door before stopping dead in her tracks. Bobby slammed into her and nearly fell backward down the stairs, but he caught himself on the railing. He looked around her to see what had happened, and his eyes fell on two burly public safety officers checking IDs of the partygoers upstairs.

"We're underage. What do we do?" Bobby mouthed.

An idea popped into Winter's mind, and Bobby nodded as if to give her permission to do it.

She discreetly reached through the door and felt around the wall for the thermostat. Without looking, she cranked it up to the highest heat, then slowly closed the door so as not to draw attention. Despite her stealth, the officers saw her and descended like doughnut-eating vultures.

"Run!" Winter whisper-yelled.

Winter and Bobby leapt down the stairs and rushed to warn Omari. They cut through the dancing bodies and found him in a corner, changing the music on a makeshift DJ station. Bobby tapped him on the shoulder and pointed at the approaching officers. Omari's mouth turned into an O, but it was too late for him to do anything. The officers flashed the lights, and the room went deathly silent.

"Whose house is this?" one of the officers, with a steely face and rust-colored beard, demanded.

Omari took a deep breath and stepped forward.

The sound of the heater kicking on in the old house echoed in the wall. Bobby and Winter smiled at each other as a burning dust smell filled the room. As the officers busied themselves with trying to find the source of the smell, Bobby and Winter tried as best they could to fade into the background, moving bodies in front of them as they searched around the ceiling. Bobby grabbed a lighter out of someone's hand and ripped the label off his beer bottle, handing them both to Winter.

Obscuring themselves in the dimly lit corner of the basement that held the hot water heater, Winter jumped on Bobby's back and lit the label near a smoke detector. An ear-splitting screech immediately filled the room, followed by a collective groan.

Winter and Omari made eye contact from across the basement. He nodded his approval, then yelled, "Evacuate!"

No one in the basement was a stranger to a party bust; they knew the drill. They helped one another out of every door and window they could find. Bobby dragged Winter into the laundry room and hoisted her up onto the washing machine so she could shimmy through the window. Using her legs, she braced herself and appeared to be using all her strength to pull Bobby through as well. His shoulders cleared the small opening, and he fell out of the house, landing on top of Winter in the wet grass. They took a moment to catch their breaths. He didn't even care that they were covered in mud and smelled like a mown lawn.

"What did we just do?" Bobby said with a deep chortle.

"Let's not think about it too much."

Suddenly, a light shone on them, bright and jarring, making Bobby wince away from it.

"Turn off the moon, Park," Bobby groaned, pawing at her. When his hand hit nothing, he opened his eyes and was met with a flashlight in his face and an officer behind it.

Bobby and Winter sat side by side in a fluorescently lit public safety office. They were left in a back room alone as the officers dealt with other partygoers who were far louder and more unruly. Winter hiccupped and then giggled. Her giggle quickly turned into full-blown, side-splitting laughter.

"I fail to see what's funny," Bobby said.

"We're going to get in trouble for the first time in our lives. What do you think that'll be like?"

Bobby smirked. "I have no idea. I might actually break my dad."

"I think Halmeoni will be proud, though."

"Good. Because we may have to move in with her after our parents find out what we did."

They both laughed and then trailed off.

"I'm kind of excited. Is that wrong?" Winter asked, barely concealing a dark smile.

Bobby contemplated the girl before him for a second. Her hair pointed in every direction, with blades of grass sticking out. Her shirt was damp and completely stretched out, askew on her body. Her cheeks were flushed and her eyes open and alive.

"Come here," he said, motioning her to him.

Her expression became serious, and she slid closer. She tilted her chin up and closed her eyes, waiting for him to kiss her.

"I've really missed you," Bobby said, holding her face in his hands.

She opened her eyes but didn't move. "We've seen each other almost daily for nearly a decade."

"I know, but I've always had this loneliness that was only for you."

Winter sat there still as stone and gawked for a moment before propping herself up on her chair with one of her legs to close the space between them. Their teeth clanged together, and they both backed up, laughing and covering their mouths.

Suddenly, the door swung open, and the two leapt away from each other and folded their hands in their laps. A man in a public safety T-shirt walked in with tired eyes and the lower half of his face dark with stubble.

"My name is Dan, and I'm a public safety officer here at BU. Are you both students?" he said, all in one breath.

"No. We were visiting friends," Winter said.

"Do you have IDs on you?"

"No," Bobby lied.

"How old are you?"

Bobby considered lying, but he knew he and Winter didn't look twenty-one. The pause he took told the officer everything he needed to know.

"Look," Dan said. "Students have already started moving into their off-campus housing, and it's a huge party month, so we're backed up here. If you call your parents and have them pick you up, then you're free to go, and it'll save me having to do extra paperwork."

"Our parents are in North Carolina," Winter said.

Dan sighed. "Fine, then I'll need to speak to them on the phone. If they clear you to go, then I'll release you. Sound fair?"

Bobby and Winter nodded.

"Okay, you," Dan said, pointing to Bobby. "Come with me."

Bobby reluctantly left Winter behind and entered the hallway. Dan gave him back his phone. As soon as the lock screen lit up and the picture of Bobby and his parents smiled back at him, his spine went cold. He found his mother's number in his recent calls, and his finger hovered over the green call button, but something within him couldn't do it. It was nearly three a.m., and according to the pin he'd dropped her earlier, he was safe and sound in his hotel room. He imagined his mother hanging up the phone and immediately breaking out her knitting needles and sitting alone in the dark, waiting all night for him to return home. In a snap decision, he pressed the number just below his mother's—Jacqueline's. She answered almost immediately.

"Hey, Mom. I got caught at a party at BU, and the campus police need to speak to you. I'm really sorry, but can you please talk to them so they'll let me go?" he said as quickly as he could.

He heard Jacqueline take a deep breath on the other side of the phone. "Fine. Hand over the phone," she said in her deep newscaster voice she used for the school news station.

Bobby bit his nails as Dan spoke to Jacqueline. Dan was a phone pacer, so he walked up and down the hall as he spoke. Bobby tried to listen, but he could only catch bits and pieces. After a few short minutes, Dan handed the phone back over.

"You and your sister are free to go," Dan said. "Just be careful."

Bobby contorted his face. "My sist—? I mean, yes, sir. Thank you."

"Your mother is still on the line. Good luck. She sounds pissed," Dan said, clapping Bobby on the shoulder and walking off.

Bobby slowly put his phone to his ear and muttered, "Hey, Jack. Thanks. I—"

"That girl is toxic, Bobby," Jacqueline spat. "You spend one week away with her, and now you're drinking and getting arrested? She's a bad influence on you."

"I didn't get arrested. We went to a party, just like you go to Carly Bishop's house every week when you think I'm not paying attention."

"Why can you have fun with her and not me?"

Bobby's anger bubbled to the surface. "Because you broke my heart!" he whisper-yelled. "And I don't mean two weeks ago when you dumped me. I mean months ago when you decided you wanted to, then never did." Bobby wiped his face but was surprised when his hand came away dry. "I have to go, Jack. I don't think we should talk again."

"Before we ever dated, we were best friends, Bobby. What happened to us?"

"You made me feel like I was nothing. Friends don't do that," Bobby said, clenching a fist. "I know I made mistakes, but I never intentionally did anything to hurt you."

"I know, and I'm sorry for the way I handled things." She paused. "I'm glad to hear you're having fun, though. Truly."

"I'm sorry too. I didn't even notice that you weren't happy for all that time. Or maybe I did notice and didn't care as long as you stayed with me. That was wrong. Thank you for helping me tonight. You didn't have to do that."

"I wanted to," Jacqueline said. "I want you to be happy, okay?"

"I want you to be happy too," Bobby replied, but Jacqueline was already gone.

Bobby crammed his phone into his pocket. He put his head down in his hands and took a few deep breaths before fixing his hair and walking back into the room where Winter was waiting. She smiled brightly and stood up when she saw him. He couldn't help but smile back.

♡

Winter Park

Winter was still buzzing. Her parents were going to be so mad, and she couldn't wait to see Halmeoni's expression when she found out.

Bobby walked in with a haunted look on his face, but he smiled as soon as he saw Winter. She stood up and waited for him to cross the room.

"Did you *miss* me?" she asked, getting on her tiptoes and throwing her arms around his neck.

Bobby let out a short laugh. "Are you mocking me? I knew I shouldn't have said that."

"No, it was really cute." Winter blushed. "I missed you too."

"I want to kiss you again, but we shouldn't in here," Bobby said, unwrapping her arms from his neck and looking over his shoulder.

Winter pouted. "So that's it? We're back to being good?"

"No, but I—"

Winter kissed him, effectively shutting him up.

Bobby immediately kissed her back, and it bothered her how good he was at it. *He's good at everything*, Winter thought. Competitive even in kissing, Winter deepened the kiss, then pulled back to see what Bobby would do. Apparently he couldn't turn off that competitive spirit either. He followed her lips and backed her into the wall, which made her let out the slightest gasp. Bobby immediately pulled away, and Winter slapped a hand over her mouth.

"We have to stop. We can't do this here," Bobby said in a frenzy.

Winter was mortified. "You're right. I have to go call my parents," she said, prepared to rush off.

Bobby grabbed her arm. "It's already handled, but we can't do this here because they think we're siblings. I'm pretty sure what we're doing is illegal in all states."

Winter winced. "Why do they think we're siblings?"

He bit his lip. "I may have called Jacqueline and had her pretend to be our mother."

She ripped her arm away. "You did *what*?"

"I panicked."

Winter was unsure how to proceed. A flood of emotions filled her up, and it tasted a lot like bile. It was easy to be with Bobby there, away from home. But the moment Jacqueline's name was uttered, Winter was brought back to reality. The reality with friends, family, whispering classmates, and ex-girlfriends who would all have opinions about their relationship. She was so caught up in the moment, she hadn't considered that the bubble they were in would eventually have to burst. Bobby just had to go rampaging through it before they even got home.

She stormed out of the room and out of the building.

"Wait," Bobby yelled, trying to take hold of her wrist, but she yanked it away. "Why are you upset?"

She whirled around and stuck a finger in his face. "Do you not realize how shady that was? Why did you have to bring Jacqueline into this?"

Bobby's jaw tightened. "It's over between Jacqueline and me, I swear."

"I think we both knew we'd go back to our regular lives when this was all over, and I guess that includes Jacqueline. It's in the rules after all."

Bobby grabbed his hair at the root, and for a moment, Winter thought he might yank it out. She pretended not to care.

Finding the car was a chore, but as soon as they did, Winter ran to it and opened her door before Bobby got the chance to do it for her. Internally she was panicking, and she didn't want him to see. Their relationship and the rules they shared had been a constant in Winter's life since she was young. Why blow up the last vestige of her childhood by trying to be more than that?

Bobby slid into the driver's seat, and the two were quiet for a moment before he said, "I only did it because I wasn't ready to disappoint my parents, and Jacqueline sounds like an adult on the phone."

"You're so transparent. Jacqueline broke up with you because she thought you were boring," Winter said, "so you called her after being caught at a college party so she'd think you were cool. Are you really that desperate?"

Bobby let out an exasperated sigh. "I didn't want to do any of this. You dragged me along on one of your crazy ideas, and now look at me! You just couldn't stick to the itinerary I laid out. You can never leave well enough alone."

Winter turned over a few times in her seat, trying to get comfortable. All she wanted to do was talk to Emmy and for Emmy to call her an idiot a few times.

"I didn't force you to do anything. You were having fun for once in your life."

Bobby sucked his teeth. "I'm not like you. I can't just have a good time. I can't just not worry about things. I care. About everything. Everything is hard for me."

"It's hard because you make it hard! What do you think is so easy for me?" Winter snapped. "We're the same. We're under all this pressure all the time, and we only have ourselves to blame for it."

Bobby ran his fingers through his hair. "Why does it always feel like you're trying to tear me down? You're this constant reminder that I'm not smart enough, not Korean enough, not worthy enough for anything! I was excited to have another Korean kid to be friends with, but you decided you hated me before we'd ever even gotten to know each other!"

Winter threw her hands in the air. "Look, I'm sorry your parents didn't teach you Korean, but that's not my fault. And I'm sorry about your constant need for approval. It must be exhausting being you."

"It is. Especially when I have to deal with you. If you want to be alone so bad, then maybe you deserve it."

"At least if I'm alone it'll be my choice."

"So is that it?" Bobby asked. "If you're going to go back to hating me, can I at least know why?"

Winter leaned her head on the window and watched absent-mindedly as students stumbled home. Her eyes stung. "I don't hate you. I just thought that you had changed and that I had changed, but it's all too much. It's all happening so quickly, and I don't know what I'm doing. Not everything has to change. Some things are allowed to stay the same."

"What are you so afraid of?" Bobby asked.

"Everything! Aren't you afraid? How can I be the only one who's scared?" Winter made herself small as she huddled against the door. "I thought that when people lose something important to them, they try their best to hold on to whatever they have left, but when Năi Nai died, it was like Emmy couldn't wait to leave me behind. Aren't you guys scared to move to new cities? Aren't you scared of things between us changing? I just want everything to go back to how it was. I don't want whatever is happening between us, and I don't even want to go to school in this stupid city. My parents should have never let me skip eighth grade. I had to start high school all alone as the weird smart kid, and I don't want to do that again."

Winter could see Bobby's reflection in her window. He hung his head and said, "You can't control everything anymore, Winter. Things need to change in order to grow, and you need to let them. You may not have written them all down like we did, but you have rules and parameters around every relationship in your life, including your relationship with Emmy. Like I said before, you're completely incapable of meeting anyone halfway. If Emmy is changing, then change with her. If things between us are growing, then grow with me. I care about you. Can't you just let me?"

"I can't be what you need me to be," Winter replied, her eyes transfixed on broken bottles on the curb. "I'm not ready for any of this."

"Please look at me," Bobby asked. He placed a hand over Winter's, but she pulled away. "Please don't shut me out, Winter. You know I can't cope."

She averted her gaze so she could no longer see Bobby's reflection in the window.

"Fine," Bobby said, his voice gruff.

Winter's eyes misted over, and she wept silently.

It felt like only a few minutes had passed before Winter awoke with the sun. She had a rotten taste in her mouth, and her face was puffy from crying.

She looked over at Bobby, who was outside brushing his teeth. He spit and got back in the car.

Winter felt sick to her stomach. All she wanted was to go home, curl up in a ball, and hibernate until she forgot that Bobby Bae existed. She didn't care if it took the rest of her life.

A call came through the Bluetooth, and Bobby picked it up. It was his parents.

"Bobby, where have you been?" Mr. Bae asked, his voice uncharacteristically stern. "We haven't heard from you in over twenty-four hours; we were worried sick!"

"I'm sorry, Dad," Bobby said, his voice lifeless and grating to Winter's ears. "I meant to call—"

"We've been calling you all night!"

"Where are you?" Mrs. Bae demanded.

"Sorry, my phone died, and I was too tired to drive, so we stayed the night. We're leaving Boston now."

"Why didn't you find a phone yesterday to call us and let us know you were okay?"

Bobby sighed. "Winter and I were exploring the city, then we met up with Kai's cousin, and we lost track of time. I'm sorry."

"This is unlike you, Bobby. You don't forget to call us. You don't lose track of time."

"Mom, relax. We're fine. We'll be home later tonight."

Winter had never heard Mr. and Mrs. Bae get angry with Bobby before. Even they seemed confused by it. She could hear them pacing around, arguing with each other in the background.

"They're only teenagers. What were we thinking letting them go that far?" Mr. Bae asked.

"They've never done anything like this. How were we supposed to know?" Mrs. Bae asked.

Mr. Bae must have picked up the phone again because his voice grew louder and clearer. "I want you to come home right now. Stop for the night if you need to, but I want you home no later than tomorrow afternoon."

"We'll come straight home."

"You will have Winter text us every hour until you're here."

"Yes, sir."

Winter rolled her eyes. She had texted her parents the night before.

Bobby hung up the phone, and it was the last time Winter heard his voice for the next twelve hours. They didn't speak at all and barely looked at each other the entire way back to North Carolina. In the original itinerary, there was a stop halfway so he wouldn't drive the whole thing in one day, but Bobby decided to power through. She was glad for it. She didn't want to be in that car any longer than she had to. They only stopped once on I-95 so Winter could vomit the residual alcohol sloshing around in her stomach, another time to take a nap at a rest stop, twice for gas, and once more for food and energy drinks.

Winter watched the day go by and the license plates change. Seeing all the same roads but doing them in the opposite direction felt like a reversal. Like none of it had even happened. Their friendship was a weeklong experiment that had failed as badly as *Mariner 3*'s mission to Mars.

When they finally reached home, Bobby wordlessly got Winter's door for her and carried her luggage to the porch. He waved at the house and then peeled out of the driveway once she was inside.

Her parents were sitting on the couch, waiting. At the sight of them, she immediately burst into tears. Her parents looked at each other, confused. Appa sat Winter down between him and Umma and leaned her head on his shoulder. She wrapped her arms around him, and her tears soaked his tartan nightshirt.

Umma's tone was gentle, but without a smile on her face, she asked, "Should we even ask?"

"Bobby and I got in a huge fight," she choked out.

"You'll make up. You two are always fighting," Appa said.

"No, not this time. This was real, and it was bad. We both said some horrible things."

Umma brushed a few strands of Winter's hair out of her face. "Did you at least try to be his friend, Soon-hee?"

"I think I tried too hard. Bobby was a mess from breaking up with Jacqueline, and he seemed to be having fun. You know, at first. I think I pushed him too hard, and I don't know . . . I got angry at him, and I'm not even sure why."

Umma put her hand on Winter's leg. "Soon-hee, I don't understand what went wrong between you two. When you first met, you were attached at the hip. It was always *Bobby this and Bobby that.* You followed him around everywhere."

"I used to do what, now?" Winter asked incredulously. She had only been in the first grade, and she vaguely remembered playing with Bobby. But attached at the hip? That felt like a stretch.

"It's true," Appa said. "He was like the big brother you never had. He'd show you his action figures, and you were into astrology back then, so you'd explain his signs and rising moons or what have you. And then he started hanging out with other boys his age more and coming around less. It made you so mad. I remember he came over one day to play with you and he asked you what the book you were reading was about. You couldn't have been more than six or seven, and you said— What did she say, yeobo?" he asked Umma.

"'How can I find out if you keep interrupting me?'" Umma said in a high-pitched, bossy tone.

Appa slapped his knee. "That's it!"

"That was the first time I ever saw him cry," Umma said. "After that, it was like the meaner you were to him, the harder he tried to get you to like him. He was a year ahead of you, so I think you figured out pretty quickly it was the only way you could get and keep his attention. We always thought all this teasing was innocent, but perhaps we were wrong."

His attention? Winter thought. Her mind was ready to burst, but she didn't let it because she was simply too tired from being on the road all day. She hadn't gotten her sea legs yet and still felt like she was in the car.

"I thought you were obsessed with him because he was Korean!" Winter cried. "You're telling me this whole time you just wanted us to be friends again? And *only* friends. You're sure you never wanted me to date Bobby Bae?" She looked at her mother from the corner of her eye.

Umma clicked her tongue. "Of course I wanted you to," she said. "Can you blame me? He's so smart and handsome, and that nose—"

"Jesus, yes. I get it. He has a great nose," Winter said with an intense eye roll. "I just don't want to see it at Sunday dinner anymore. Can I skip it this week?"

"If that's what you want."

"Of course it's what I want! I've been telling you that for years!" Winter said, throwing her hands in the air. "You both don't take

237

any interest in my education. Now *you're* the ones who are always *Bobby this, Bobby that.* The only thing you come to are my orchestra concerts."

"It's because we never understand what you're talking about," Appa said. "We're supportive of everything you do, but we don't understand robotics terms. We come to the concerts because we know what a violin is."

"We admire your ambition. We always have. But you're younger than everyone in your grade. We've always been concerned you wouldn't socialize. And with Emmy in another country, can you blame us for wanting you to have friends and maybe even a partner?" Umma asked.

"I guess not, but I can choose my own friends."

"Maybe you're right. We'll try not to interfere."

"You should probably get some rest," Appa said as he eyed the clock. "I want you to drop some things off for Halmeoni tomorrow."

Winter said good night to her parents and ran upstairs, where she slid into her bed. She didn't trouble herself with changing her clothes or brushing her teeth. She thought about calling Emmy, but she didn't want to bother her. Instead, she turned on the TV, and within minutes, she was fast asleep.

♥

Bobby Bae

36. WE WILL NOT DISCUSS SERIOUS TOPICS

Bobby threw his bag down in the living room and dove onto the couch. He was way too tired to make it all the way upstairs. His back ached and his neck was stiff from sleeping in the car, and he smelled, but he didn't care. His eyes only wanted to rest.

Bobby's parents came down the stairs, tying their robes. He sat up but couldn't think of anything useful to say. Diana's sweet face was solemn, betraying only a hint of uncertainty. Robert Sr. was expressionless.

"You shouldn't have driven all that way in one day, Bobby," Diana said.

"I know, but I needed to come home," he replied, folding his hands in his lap.

Robert Sr. didn't speak, silenced by maybe anger or confusion. Bobby had never been in trouble before. It was new to all three of them, but Diana was the most daring and was at least trying to make an effort at lecturing her son.

"We need to talk to you about something, Bobby," Diana said, and she and his father took a seat on the couch opposite him. Bobby looked at his parents expectantly. "We know you visited your uncle Eugene. He called us."

Bobby wrapped his arms around himself. "Are you upset with me?"

"Why didn't you tell us you wanted to see him?"

"Would you have allowed it?" he asked, and his parents looked at each other. "Exactly. He's always been a shadow in the back of my mind. But then I met his daughter, and he has all these issues. I'm sorry I stirred the pot, but it's also not fair that you never told me what happened."

Robert Sr. looked down at the floor. "Eugene has children?"

"He has a stepdaughter a few years older than I am."

"He's married?"

"Widowed."

Robert Sr. went silent again.

"You were so young when we left New Jersey. We didn't realize you even remembered Eugene," Diana said.

Bobby jostled his hair and pushed it back. "It wasn't Eugene I wanted to see. I wanted to see more of our family in general. You don't share our culture with me, and I feel like this fraud all the time. I look like a duck, and people expect me to quack like one, but I can't. I didn't know how angry that made me until Win— Until a few days ago."

"We only wanted to protect you."

"From what? A sad man with a dead wife? Maybe he wouldn't have ended up that way if you hadn't abandoned him. Or you could have at least convinced him not to buy back the farmer's market," he replied.

"What happened with Eugene is between him and me."

"And you're American, Bobby," Diana offered. "You were born here. Just tell people that."

"Mom," Bobby barked. "It doesn't work that way. I tell people I was born in New Jersey, and they ask me where I'm *really* from. Then I tell them my grandparents were born in Korea, and they ask me North or South. Sometimes I tell the truth, but sometimes I tell them we're refugees who swam from Pyongyang to Alaska, and they believe it! And you know what? It doesn't matter. They end up telling me I'm really tall for an Asian, and they move on. Sometimes they ask me to say something in Korean, and I can't. Do you know how embarrassing it is to have this face and not be able to say a single word or even name a dish? In second grade, in geography class, my teacher called on me to identify a country by the shape, and I had no idea what it was. Turns out it was South Korea."

Bobby's parents kept looking at each other for answers, but neither of them seemed to have any.

"Bobby, it doesn't matter what people say," Diana said finally. "You're responding to their image of you. Ignore it."

"Mom, I can't ignore it if it's literally everyone," Bobby said, exasperated. "And how can I have my own image if I don't know our history? Can you tell me why? What did you both run away from? What are you hiding from me?"

Bobby's mother and father were like strangers to him. He didn't know at what point their relationship became so fractured. There was an incredible amount of love, but they lacked a closeness. They were like ghosts in his life. Robert Sr. always hid something darker behind his smile, and Diana constantly dodged questions and defused any remotely tense situation. The last personal thing he remembered telling them was that he had a crush on Winter when he was eight. They'd created an environment with strict parent-child boundaries, and he respected his parents for it, but it'd only driven them apart slowly as he learned to resent their fake happiness and the pretense that everything was okay. It was probably the reason he hadn't noticed Jacqueline pulling away from him for months.

"It seems you've been angry for a long time," Diana said. "We want to apologize for not noticing. It's just that you're so indepen-dent. You push yourself and you never act up, so we've always let you make your own decisions. But we made the decision to bring you here and withhold our families from you. You are far more mature than we were when we made these decisions, but it's no excuse."

"I don't want to feel like this anymore," Bobby said, his hands clasped behind his neck as he stared at the floor. "You both are unhappy, and I hate that I can't do anything about it, especially with me leaving next year."

"We're fine, sweetheart. What are you talking about?" Diana asked.

"You both are *not* fine. Did you never notice that your scarves have been knitting themselves?" He shot to his feet. "Look, I'm tired. We'll talk about this tomorrow. Or maybe never. Maybe there's some room left under our rugs for this one."

Bobby peeled himself off the couch and zombie-walked upstairs with his parents' eyes burning a hole in his back. When he was in his room, they immediately started talking about him in hushed voices. He pulled a pillow over his head and did his best to ignore the chatter until he fell into a deep, dreamless sleep.

♡

Winter Park

37. WE WILL NOT TELL ANYONE DETAILS ABOUT OUR TRIP

One Sunday a few weeks after Bobby and Winter had returned, they were supposed to have dinner with the Baes. Winter was ditching it. Instead, she was lounging in the grass at her grandmother's apartment. She had her eyes closed and her palms turned up toward the sun in an attempt to tan the insides of her arms. Halmeoni was cooking a vegetable-and-tofu soup. Winter could smell the spiciness in the air.

She lay in the grass a while longer until the screen door was suddenly yanked open with a screech and Halmeoni poked her head outside. "What are you doing other than not helping?" she called.

"I'm trying to get a tan so people think I did something interesting with my summer," Winter replied, turning her head to Halmeoni's flower box, where the two petunias had wilted and died.

"You did do something interesting."

She'd let her paper walls down for the briefest of moments before fortifying them with steel. That didn't count.

Winter got up, dusted off her clothes, and went to the fridge. "What kind of vegetables do you need?"

"Doesn't matter. All of them."

"But, like, specifically. What vegetables does this recipe call for?"

Halmeoni sucked her teeth. "You think I'm using a recipe? The ancestors tell me what to put in the pot, and I listen."

"Okay, but the ancestors aren't really saying anything to me right now, so can you just tell me what you want?"

Halmeoni stayed silent.

Winter took to going through Halmeoni's fridge. Most of her dairy products were nearing their expiration date. She stared at the milk jug for a moment before gathering a zucchini, a squash, two carrots, and a cabbage for the soup. Somehow Halmeoni disapproved despite her vague instructions.

Winter lined the vegetables up for slaughter, then systematically sliced them and put them in separate glass bowls, taking extra care with the carrots. Halmeoni unceremoniously dumped everything in a giant pot with the tofu.

"Are you upset with me, Halmeoni?" Winter asked.

She gave the pot a stir and put on the lid. "You have been here for weeks, Soon-hee. School starts tomorrow, and you've become lazy."

"*Lazy?* Do you not want me here?"

Halmeoni went to wash dishes. "It's not that. You're moping, and your long face is starting to annoy me. You've been frowning all over my house since you got home. Your face will stay that way."

"Whatever."

Winter went to sit on the couch, but Halmeoni stopped her. "Clean up before you sit on my couch. You smell like outside."

Winter didn't understand why Halmeoni was being so mean to her. If she couldn't sit on the couch, then she would have to just lie in the middle of the floor.

"Why is the gravity so . . . gravity today?" Winter mumbled.

"Can't you go sulk at Emmy's?" Halmeoni asked.

Winter spread out her limbs like a starfish and stared at the ceiling. "No. We keep missing each other."

She had seen Emmy only a few times in passing since she got home. There was always a box to pack or a dance practice to go to or some random person with a German-sounding name on the other line who needed her attention. She hadn't gotten to tell her about the disaster of a road trip yet. But even if she could fit herself into Emmy's schedule, it wouldn't matter anyhow. How could she complain about her silly little problems while Emmy was still grieving? She wasn't that selfish. Or at least she was trying not to be.

Winter remained on the floor until Halmeoni stood over her with a judgmental glare. She was impervious to Winter's pout.

"Fine," Winter groaned, "I'll get cleaned up for dinner."

♥

Bobby Bae

Bobby's parents had been running around since church ended, making salads and cleaning wineglasses. Normally he would offer to help, but he had restarted *Riverdale* and was halfway through season four, and he was sure that he was experiencing muscle atrophy. He didn't think he could pick himself up, much less a stack of plates.

Bobby curled into a ball and listened to his parents talking about him downstairs. He wanted to tell them that everything was fine, but that would have been a bald-faced lie. He felt worse than he did before. Losing Jacqueline was hard, but losing himself and Winter in the process was harder.

A car door in the driveway slammed, signaling the arrival of Mr. and Mrs. Park. Within moments, his parents and the Parks were doing their usual over-the-top greetings, followed by wine in the den. Bobby could tell they were trying to be quiet, but he could hear everything because of the way sound traveled through his house. The only quiet place was the bathroom.

"How has Bobby been doing?" he heard Mrs. Park ask. "Winter is upset with us and won't talk about what happened between them at all. Every time we bring up the trip, she runs over to her grandmother's house. She's basically been living there."

"You know how Bobby is," Robert Sr. said.

"He's taking it hard, is he?"

"Have you ever known him not to take something hard?"

Bobby didn't expect to feel attacked like that in his own home.

"He keeps . . . showering," Diana said, dropping her voice.

"That's okay, isn't it?" Mrs. Park asked. "Winter hasn't even unpacked her bag yet. Her room is a disaster."

Diana whispered, but Bobby could still hear. "He stays in there for hours at a time," she said. "School is starting tomorrow, and I'm worried about his skin. His eczema is getting out of hand. I don't want to tell him, but I'm worried about what the other kids will say."

"Send him to the office after school tomorrow. Soon-ja and I have a few open appointments. It's always slow the first week of school," Mr. Park said.

"Thank you," Diana replied. "I just don't know if we'll be able to get him out of bed. Whatever disagreement they had must have been serious."

"That is, unless you think it's possible they got . . . a little too close?" Robert Sr. said.

"Of course not," Mr. Park asserted. "They haven't gotten along in years."

They stopped speaking for a moment. Bobby thought it was because they wised up and realized he could hear them, but it was really for a wine refill. He realized it when they clinked glasses and continued gossiping.

"Would it be the worst thing in the world if they got together?" Diana asked. "They would be such a power couple. She's very bright and strong-willed but not too overbearing for our Bobby like Jaqueline was."

"Bobby always had an eye for strong women," Robert Sr. said. "I wouldn't be surprised if his crush on Winter returned."

Bobby had heard enough. He ran to the bathroom and locked himself inside. He looked at his reflection in the mirror. His parents had been right; his skin was a mess. He had dry red patches everywhere, and he was impossibly itchy. It hadn't been that bad in years. He forewent the shower and crawled back to bed, cranking up his air conditioner and his TV so he couldn't hear the dinner gossip anymore.

♡

Winter Park

39. WE WILL NOT BE SEEN TALKING TO EACH OTHER AT SCHOOL

Brown, brown, brown. Everything at school was brown, including things that weren't supposed to be, like the ceilings, which were water-stained. It wasn't even a nice brown—it was like an orthopedic-shoe brown. Someone in the seventies had to have been going through something to pick the color scheme or rather lack thereof.

Winter walked into her last first day of high school with an iced coffee in one hand and a granola bar in the other. She was already late, so she didn't see the sense of being late *and* hungry.

She passed her robotics coach, Mr. Metzler, on the way to class.

"Late start, Miss Park?" he asked. He wrinkled his nose, causing his razor-edged mustache to rock back and forth. Winter could almost hear the *snip snip snip* of his needle-pointed scissors.

"Giving internships to people who don't deserve them again?" Winter muttered under her breath.

"Excuse me?"

"I said good morning, Mr. Metzler."

"Good morning, Miss Park. Get to class."

Winter rolled her eyes.

Ambling through the halls that were lined with outdated red

lockers, she arrived at her first-period class, AP Gov with Mr. Andrews. Winter didn't know him, but she'd seen him in the hallways, his thick beard sitting prominently on his laugh-lined face. He customarily wore a knit sweater-vest, sometimes adorned in cats, that he buttoned over the charming curve of his belly.

Mr. Andrews looked at Winter over the top of his horn-rimmed glasses as he rapped his nails against the desk. "You're late, Miss Park," he said.

Winter wanted to ask how he knew who she was, but in a school with only a handful of non-white kids, it probably wasn't hard to use the process of elimination, especially since Bobby Bae was in this class too.

"I had locker trouble," Winter lied.

"Take a seat."

Winter looked out over the sea of heads staring at her. Kai waved at her excitedly. He took his bright yellow Fjällräven bag off the seat he'd saved for her, which was right behind Bobby Bae. It was the first time she'd seen him in three weeks. It was actually quite easy to avoid him if she really put in the effort. She settled into her desk and tried to make herself disappear. Bobby didn't look at her once, not even when she knocked her thick history textbook against the back of his chair by mistake and it made a loud clang.

"I figured you'd want to sit together," Kai whispered with a wink.

"I told him we wouldn't," Bobby muttered.

"Bobby isn't that bad of a kisser," Kai said with a chuckle.

Mr. Andrews cleared his throat. "Mr. Barbier," he said, his lips in a flat line. "What amendment protects interest groups?"

"All of them?" Kai replied.

"If you don't know, then please don't talk in my class," Mr. Andrews said.

Kai shrugged.

"Does anyone else know the answer? Whoever gets it right gets an extra point on the next pop quiz."

Bobby's hand twitched. He was offended, like it had moved without his permission. He stuffed both his hands into his hoodie pocket and put his head down.

Winter didn't want to answer either. Brandon Long was sitting all the way in the back of the classroom as low in his chair as he could without spilling onto the floor, his glasses resting unused on his desk. He beat Winter in getting an internship, so why didn't *he* answer the question?

Winter took a deep breath and tried to focus on anything except for the twenty-some-odd pairs of eyes looking at her when she raised her hand after Bobby, Brandon, and everyone else failed to. Mr. Andrews nodded in Winter's direction.

"Interest groups are protected by the First Amendment, which states Americans have the right to assemble and petition against the government."

Mr. Andrews was pleased, but Winter wasn't. She knew Bobby had the answer to that softball question. Her eyes settled on the boy in front of her. Despite the heat, he was wearing a hoodie and long pants. He appeared to have cut his hair as well. Since she'd sat down, he hadn't brushed his bangs back once. She tried to pay attention as Mr. Andrews went over the syllabus, but she couldn't help it; Bobby was right there. The back of his chair was resting against the front of her desk, and he was one of those men who smelled good without the help of fancy soaps and cologne. Winter was barely breathing, trying to ignore it.

"Winter, you good?" Kai asked in his low drawl. His voice was like smoke rising from a fire. Winter looked over. "You're biting your nails."

Winter looked down at her nails. They were short and uneven. She took to bouncing her leg instead. "I'm fine," Winter said, taking a few long sips of her iced coffee.

Mr. Andrews gave them a look that told them to be quiet. Kai went back to his notes, and Winter went back to trying to ignore the static in her brain. She kept bouncing her leg until a hand suddenly grabbed her by the calf. A cold snap ripped through her body, and she gasped. She played it off as a cough. Bobby hadn't turned around, but his arm was reached back, and his hand was firmly gripped around her leg. She must have been shaking his chair. It instantly reminded her of those hands cradling her neck and tilting her head back for that first kiss at Omari's party.

Bobby took his hand away, and Winter didn't move a muscle for the rest of class.

When the bell rang, she shot up to leave but was hindered by Bobby putting on his backpack. They did that awkward dance where they each attempted to move out of each other's way but ended up blocking the other no matter what they tried. Bobby finally grabbed Winter by the shoulders and moved her to his other side, causing her to swoon. The rest of the class cleared out as they stared at each other for a moment.

"Can we talk?" he asked flatly. Kai got the hint and went ahead without him.

Winter wrapped her arms around herself. "About what?"

"I think you know what." He stepped in closer and reached for her hand, but she jerked it away before he could take it. His eyes were intense. "If our trip was only a onetime lapse in judgment, I'll

252

leave you alone, but I can't stop thinking about it. Can you?"

Winter noticed rough patches of red skin on Bobby's neck. She gently traipsed her fingertips along the side of his face. "*Where* have you been thinking about it?"

"You know where I do most of my thinking."

"You mean most of your crying?"

Bobby growled. "You're deflecting, but I don't care. Can I kiss you?"

Winter blushed. "We're not supposed to be seen talking to each other, and you want to make out in the middle of a classroom?"

"Kind of. Yeah," he said, smirking.

Winter was chewing the insides of her mouth to shreds as she looked up at Bobby expectantly. She closed her eyes for only a split second and felt his hands at her neck again, like she'd been dreaming about since they'd kissed. When she opened her eyes, she realized it had only been in her mind.

"I'm sorry. I don't care who was right or who was wrong," Bobby said, taking a step closer. "And I don't care what was said. Let's forget about the whole fight and move on."

"Don't," Winter whispered, putting her hand on Bobby's chest to put distance between them. As much as she wanted to, she couldn't bring herself to accept the apology or give one of her own. She wasn't even sure there was anything to forgive him for. As angry as Winter had been learning that Bobby called Jacqueline, she hadn't really wanted to get in trouble with her parents. The way in which he chose to avoid the trouble—Jaqueline—left something to be desired, but she wasn't upset he'd done it.

Winter dropped her head. "I like you, Bobby, but maybe we're not the best for each other. I don't know who I am lately. We're doing and saying things that aren't us."

Bobby once again tried to close the space between them. "Isn't that a good thing?"

"I honestly don't know," Winter replied, and she took a step back, but it wasn't far enough. She left the classroom without another word.

♥

Bobby Bae

40. WE WILL NOT INVOLVE OUR PARENTS IN OUR BUSINESS

Bobby darted for his car after school without looking up. He was moving as briskly as he could, but with the hoodie he had on to hide his eczema, he nearly turned into a ball of sweat and evaporated into the hot September day.

He pulled up to Park Dermatology, which was in a converted house on their town's main road. According to Mr. Park, their location brought in half their customers. Though Bobby attributed most of their business to him helping them set up their online presence.

"Bobby!" Mrs. Park said as he walked in. She threw her white coat over her blouse and fixed her hair. "You can come on back."

Bobby followed Mrs. Park back into the exam room. Mr. Park was sitting at a desk in the corner. Bobby took his jacket off and threw it on the couch, then settled into the exam chair. The Parks looked at his irritated skin, but he knew the visit wasn't entirely necessary. They were familiar with his skin after nearly a decade of being their patient. They could have prescribed him creams at home.

"I'm sorry for everything," Bobby said without any prompting from the Parks. "You trusted me with your daughter, and I upset her. Is she . . . okay?"

Mr. Bae looked up from his desk. "You could ask her yourself."

"Right. I'm sorry, sir."

Mrs. Park gave her husband a look, and he shrugged.

"Winter has been hiding out at her grandmother's. We truthfully don't know how she is," she said. Mrs. Park had her gloved hands on his cheek. "How are you, dear? Are you back together with Jacqueline?"

"No," he replied resolutely. "We've broken up for good."

"That girl must have done a number on you. Skin doesn't lie. Winter knows. She's been breaking out lately," Mr. Park said.

"Young-gil, she wouldn't want you telling him that!" Mrs. Park snapped as she went to a drawer and handed him a few sample-sized creams.

Bobby hadn't noticed. Winter looked as beautiful as ever at school earlier.

Mr. Park cleared his throat. "We're glad you're here because there's something we want to talk about. We spoke to your parents, and they told us you've been having some questions about your culture. As you know, my mother is getting older and doesn't always accept our help. So if you'd like, you can visit maybe once a week and check on her? She'd love to share what she can with you too."

"Really?" Bobby's chest swelled. Mr. and Mrs. Park had always felt like his uncle and aunt. He was grateful they weren't upset with him. "I'd love to spend time with Halmeoni. Thank you."

"It was actually Winter's idea. She and her grandmother already discussed it."

"She told you not to tell him that," Mr. Park barked.

Bobby stiffened.

"And one more thing before you leave," Mrs. Park said. "Winter is headstrong, but she's more sensitive than she lets on. She's always put her studies and her passions above everything else because she wants to be taken seriously. As a woman and a doctor, I can respect

256

that. It's no coincidence Mr. Bae has more patients than I do."

"Why are you telling me this?" Bobby asked.

"Because you both are so mature and so responsible, we forget how young you are sometimes. We want you both to be happy, and it's clear you aren't right now," she said. "We don't know what happened between you, but I think she misses you."

Bobby put his jacket back on and stuffed his medication in his pockets. "I miss her too," he said. "And I'll visit Halmeoni tomorrow after school."

Mr. Park got up and clapped him on the back. "Good boy."

Bobby's eyes stung, and his lip quivered. He didn't feel like a good boy lately.

"Look what you've done!" Mrs. Park said.

"I didn't do anything!" Mr. Park exclaimed.

A full wail emanated from somewhere deep within. "I'm. Sorry. I'm. Just. So. Itchy. And. Hot. Thank. You," Bobby said between sniffles.

"Get the boy some water, Young-gil. Quickly!" Mrs. Park snapped.

Mr. Park whirled around in his swivel chair and grabbed a paper cup from the dispenser by the sink. He filled it up with tap water and handed it to Bobby. Bobby downed it in one gulp and placed the cup on the counter.

"I'm. Sorry. I. Should. Probably. Get. Going," he choked as he slipped out of the room.

There was one Black-owned indie bookstore in town, and it was the perfect place for Kai to work. He'd had many odd jobs over the years, but none had ever stuck. Uncle Moodie's Books was the first.

Bobby found himself there. He walked in, and the bell alerted Kai to his presence. He was behind the café counter with his sketchbook. He smiled and waved Bobby over. The smell of coffee got stronger as he approached. In the case, there were comic book–themed cookies and cakes. Kai must have instinctively known Bobby was in crisis, so he handed him a Wookiee Cookie in wax paper. He then poured him a frothy oat milk cappuccino and drew a heart in the foam.

"Kai, how are you still single?" Bobby asked, taking the mug in both hands.

"You'd think my options would be wide open, but not so much," he replied with a sad smile. "The guy I went out with was rude to the server and left a terrible tip, so it's safe to say there will be no second date. Got anyone else for me?"

"After all these years, I still have no idea what your type is."

"Zoë Kravitz . . . also Lenny Kravitz. Actually, Lisa Bonet too, now that I think about it," he said with a dazed look on his face.

Bobby laughed. "Okay, maybe I can't help you."

"Shame."

The two of them sat at the table by the window. Bobby nibbled his cookie and sipped the cappuccino as Kai opened a fresh page in his sketchbook and took his time selecting which pencil he wanted to use.

"You finally going to tell me what happened?" Kai asked, touching his pencil to the paper.

"I think you already know," Bobby said as he looked out the window.

Kai's shoulders shook with laughter. "You've been down bad for that girl for years."

Bobby sank into his chair. "She says she likes me but doesn't think we should be together."

Kai put his pencil down for a second and asked, "Do you remember how we became friends?"

"Mr. Melton's fourth-grade class," Bobby replied. Kai's last name is Barbier, and they sat alphabetically. Theodore Bach almost became Bobby's best friend, but he liked to cheat off his tests, so there was really no competition.

"That's when we met, but we didn't become best friends until after I told you I liked you. Instead of being weirded out, you kissed me and cured us both of any delusions we may have had."

Bobby blushed. He'd almost forgotten how candid Kai could be. It had been a while since they'd had a proper conversation because he'd been so mopey.

"Look," Kai continued, picking up his pencil. "You're a strange dude. I don't know anyone else who would do what you did. You just have to show Winter a little bit of that."

"She's so guarded. I don't know if I can break through again. I ruined my chance."

"You mean you put the Bobby Bae charm on her, and she didn't immediately press 'add to cart'?" Kai asked sarcastically. "Did you even apologize?"

"Yeah. I mean, sort of. I tried to apologize at school, but she walked off."

"Then try harder."

It was odd, but Bobby had always been proud of his friendship with Kai. He had oceans of depth to him, and Bobby didn't think he intended to be funny at times, but he was so honest and plain in his thinking that he made it so you had to laugh at the absurdity of life. Any of the pretenses Bobby kept up with everyone else weren't possible with his best friend.

"I think I have an idea," Bobby said, suddenly lighting up. "You're going to have to start billing me for your time."

Kai smirked. "You couldn't afford me."

Bobby buried his face in his hands. "Speaking of things we can't afford—I'm considering visiting Berkeley with you."

Kai stopped drawing for a moment. "What about Harvard?"

"Not everyone gets accepted to Harvard, and I've been thinking about our app a lot lately."

A smile took over Kai's face. "We could really get into some trouble out there."

"I look forward to it. In moderation of course," Bobby said, taking a bite of his cookie. He grinned with it between his teeth.

Kai gave one of Bobby's ears a playful tug and said, "You're such a flirt. I can't stand you."

"Maybe you could learn a thing or two from me," Bobby replied with a shrug.

"And ruin my historic run of striking out with all the ladies, theydies, gentlethems, and gents? Never. I'll give up now while my dignity is still intact."

"You just have to put yourself out there. You're the best person I know."

Kai's social anxiety usually had him seeking out his sketchbooks for comfort. However, on the rare occasions he would third wheel with Bobby and Jacqueline, Kai's sadness over not having someone special of his own was obvious.

Perhaps all he needed was a push.

Bobby spotted a group of girls across the street. He gave them a smile and waved them over.

"Dude, what are you doing?" Kai growled.

"You only have one customer, and I'm not even a paying one."

"Bobby, I know what you're doing. Stop it."

"Too late!"

The bell over the door jingled, and the group of girls walked in. Kai begrudgingly stood up and went behind the counter. He left what he had been drawing on the table, which was a rough sketch of the latest panel of his Milquetoast comic.

Bobby glared at Kai, who smirked at him over the heads of the girls.

Dropping a large tip on the table, Bobby made his way outside. As he walked by the shop window, he aimed a finger heart in Kai's direction but raised his middle finger as soon as Kai started to look too pleased with himself.

With a plan in its infancy swirling around in Bobby's head, he rushed home to see it through.

♡

Winter Park

41. WE WILL NOT INTERFERE IN EACH OTHER'S PERSONAL MATTERS

Halmeoni invited Winter over for dinner. When she arrived, Halmeoni was waiting on the patio. She had on one of her snappy outfits and a bumblebee brooch. She motioned to the other chair and started the conversation with everyone's least favorite words. "We need to talk."

"Is something wrong?" Winter asked.

"I think that enough is enough, Soon-hee," Halmeoni said. "I've given you your space, but it's been weeks, and you're still sulking."

"I'm fine, Halmeoni."

"No, you're not. But it's okay. I got something for you that will raise your spirits."

Winter clapped her hands together. "A present?"

"Sort of."

Halmeoni swung open her apartment door, and there was Emmy with a huge smile on her face. She had her signature slicked pony-tail that went almost down to her waist. Her outfit was effortless but intentional. In front of her were mandu-making stations set up with bowls of the filling in one corner, the wrappers in another, and the finished products at the end of the table waiting to be panfried. Winter peeked into the filling bowl. It was full of smashed-up clear noodles, chives, pork, and every seasoning in the cabinet.

Winter went through a roller coaster of emotions. "I used to love those days we made mandu together—you, Halmeoni, Nǎi Nai, and I," Winter said.

Making mandu started out as a monthly ritual, but due to high demand, it became biweekly and eventually weekly. Winter and Emmy would come from playing outside, their noses running, lungs raw, smelling of sweat and earth. They'd wash their hands up to the elbows and tie their hair back before sitting down with bowls of cool water and floured plates. Nǎi Nai and Halmeoni would gossip in their own special language, their practiced hands splitting their time gesturing and forming restaurant-worthy dumplings while barely looking, and Winter and Emmy would enter their own little world, mixing Korean and Chinese ingredients into only mildly edible concoctions.

Winter realized this was probably the last summer she would spend with Emmy at the senior community. It was the end of an era marked by scraped knees, grass stains, slurped noodles, awkward phases followed by even more awkward phases, dancing under the sprinklers, bottling lightning bugs, giggling past bedtimes, and other endless summer memories.

Emmy dipped her fingers into one of the bowls and flicked droplets of water at Winter, breaking her out of her stroll down memory lane.

"Sit with me," Emmy said, and Winter took a seat next to her at the table.

Halmeoni, looking pleased with herself, left the room, busying herself in the kitchen with folding dish towels Winter had never known to be folded.

Leaning back in her chair and crossing her arms, Emmy said, "We should talk about me not going to college."

"It doesn't matter. I'm not going either."

"MIT has been your dream since we met. Don't joke like that."

"I'm not joking," Winter replied, leaning all the way back in her chair and staring up at the ceiling. She couldn't bring herself to care about anything these days, much less MIT. "I don't want to go. I probably can't get in anyway."

"You can't be serious."

If Winter's time visiting schools taught her anything, it was that MIT was not a done deal. With an acceptance rate of about 7 percent, she had a better chance of seeing a shooting star in the middle of Times Square. And what was the point in busting her ass to go to a school in a city with no Halmeoni, no Emmy?

"I just want to enjoy my senior year and have modest expectations for college," Winter said.

"You? Since when?" Emmy said with a snort.

"Since I got passed over for an internship. Since I've exhausted all my waking hours with my nose in a book. Since—"

Emmy suddenly smacked Winter on the arm, which stung like a bug bite.

"Ow! What was that for?" Winter asked, cradling her arm.

"Respectfully, Winnie, the spine has twenty-six bones, and you're not using a single one of them."

Winter gasped. "Emmy Lin!"

"I said *respectfully*! College is the time to get out of your comfort zone. Woman up!" Emmy smacked her again. "Halmeoni filled me in on everything. Why didn't you tell me what was going on with you?"

"Because you're busy and you're grieving. My problems are so stupid."

"I'm sorry I haven't been there for you recently, but you can always come to me."

"Don't apologize. You just lost Năi Nai, and you're starting this whole new chapter of your life. I'm the one who hasn't been there for you. I've been selfish, pushy, and needy," Winter said, counting her sins on her fingers.

Emmy smirked and raised an eyebrow. "Go on."

"I'm happy for you and so proud. You're beautiful and talented, and your body moves in ways that are probably illegal in some states. I want to see your face on every billboard and magazine in the entire world."

"I'm doing high fashion."

"Then I want you on every runway. I'm not kidding when I say I want to be you when I grow up."

Emmy's eyebrows drew together. "Look, Winnie. You're an only child, and ever since you skipped a grade, you've always been the youngest one in the room. You're just getting used to the fact that you won't be everybody's baby anymore. But you're going to MIT if I have to drag you there myself."

"*Baby?*"

"You whine and pout and get whatever you want."

Winter opened her mouth to argue, but her rebuttal was without merit. She folded her arms and stuck out her bottom lip. "I'm not a baby."

"You're *my* baby," Emmy said with a laugh, threading her fingers through the length of her ponytail. "What internship did you get passed over for?" she demanded.

"There was only one slot available at Convergence Robotics, and the robotics coach, Mr. Metzler, offered it to Brandon Long."

"*Brandon Long?*" Emmy said with disgust. "The kid you told me used to bite people in elementary school?"

"Yeah?" Winter replied, feeling more and more ridiculous the longer she thought about it.

"You see how this is a problem, right?"

Of course she knew it was a problem. Brandon Long did his equal share of the work, but when it came time to present, he spoke so quickly and loudly that Winter could hardly get a word in. It was like trying to yell over a rocket launch. Winter tried to double Dutch into the conversation and failed miserably, causing Mr. Metzler to believe Brandon contributed more to their projects.

Winter squirmed under Emmy's gaze. "You may have a slight point."

"Then why are you doubting yourself?" Emmy glared at Winter, and she leaned away. "Look at who you are and everything you can do! You're amazing! You're like a walking almanac, and I've seen you build a robot out of an electric toothbrush! I don't want to hear you doubt yourself ever again," Emmy said, giving Winter another swat. "You tell this Mr. Metzler he better give you that internship, or he's going to have to deal with me."

"Okay! Okay! I will! I'll go to his office tomorrow," Winter said, cradling her arm. She then dug a finger into Emmy's thigh, and she cried out and folded to the ground, pulling Winter down with her.

Emmy was right. She owed it to herself to at least try to get into her dream school. Of course it would be scary to be without her family in a new city for the first time in her life, but it was time to grow up, whether she liked it or not. If she gave it her all and still didn't get in, at least she would know for sure that it wasn't meant to be.

The girls laughed on the floor together for a moment before

266

Emmy said, "Can we stop talking now and make some mandu? I'm starving."

"Me too," Winter said, pulling her best friend into an awkward floor-hug. "Just promise we'll always be friends, okay?"

"I promise."

The two then reclaimed their seats, took their first wrappers, and prepared to bring disgrace to their family names as Halmeoni rejoined them at the table.

♥

Bobby Bae

42. WE WILL DISCONTINUE FAMILY MEALS

Homecoming was soon, and Bobby was pleased to be nominated for homecoming court along with half the lacrosse team, a few cheerleaders, and some theater kids. Only the best and brightest were nominated every year.

Bobby took a deep breath and smiled to himself.

He'd been starting every day with a coffee and ending it with another. He'd never been so focused in all his life, running solely on caffeine and intrusive thoughts. If he kept himself busy, he didn't have time for shower cries. He also hadn't had time to visit Halmeoni as often as he'd promised, so he was glad to finally have planned a visit.

After sitting for dinner with his parents, Bobby changed into an aubergine-colored blazer and pants and picked up a potted money tree to gift to Halmeoni. He never went anywhere empty-handed.

When he knocked on Halmeoni's door, he heard voices inside, which immediately caused his palms to sweat.

The door swung open, and Bobby handed Halmeoni the plant. "Halmeoni, annyeonghaseyo."

"Have you eaten? Make some mandu," she said in English, taking the plant and leading him to the table.

Halmeoni moved out of the way, and Bobby's eyes fell on Winter and Emmy rolling dumplings at the dining room table. He wanted to run away, but Halmeoni had already shut him in with the door and her death glare.

"Hey, Emmy," Bobby said with a nod. "How are you?"

"Wonderful." Emmy looked him up and down. She wasn't even trying to be subtle about checking him out. "And you?"

"Never better."

Bobby sat and stared at Winter, waiting for her to speak first. When they both failed to say anything, Emmy burst out laughing. "I'm sorry, this is just so awkward," she said.

Bobby blushed and silently started making dumplings. Halmeoni joined in, and they all rolled dumplings in silence. Bobby's looked even better than Halmeoni's, Emmy was rolling hers like blunts, and Winter wasn't even looking at what she was doing because she was too busy not staring at Bobby. She was rolling hers between her palms, which made the filling burst from the wrappers.

A long while went by in silence. Too long. Halmeoni sucked her teeth. "I hope my funeral isn't like this."

"Halmeoni!" Winter gasped. "Don't say stuff like that. It's bad luck!"

Halmeoni sighed. "I have all my grandchildren together, and you can't look at each other. Do you think I had family to spare when I came to this country? You are all so spoiled."

"I'm just surprised to see Bobby is all. You didn't say he'd be here," Winter replied.

Halmeoni considered her words for a minute. She put down the wrapper in her hands and commanded everyone's attention. "Do you all know how I ended up in America or why?"

The expression on Winter's face twisted. "Why are you bringing this up all of a sudden?"

"You should hear this."

Emmy, Bobby, and Winter looked around at one another and shrugged.

"You've never really spoken about this before, Halmeoni," Winter said.

"I'd really like to hear the story," Bobby interjected, still unsure of the relevance.

Emmy, Bobby, and Winter kept folding dumplings as Halmeoni leaned back in her chair and looked at the three of them.

"Many moved to America for jobs or school or to avoid serving in the military," she began. "Winter's grandfather and I moved to start our family. He bought into the American dream, but I wasn't convinced. I had a big family with lots of sisters, and they all urged me to go, so we left Korea.

"The airlines used to serve real food on planes back then. On the flight over, they asked us how we wanted our steaks prepared. I had no concept of raw steak. In my household, we always fully cooked our meat, the ghost too. Everything starting from then was an adjustment."

Bobby smiled. He didn't want to laugh because he thought it'd take Halmeoni out of the moment and she'd stop. He'd always wanted grandparents, and she was the closest he had.

Halmeoni cleared her throat. "We could all read and write in English, but speaking took work," she continued. "It was hard for me. I considered going back to the Korean countryside with my parents, but my husband and I decided to do this together. I tried harder. *The Price Is Right* and American soap operas still haunt me. It's a wonder I don't sound like Bob Barker."

Emmy nudged Winter and whispered, "Who's Bob Barker?"

Winter shrugged.

"Do you regret coming here?" Bobby asked.

Halmeoni steepled her fingers under her chin. "Seeing you three together tells me I made the right decision. You are going to have beautiful lives, surrounded by different people. You can do anything you want, but I don't want you to rush to get there. I wouldn't have made it without family, and neither will you," she said, and then held her hands out to Emmy and Bobby. "Emmy, Soon-hee, Dae-seong, you are family. Remember that."

"She wants you two to kiss and make up," Emmy whispered, nudging Winter in the side.

"Shut up, Emmy," Winter said under her breath.

"A kiss isn't going to fix ten years of animosity," Bobby said.

"And how long has your father not talked to his brother?" Halmeoni asked.

Bobby looked down. "Ten years."

"And are they better off for it?"

Bobby looked over at Winter. She had her hands folded in her lap and her eyes cast down at the floor. He shook his head.

Halmeoni went to check on the stove. "You are all smart enough to make your own decisions. Make up or don't. I'm still inviting you to bingo tonight."

"Bingo?" Emmy laughed.

"Why would you invite us this time?" Winter asked.

"Because now I know you both like to break rules," Halmeoni said. "And did you know in North Carolina, it's illegal to play bingo for over five hours in a row?"

Bobby's eyes snapped to Winter's. She was holding back a laugh.

"You planned a five-hour game?" she asked.

"No. I planned a five-hour-and-one-minute game. What did you think these mandu were for?"

"I thought they were for me!" Emmy exclaimed. "I'm leaving tomorrow!"

"Then it's for you," Halmeoni replied. "We still need food."

Bobby snorted. Halmeoni was always up to something. He excused himself from the table and texted Kai to join.

♡

Winter Park

43. WE WILL NOT COMMENT ON EACH OTHER'S APPEARANCE

Hour One

Halmeoni picked up her bingo card and took a seat at a table with some gossiping grandmothers and bottles of champagne. She called everyone's attention. "Say hello to my granddaughter and her friends," she said, as if Winter were a show pony.

Mrs. Fowler rolled her eyes. "We know Winter. We see her every week."

"Tonight she's the guest of honor. The stakes will be the highest they've ever been."

"We're all going to go broke being friends with you."

Winter laughed and bent down to give her grandmother a hug.

Kai ran straight for the stage and took the mic over from Archie, one of Mrs. Fowler's kids, who often volunteered for the senior center events. Archie didn't know what to make of Kai, but he moved over and handed him the microphone. Kai turned the handle on the ball spinner and pulled the next number. "Gluten-free, G fifty-three!" he called, and a few seniors moved their plastic pieces onto their bingo boards.

Emmy leaned into Winter, her eyes fixated on Kai. "I'm going to miss this place."

Winter was distracted by Bobby. She was aware of him wherever he went in his deep burgundy suit and tie. He was sitting at a table a short distance away.

"What are you staring at?" Emmy asked, waving a hand in front of Winter.

Heat rose in Winter's cheeks despite herself. "Nothing. Not Bobby and his stupid haircut."

"You don't mind if I shoot my shot? Technically I had a crush on Bobby first." Emmy's red lips split into a crazed smile when Winter grimaced. "So you do care! Did you guys kiss?" Winter again said absolutely nothing. "I knew it! How was it? I used to dream about it . . . a lot. He seems like he'd make you do something weird like slap him in the face."

Winter hid her fiery cheeks in her hands. "You're disturbed."

Emmy flipped her ponytail behind her shoulder. "Maybe, but the fact that you're dodging my question makes me feel like I'm right."

"I mean, he did do this one thing."

"I knew it! I always knew he was the type of guy who did *things*."

Winter thought of Bobby's thumb brushing her lips open, and she shivered.

"Oh, so it was like that," Emmy said with a devilish smile.

Winter didn't see the sense in trying to hide what was going on with her anymore. She clearly wasn't fooling a single person, including herself. She put her hand on Emmy's shoulder. "It's bad, Em. I thought it would go away, but it's worse than ever," she said, biting her lip.

"How bad?"

"I had a dream where all I did was watch him refill fountain pens."

Emmy was dying laughing. "That's hot."

"I shouldn't be dreaming about boys who make ten-page itineraries in military time."

"What, you don't support the troops?" Emmy snorted. "I'm so glad you have your first crush."

Winter's immediate impulse was to deny that she had a crush, but it'd been long enough. She did. She loved that he collected pens and obsessed over milk even though he couldn't drink it. She liked that he cried. He didn't have them anymore, but she even liked his stupidly long bangs and the way he used to toss his head back to get them out of his eyes. She liked that he ordered waffles at pancake houses and that he cared about absolutely everything and everyone, sometimes more than he cared about himself.

Admitting it felt good.

When Bobby noticed Winter looking at him, he stood up and started walking over.

"You know when guys in suits unbutton their jackets as they sit down so they don't, like, split it in half?" Winter asked Emmy, and she laughed. "I like when they stand up again and rebutton it."

"Congratulations. You've unlocked one new kink," Emmy said, clutching her sides.

"Shut up."

They were sitting with Mr. Graham, Miss Evelyn, and Miss Sue. Bobby sat down between Winter and Miss Sue. He took Winter's gaze hostage with his own and said, "Hey," quietly so only she could hear.

"Hi," she replied, pushing some of her fallen hair behind her ears.

"Is this your boyfriend, Winter?" Miss Sue asked.

Winter snapped her head around. "No, no. He's not."

"Are you dating anyone, sweetheart? Do kids these days still date?" Miss Evelyn asked.

"No, I mean, yes, people date, but I'm not dating anyone."

"Leave these kids alone," Mr. Graham cut in. "They're young. They'll have time for all that later."

Kai was still onstage being the best emcee bingo had ever seen.

"I so badly want to make a joke that's out of line, but, honey, the way Mrs. Fowler is looking at me, I must decline. O sixty-nine!" he called out.

Winter took in her surroundings. There was a tacky disco ball hanging in the center of the room and multicolored strobe lights bouncing off it. Cheap pink and lime-green streamers hung all over the room, as well as sparkling tinsel left over from Christmas. There were remnants of every holiday strewn about and champagne bottles on every table. If this was what getting old looked like, Winter might not mind it. Each person in that room had lived such a life. They had had kids and grandkids and heartache and happy times. They had probably seen every peak and every valley the world had to throw at them. If she was going to learn how make the most of her life, rather than just survive it, it was going to be from them.

♥

Bobby Bae

44. WE WILL NOT DANCE TOGETHER

Hour Two

If you are a young man at a nursing home, it's customary to dance with absolutely every single elderly woman in the room. Bobby was dancing middle school dance-style with Miss Joanne. She smelled like old-lady perfume and had on a sweater with a feather collar that made her look like someone who may or may not have at one time killed one of her ex-husbands.

"You're such a handsome boy," Miss Joanne said. "If I were fifty years younger . . ."

Bobby always found it interesting that when people said creepy things like that, they always trailed off at the end because they wanted you to make the creepy inference yourself. They wanted you to be complicit in your own gross-out.

Miss Joanne pulled him closer. Kai had the right idea. Bobby should have gotten up on that stage instead.

He politely excused himself from the dance floor and took a breather next to the stage. He couldn't help but feel ignored by Winter. If he sat next to her, she went to the bathroom. If he brought her a drink, she already had one. It was driving him crazy.

"You good, dude? You're moping," Kai said as he wolfed down a slice of pizza with the cheese picked off.

"Winter's been avoiding me."

"Dance with me, then," Kai said, wiping his hands on his pants. He pulled Bobby up, and they took a spot in the middle of the make- shift dance floor. Kai bear-hugged Bobby and held his head to his chest as they swayed. Bobby laughed for the first time all evening. Kai's gangly limbs draped over him as he patted Bobby's back and made a shushing noise.

"You're wrinkling my jacket," Bobby said.

"First of all, watch your tone. Second of all, you're right."

Kai extended his arm and spun Bobby. Right into Winter.

"Kai!" Bobby said, grasping after him.

Kai jumped back onto the stage and waved. "Have fun!"

Bobby turned to face Winter. She'd changed into a white dress, the first he'd seen her wear in years. It was no doubt one of Emmy's.

"You look nice," he said.

She let out a short laugh. "You can't say stuff like that to me."

"You've been avoiding me," he said as he pulled her into a slow dance. "I wanted to tell you something."

"Tell me what?" she said as she looked up at him, her dark eyes shining and expectant.

"My parents have been speaking with my uncle, and I think we're going to spend Thanksgiving together."

Winter lit up. "Bobby, that's amazing."

"Yeah, and also . . . I think I may consider computer science. I put the beta version of Uyu in the app store, and it's gotten some positive reviews, so I booked a tour at Berkeley. Kai and I are flying out to California next month."

Winter put her head down against his chest. "No Harvard?"

"I considered GW for Jacqueline, Princeton for my uncle, and Harvard for my father. I may choose Harvard, but maybe I won't. I don't know yet. I've always had this life planned out for myself, and

I worked so hard to get it, I didn't even realize I didn't want it," he said. "I have you to thank for helping me see that."

Winter laughed. "I made you realize you were unhappy? Great."

"You know what I mean." He cradled her against his body. "You going to be okay without me in Boston?"

She didn't have time to respond. Kai and Emmy cut in. Kai got Bobby in a headlock, ruffled his hair, and gave him a rough kiss on the forehead. Bobby wiped it off, and the two broke into a contact-less boxing match. Emmy took Winter by the hand and twirled her. The four of them danced like idiots in the middle of the room with their arms in the air while the strobe lights hit them and disco music blared.

Truthfully, Winter didn't know if she'd be okay in Boston without her friends and family, but the prospect of having them to come home to filled her with an immense joy.

♡

Winter Park

45. WE WILL NOT MAKE IT WEIRD

Hour Three

The room had thinned out considerably. It was past midnight, so it was far beyond some of the seniors' bedtimes. It was after Winter's bedtime too, if she was being perfectly honest. When she stayed up, it was only to sit outside and watch the stars. She decided to do just that for a moment.

Looking through the windows of the senior center, her eyes fell on Bobby. He was back-to-back with Kai as Emmy stood on a chair to compare their heights. Kai was very obviously at least five inches taller than Bobby, so she didn't know why he needed to hear it from Emmy's mouth before he accepted the truth. The three of them laughed, and Kai scooped Emmy off the chair and placed her back on the floor.

Winter enjoyed a few minutes of peace, breathing in the thick, humid air that smelled of mown grass and moist earth before she heard Emmy call, "Winnie!" Emmy made her way outside and locked Winter in a protective back hug. "What are you doing out here?" They swayed with the trees as the warm wind blew them back and forth. "Are you hiding from a certain well-dressed Lactaid ad who is completely obsessed with you?"

"I freaked out on him in Boston. I don't see why he isn't furious with me."

"Easy. Because that boy is clearly in love with you."

"Oh, shut up," Winter said with an airy laugh.

"I'm serious," Emmy said, flipping Winter around and holding her by the shoulders. "Bobby swore me to secrecy, but you're my best friend, not him. He called me yesterday and told me about how you seemed really scared of losing me as a friend, so he bought us plane tickets to Nascar Kuja . . . Kullajeq? Umm . . . I don't know how to say it, but it's somewhere in Greenland."

Winter blinked, confused. "I'm sorry. What?"

"'Narsaq Kujalleq,'" Emmy said, reading it from her phone. "I don't know. He said something about you meeting me halfway? I zoned out when he started listing off coordinates."

The conversation Winter had with Bobby on the balcony their first night in a hotel came to mind. He told her she needed to meet people halfway. Why was he so literal? At least he wasn't sending her to the middle of the ocean.

Winter looked pleadingly into Emmy's eyes. "Emmy, I want him . . . like, bad," Winter said, clenching her fists.

Emmy nearly choked. "Girl, you've been giving him mixed signals all night. What are you so afraid of?" she asked, smoothing out Winter's unruly hair.

"I don't know! I've never felt like this before. And now he said he might be moving to California next year. Is there even a point? There are plenty of other fish in the sea, right?"

"Yeah, but you'll never catch any of them if you don't grab a pole."

"Emmy!"

Emmy laughed. "You need to relax and let him know what you're feeling. I've seen the way he's been looking at you. I don't even think he realizes there's a party going on."

"I can't. It's too weird."

"Ugh. Come with me."

She pulled Winter back inside, down the hallway, into the supply closet where the bingo cart was kept. Kai and Bobby were sitting on the floor with a few bottles of champagne. Winter turned around to leave, but Emmy pulled her back inside by the collar. She grabbed the nearest bottle, took off the cage, and the cork hit the ceiling.

Winter sat next to Bobby. They briefly made eye contact but quickly looked away. Her body warmed like she was sitting under the sun on that beach in Maryland again.

"It's been a while since I was in a good cuddle puddle," Kai said. He was using Emmy's stomach as a pillow.

"I wish you could all come to Europe with me," Emmy said, her head in Winter's lap.

Winter stroked Emmy's hair. "Didn't you threaten my life recently for saying I didn't want to go to MIT anymore?"

"Maybe, but university in Europe is free, and we have space there too."

Emmy tried to pass Kai the bottle, but he refused. He didn't drink. He only smoked, but he had taken the night off.

"Let's go check on the game, Kai. I think it's almost time for some more numbers," Emmy said, abruptly getting to her feet and shoving the bottle into Bobby's hands.

"All right. Being in a closet was bringing me back to a dark time anyway."

Emmy pulled Kai up, but being nearly twice her size, he almost pulled her down with him. She shooed him out of the room, and Winter was left awkwardly leaning on Bobby without the safety blanket of their best friends.

"This is sparkling cider," Bobby said. "She set this up, didn't she?"

Winter sighed. "Yup."

♥

Bobby Bae

46. WE WILL NOT GET CONFUSED

Hour Four

Winter took a swig of sparkling cider from the bottle Bobby was holding. She wiped her mouth with the back of her arm.

"Can you turn around?" she asked. "I have to say something, but I can't with you looking at me like that."

Bobby turned around, knocking over a broom.

Winter took several deep breaths. "I like you, Bobby. Like, a lot," she said. "And the truth is that I never hated you. I hated what people would think. I hated that our parents would have loved it. I hated how uncomfortable you made me, but I never hated you."

Bobby turned back around. Winter's pupils were large like dinner plates as she stared at him intently. He was thankful he was already on the floor because he would have made quick friends with it if he hadn't been. He tried to find the courage to move closer, but he was frozen.

Winter reached out and straightened his collar, but then lingered there for a moment before she pulled him into a rough embrace. His arms wrapped around her waist, and he nuzzled into her neck, finding a safe place for himself above her collarbone. Her hair tickled his cheek, but he didn't care. He couldn't let go.

"I've missed you too," Winter said.

They pulled away to look at each other but didn't drop the embrace.

"If I asked you to the homecoming dance, would you say yes?"

Winter's eyes crinkled at the corners. "Would you wear that suit?"

"I'd wear whatever you wanted. I'd go naked if you asked," Bobby said, and Winter blushed.

The surrounding air was tense. The stars were waiting for Winter's permission to align.

"Can I ask *you* something?" Winter said, just above a whisper.

"Anything."

"You don't have to fly me around the world, Bobby. I already like you. Do I really have to go to Nasdaq, Greenland?"

"It's *Narsaq Kujalleq*," Bobby corrected. "And no, you can go wherever. I just want to make you happy. That's all—no strings."

Winter put a finger to her chin. "I've always wanted to visit Spain."

"Done," Bobby said.

"Great. And let me think about homecoming. Right now, I want to get back before the countdown."

Bobby straightened himself out. He stood up and redid the button on his jacket. He then helped Winter up, and for a moment, he thought she might kiss him.

Back at the party, Kai was blasting "No Woman, No Cry." Everyone was cheering and clapping, camera flashes were going off, and everything that was good before became better with the knowledge that Winter was open to giving him another chance.

The Baes and Parks finally showed up, and despite being late by several hours, they grabbed fresh bingo cards. Bobby and Winter greeted them, then took their seats in front of their long-abandoned bingo cards, the old metal chairs squealing under their weight. Mr. Park, spotting his mother across the room, rushed past them, straight toward Halmeoni. The other parents shook their heads. Bobby's mouth curved into a smile as he watched Halmeoni wave her son away like a pesky fly, trying to focus all her attention on her bingo card. The hall was alive with the sounds of clinking chips and animated voices echoing off the walls in a symphony of excitement and anticipation as Kai prepared to call the next number.

"O sixty-six, because old Nat King Cole knew where to get his kicks!" Kai yelled over the crowd as the players continued shuffling their plastic red pieces over their boards.

After a few more lucky rounds, Bobby only needed B and G to win.

"Our time is almost done. Who in here has got N thirty-one?" Kai said, brandishing the little white ball. He cranked the ball turner and pulled out another. "Britney says gimme gimme more, so gimme more for G fifty-four!"

Bobby was able to get his G. He was one letter away from bingo if he got a B.

"How are you doing over there?" he asked Winter with a smirk. She tried to hide her board, but he pulled her arm away. "You could still win."

Winter scoffed. "*I could still win?* Where is that competitive spirit, Robert? Or are you going to lie down and let me win again?"

Bobby blinked hard. "Do you want me to let you win?"

"I want you to beat me if you're going to beat me. None of this gentleman bullshit. What happened to the Bobby Bae who made Angela Warren cry during a class debate about the dangers of self-driving cars?"

There were only a few minutes left until the five hours and one minute was up. Bobby and Winter never broke eye contact as they played against each other like they were the only ones in the competition. He regarded her through narrowed eyes, nearly forgetting anyone else was around.

"Beautiful people, I know you all can control yourselves, but, Ms. Betty, it may be time to put the champagne down and take your B twelve!" Kai called.

Bobby's eyes grew wide. That was the last letter he needed. He slowly pushed the red piece toward the spot as Winter followed his hand with her eyes.

"You know what this means, right?" he asked. "It means you're not the best anymore."

He could almost see steam coming from her ears. Her eyes darted between the playing piece and his grinning face several times before she finally swept his entire board onto the floor, sending the pieces flying.

"Who's the best now, bitch?" Winter exclaimed.

Bobby didn't know whether to laugh or cry.

"We're almost at the end," Kai said, "so I just want to bring Miss Emmy Lin to the stage to say a few words."

Emmy stepped up onto the platform with Kai's assistance. She stood with her feet turned outward in second position and smoothed out her skirt. She lowered the microphone almost a foot and tightened it.

"Hello, everyone," Emmy said quietly. She cleared her throat. "I'll make this quick so we don't miss our five-hour-and-one-minute mark, but I just wanted to say how much I love everyone here. My grandmother was so happy to be with you all, and I wanted to dedicate this night to her memory. She would have loved it. With me moving soon, I may not come back here as much anymore, but I wanted to let you know how much I cherish every second I've spent here." She gestured to her father, who was watching her with a sparkle in his eyes. "Baba, do you want to say something?"

Mr. Lin crouched down to the mic and squinted at the lights. "I'd like to read you all a poem from my personal collection." Winter laughed as everyone in the room tried to hide their displeasure. Mr. Lin threw a finger gun. "I'm just kidding. To Năi Nai!" he said, raising his glass, and everyone followed, relieved.

"To Năi Nai!" the entire room chanted in unison, their glasses in the air, Halmeoni seemingly raising hers the highest.

"Now let's all count down our last ten seconds together!" Emmy yelled over the crowd.

Everyone prepared to count down, but the only thing Bobby could focus on was Winter. He had never been more attracted to her than he was in that very moment.

Ten seconds felt like forever as everyone in the room grabbed sparkling cider bottles and got ready to pop the corks.

With nine seconds left, Bobby stared deeply at Winter, who was daring him to take his revenge for turning over his board.

Eight seconds didn't feel like long enough to come up with a plan. Was revenge even what he wanted? Was it even necessary for them to compete anymore?

Seven seconds quickly turned to six.

Six seconds quickly turned to five.

Five seconds quickly turned to four.

Three meant they were close to breaking their biggest rule yet.

Two seconds meant he hadn't breathed in eight whole seconds.

One.

Emmy fired a confetti gun from somewhere behind the stage, and the metallic bits flitted to the ground around them. Some of the seniors sent corks flying, frothy bubbles spewing out of the bottles into the air.

Zero.

It felt like New Year's Eve, so Bobby did the only thing he could think to do—he kissed Winter in front of his friends, family, and about thirty-five elderly strangers. They whooped and hollered as the two embraced each other.

Kai spun the bingo cage and selected the last ball. "Give it up for Winter Park and Bobby Bae! The last number is . . . G fifty-eight!" Kai said, and everyone went quiet. "Come on, someone has to have bingo by now."

Bobby glared at Winter. The way she shrugged and looked back at him with smug indifference was maddening.

"Bingo!" Halmeoni yelled, brandishing her hands in the air.

Kai and Emmy ran up to Halmeoni and informed her that she'd won the pot of almost ten thousand dollars.

"You mad?" Winter asked with a devilish grin.

Bobby bit his lip. "Can I take you home?"

"You're not sick of being in the car with me?"

"I'll find the strength to manage."

♡

Winter Park

47. WE REALLY, SERIOUSLY, WILL NOT BE FRIENDS

Winter was picking her fingernails and biting her lips raw. All she wanted was for everyone to stop kissing her on the cheeks and shaking her hand and telling her how much fun they had. She only wanted them to leave and for all the confetti to clean itself up and all the chairs and tables to put themselves away.

Eventually, it was only Bobby, Winter, Emmy, Kai, and Halmeoni.

"Thank you, Halmeoni, for putting this together," Winter said, throwing her arms around her grandmother.

Bobby bowed low. "I'm grateful."

"Geumanhae!" Halmeoni said, dismissively waving her hand. "Flatter me when I'm dead."

Emmy stepped from behind Halmeoni. "I will never get used to this," she said, motioning to Bobby and Winter. She hugged them both and walked Halmeoni home but not before making plans to hang out with Winter the next morning before she left for Germany.

Kai was the last holdout.

"This was dope," Kai said as he looked wistfully at the stage.

"I'll call you later, man," Bobby replied, giving Kai a sharp pat on the back.

"Have fun in Nards-sack, Winter!" Kai shouted with a wave as he disappeared through the glass doors. Bobby clenched his jaw.

Finally, Bobby and Winter were alone.

Winter stood by the large windows, looking at the full moon. It was like a hole puncher had been taken to the sky. Bobby came up next to her.

"Did you know the moon only shows us one face?" Winter said.

"And yet it's never less beautiful," he replied, and kissed her on the shoulder. "Ready to get out of here?"

They walked down the senior center's lawn to Bobby's car. The sky was a black sheet littered with perfect sparkling diamonds. It was so dark that when Bobby drove off, it felt like they were driving right into space. Winter couldn't stop fidgeting. She pointed to the Village Park on their way to her house. She wasn't ready to go inside yet. That would have meant the night was over.

"Last time we were here, you were worried that the park was closing in ten minutes, but now it's definitely been closed for at least six hours," Bobby said.

"You're still worried about rules?" Winter asked. "We haven't gotten in trouble once. The odds are in our favor."

Bobby glared. "Technically, we did get in trouble at the party, and that's not how odds work. Statistically, our chances of getting in trouble increase every time we do something risky."

"Will you shut up and pull over?"

Bobby obeyed, and there they were, parked in front of the basketball courts once again. There was nothing but a symphony of cicadas and the blanket of night to obscure everything. They stopped under the one streetlight in the lot.

"Don't you think it's funny we never got in trouble for all the stupid stuff we did? My parents didn't even punish me. Did yours?" Winter asked.

"Nope." Bobby was twisting his fingers into knots. "Breaking all these rules with you was fun, but I think I'm retired. Back to the straight and narrow for me. No more Bonnie and Clyde."

"You mean Soon-hee and Dae-seong."

Bobby smiled and pulled his notebook from his back pocket. "Did you want to roundtable ideas for our first date? I have some suggestions you might like."

"Is that why you were so eager to drive me home?" Winter asked, dropping her voice.

"No," he responded resolutely. "But I didn't want to assume anything . . . lascivious."

She smoothed down his jacket lapel. "Don't you want to wait until our first date? Or homecoming? It's not too late to make an honest boy out of you," she said in a mocking tone. With adrenaline pumping through her body, she leaned over the center console until she and Bobby were face-to-face.

Bobby shook his head. "I hate you."

"You're a terrible liar."

Bobby cupped Winter's face. She nuzzled into his hand.

"I'm going to kiss you now," Bobby said. "Are you ready?"

"Are you going to keep talking?"

"If we start dating, you're going to have to be nicer to me."

"Will I?" Winter asked, and moved closer so that there was only a breath between them. "You like—"

Bobby stopped the incoming insult by pressing his lips to hers. She gasped into his mouth. Her mind instantly became a vacuum. Bobby pulled her into him and then onto him. They were dueling with each other, both trying to win their kiss. Some habits never die.

Winter could feel his ragged breath in her body as he kissed her underneath the stars. Who was this boy in front of her? This eager, commanding kisser. This couldn't be the same Bobby Bae who frequently roved Wikipedia looking for discrepancies to fix or had a safe word with his best friend for when he was talking about the political structures in Star Wars too much. He couldn't be the same boy whose Instagram profile picture was a landscape and only posted twice before abandoning the profile altogether. He was the most serious goofball she'd ever met, but she couldn't stop kissing him.

She wasn't sure what part of the car they were in anymore. They could have been on the roof for all she knew, or higher, among the cosmos.

A sharp tapping at the window was the only thing that brought her back to Earth. Winter yelped, and her eyes shot open. Everything was swirling with red-and-blue lights, and there was a park ranger standing there with a long flashlight and look of judgment on his face.

"Oh—" Winter said as she touched her fingertips to her lips.

"Shit," Bobby finished for her.

"'Shit' is right," the ranger said. "Are you aware the park is closed?"

Bobby was looking at her with an expression that said, *I told you so.* She considered calling a moratorium, but his face told her she wouldn't be getting one.

Acknowledgments

First, I'd like to thank myself. Yes, this was a collaborative effort, but we all know why we're here.

That said, a thank-you to myself isn't just a thank-you to myself. When you're a woman, when you're a person of color, when you're this, that, or the other thing, a win for one is a win for us all. So, in thanking myself, I'm also thanking you and everyone who came before us, whose pain and resilience carry on through our food, music, traditions, and stories. The same stuff that lives in me. This book is a celebration of the immense joy that comes along with just waking up and getting to be us despite all the hardships we may face.

This is why I feel so fortunate to have worked on this book with Kokila. Thank you to Namrata Tripathi, whose mission of bringing diverse titles to bookshelves is more than just talk. Thank you to the entire Kokila editorial team for your feedback, support, and extreme attention to detail. To Kaitlin Yang, Theresa Evangelista, Asiya Ahmed, and the rest of the design team for making this book so eye-catching inside and out. A special shout-out to Minji Kwon for my cover, which I know will stand out on a shelf. (Why are people allowed to be this talented?) And to the marketing, sales, and publicity departments, and the entire Penguin Young Readers family—thank you for all your dedication and hard work!

Everyone at Kokila is a wonderful human for seeing something special in *Rules for Rule Breaking*, but I need to give the biggest thank-you in the world to the lovely Joanna Cárdenas. The only thing I was looking for in an editor was someone who understood the heart of my novel, and Joanna just got it.

Special thanks to JIM MCCARTHY. Thank you. Thank you. Thank you. As soon as I got you in my corner, I knew this book was going to reach levels beyond what I even imagined for it. Thanks to the whole team at Dystel, Goderich & Bourret as well.

Thanks to the API writing Discord, now tentatively named the APIary. Especially Isabelle Wong, Paul Jeong, and of course the amazing Jessica Yoon. I'll see you in the hive mind later, Jess!

Thank you to my precious little steamed bun, Tina Moon. You are my best friend, my dongsaeng, my chosen family. May you forever forget your wallet when we go to lunch. This book is dedicated to the memory of your dad, Kenny Moon, who told me I should write a story like *Kim's Convenience*. I'm not sure I did, but I've never taken direction well. Shout-out to Simu Liu too, because why not. Thank you as well to my soulmate, Joanna Prusinska, who gave me the best career advice I've ever gotten:

Me: I don't know what to do with my life.

Joanna: Don't you like to write?

Me: Yeah . . .

Joanna: Then write.

This exchange has been heavily edited for language and explicit content.

A special shout-out to Rashad Davis, who has been my loudest advocate in writing and in life for over two decades. I'd also like to thank the rest of my friends who I will not mention by name because I want to inspire some insecurity.

A huge thank-you to my family. Thanks to my big cuz Tasha for being my number-one fan. My sister, who is my main supplier of curated TikToks. From saying good night and then texting each other from across the hallway, to fangirling over Chewbacca in Disneyland, to our weekly pho meet ups, there is literally no one closer to me in my life. Thank you to my wonderful parents, who have never discouraged me from doing anything despite having constant question marks floating over their heads every time I express one of my ambitions to them. Sorry not sorry I didn't become a doctor. Thank you as well to my beautiful cat, Bowie, who was the best writing partner ever. Your fur is still in my laptop's keys. Every time the fan starts blowing like a jet engine and my lap starts burning, I miss you more.

Lastly, thank you to Winter and Bobby. I spent so much time with you both, it's like we're old friends. Sometimes I pick up my phone to text you, but then I text my therapist instead.

Lastly, lastly, I want to thank myself again. We did it!